ALSO BY M. J. SULLIVAN

Seihō's Kanji Workbook

Sword and Psyche

WAZA

Japanese Calligraphy: Practice, Learning, and Art
(with the calligraphy of Harada Kampō)

Japanese Calligraphy: A First Year Curriculum
(with the calligraphy of Harada Kampō)

Velvet
(with Alec Kalla)

Silk and Steel

Shingyō: Reflections on Translating the Heart Sutra

In This Living Body

THREE-STRAND CORDAGE

M. J. Sullivan

Three-Strand Cordage
M. J. Sullivan

colophon from Peter Matthiessen's *Far Tortuga*
(used by permission of the author)

Cover painting
"From an aerial photograph of the Bahama Banks"
by Rowena Batteau, ca.1986.

Cover design by Tōshoin Studio

This is a work of fiction. Other than the descriptions of sea and wind conditions, courses and fixes, all the names and events are fictional or are used fictionally.

ISBN: 978-0-9829920-6-7
LCCN: 2015955719

Silverback Sages Publishers LLC,
P. O. Box 1408
Abiquiu, New Mexico 87510.

SILVERBACK SAGES

THREE-STRAND CORDAGE

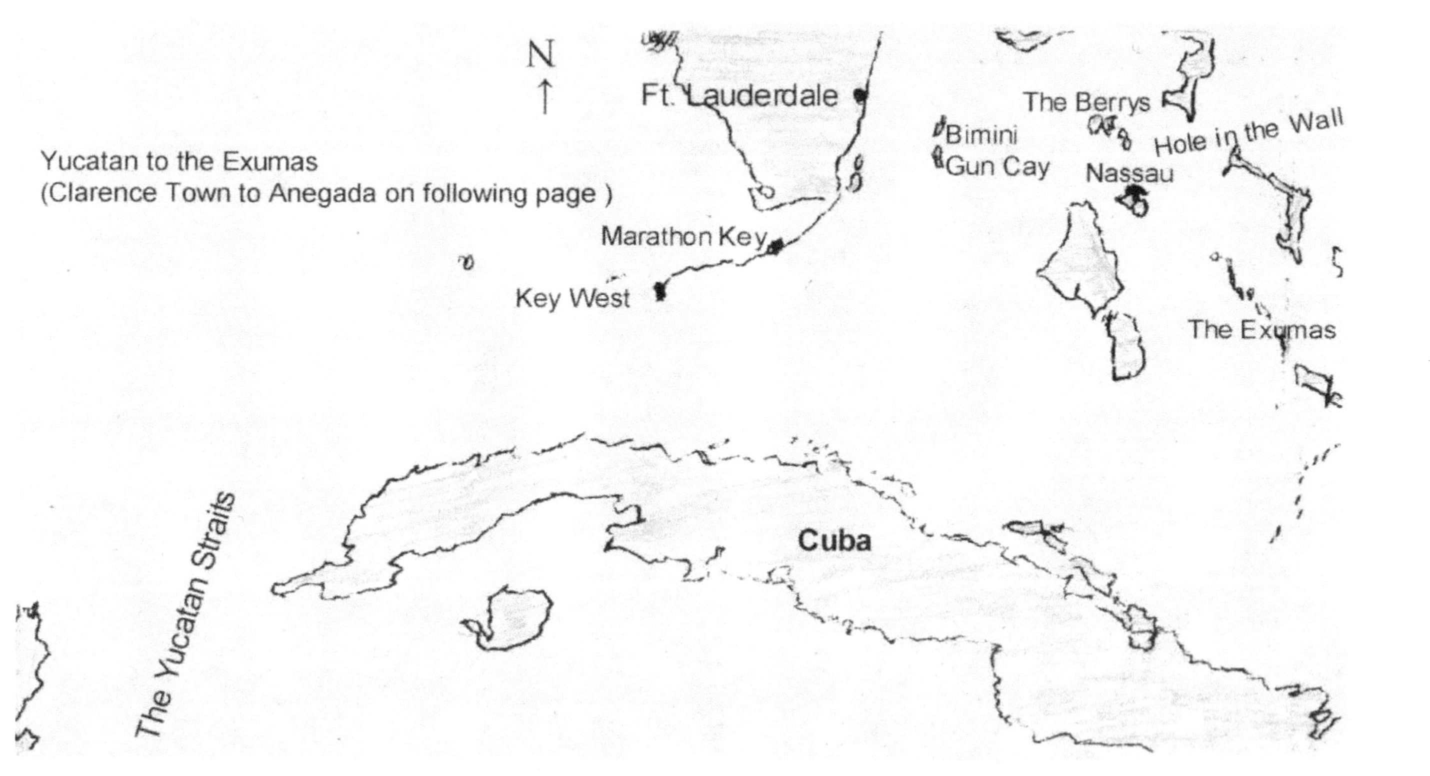
Yucatan to the Exumas
(Clarence Town to Anegada on following page)
N
Ft. Lauderdale
Marathon Key
Key West
Bimini
Gun Cay
The Berrys
Nassau
Hole in the Wall
The Exumas
Cuba
The Yucatan Straits

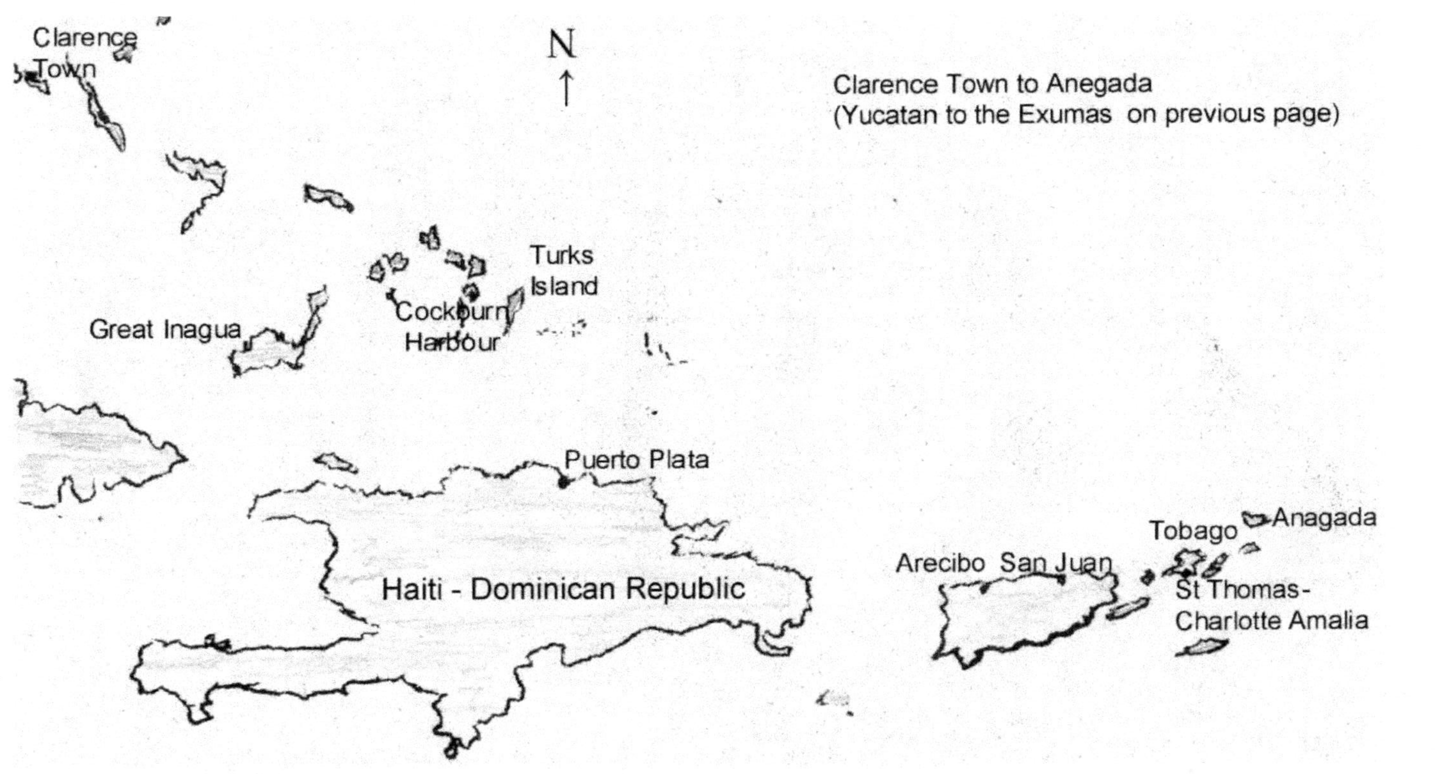
Clarence Town
N
Clarence Town to Anegada
(Yucatan to the Exumas on previous page)
Turks Island
Great Inagua
Cockburn Harbour
Puerto Plata
Tobago
Anagada
Arecibo
San Juan
Haiti - Dominican Republic
St Thomas-
Charlotte Amalia

"He a wind coptin, dass de trouble. He a sailing mon, and he used to the old-time way. All his life he been ziggin and zaggin, he don't know how to go straight."

Peter Matthiessen, *Far Tortuga*

PIRATES OF PENANCE

Watching the kids in their dinghies, the old man remembers how it felt to be ten, remembers it exactly, the sun hot on his back, the wind in his hair, the flash and sparkle and glitter of ever-changing silver and gold and green and blue of sea and sky, the taste of salt, the smells of sea-wet wood and sea-tarnished brass and sea-musted canvas. He feels the varnished mahogany tiller warm and glowing in his left hand, wet manila mainsheet in his right, his body moving with every twist and tendency of the tiny boat as it reacts to the breeze and the waves, no thought, no planning, no computation, just the joyous balance that follows the natural equation of wind, water, sail, boat, boy.

Purity. Even after all that happened, the purity of it.

He is amused by a memory from early childhood, of having been taken to a theater to see Pirates of Penzance*, probably a high school production, and believing every silly word of it. For days afterward he played pirate, drawing a skull and crossbones on a paper hat and wielding a cardboard cutlass. "We are the Pirates of Penance!" he would cry. "Here come the Pirates of Penance!" Well, he thinks, pirates we surely were, and maybe that was penance enough in itself.*

aboard *Femme Fatale*
Clarence Town

Nineteen fifty-five, we were in our twenties, Jack maybe a year or two older than I. Apparently the idea of going off to sea had looked to him like his true salvation, his chance to rebuild away from the land's endless inducements to disappointment in oneself. When I met him he was tending bar in Sag Harbor, broke, dangerously thin and pale. He didn't have a girl, seemed not to want one. I was running a nice little yawl there, got him into the racing crew, liked his way of covering his sadness with humor. At the end of the summer that job ended. I promised Jack I'd take him on as crew as soon as I could, preferably somewhere in the islands.

Anyway, I got myself down to Lauderdale and took over *Femme Fatale* for a couple who wanted to cruise the Bahamas. She'd been named *Allegretto* originally, re-named again since, an old Kinney sloop of forty-two feet overall.

At Clarence Town on Long Island the owners tired of the mosquitoes and found they couldn't get fresh ice that far down the Exuma chain, so they left me there with the boat. They planned to cruise the Virgins the following winter, so I was to take her on to St. Thomas to be hauled, which she badly needed. I would need crew for that, so I got them to call Jack for me.

It took him four days to get there. He arrived in a rusted-out jeep, laughing and back-slapping the driver, his craggy face and sweated khakis pallid against the almost blue black of the shirtless giant behind the wheel.

Hey, Bren! he called. Meet Georgie, the fastest driver on all of Long Island!

As if it had been just days instead of nearly a year since that other Long Island, where we'd raced that pretty yawl out of Sag Harbor. It was late afternoon, hot and bright, the steady southeasterly a blessing. I was cleaning a varnish brush in turpentine aft over the transom.

Hello, Georgie. Hey yourself, Jack.

I heard him invite Georgie aboard for a rum.

No mon, thanks. I got to get back.

So Jack pulled out his wallet and gave Georgie some dollars, shifted his duffle out of the jeep. Georgie said Thank you sah, revved the little engine, ground gears and backed the jeep off the dock. As the jeep was turning around up on the shell road, Jack waved. Georgie didn't wave back.

Jack's face was hard as he stepped aboard. He said nothing as he took his bag below. I'd finished my clean-up and had the varnish stuff stowed before he came back up.

I guess I don't make friends, he said, sitting and pulling out smokes.

I thought we were friends, I said, lightly as I could.

He smiled a little, offered his hand. Right. Sorry. Good to see you, Bren. Thanks for the call.

Then, as we clasped and shook, he said, We do have rum aboard?

So we drank to the sunset, such as we could see of it behind the hill to the west. The rum hit him faster than usual, tired, I'd guess, from the airplanes. He started talking, more than I remembered his ever doing at Sag Harbor.

He told me that he loved Scott Fitzgerald, especially *The Great Gatsby*. He thought of himself as of that generation and in that society, though he'd never had the money for it. Champagne and tuxedos, fast cars and daring women. There was one, he told me. She's in London now.

Her name Daisy? Light on the dock across the bay?

It was somewhat like that, only worse. And not the worst thing of all.

Going to tell me the story?

My father was a doctor in the Hamptons. Had the family but not the money. The name would have brought the rich patients, you'd think. My mother ruined that. She was Catholic, you see, and Irish. Not acceptable in that society. And she was crazy.

Crazy?

Yes. Thoroughly, not at all charmingly, cracked. Bathrobe all day, no housework, booze and pills. No society possible. Had to get out. The name got me into Princeton. Planned to marry, work for the main bunch of Morgans in New York. Didn't work out. Got a job with another firm.

Daisy?

She married a Brit, went to England. No warning. I went to OCS.

Bitch.

We drank some more, made a supper out of leftover sandwiches.

As we were eating he said, Wasn't the worst.

What wasn't?

Daisy.

He finished his sandwich, wiped and cleaned plate and table. Sipped. Lit a cigarette. Poured another and gulped it. Stared at the table.

My mother tried to kill me. Kitchen knife. Just before I left for Princeton.

Jeez. Why?

He shrugged. Cracked. Because I was going, I suppose. She always hated me.

Why?

Shrugged again. Why not? My father's son, after all.

Great Inagua

We waited two more days there in Clarence Town, for stove fuel. We drank with some locals in their rudimentary bar, worked on the brass and the varnish. The engine was sputtering as we put her out into the sound. Squalls that night. In those days before civilian Loran or GPS, without the sun we seldom knew quite where we were. When we tried to crank the engine later it grunted and groaned a little, then screeched and was gone. We got her into the basin at Inagua under sail the next afternoon. No easy trick.

A rotten time aboard poor old *Femme Fatale,* the engine seized up, no fresh food, no ice. The island is pretty much owned by Morton, and most of its surface is taken up by ponds for the drying of sea salt and the breeding of mosquitoes. It was a walk of about a mile in still heat and those mosquitoes to the settlement and the salt factory. We took turns doing it, I first with enough money for the cable to the owners, then Jack a few days later with money for groceries and to check on the cables, hoping for the arrival of the engine parts. I'd read everything aboard at least once, and Jack had almost finished my last Conrad. He was on *Heart of Darkness* and grumbled irritably about all the quotes upon semi-quotes.

The only ritual we were able to establish was the evening spraying of insecticide to protect ourselves from the sand flies, or no see'ums, some sort of gnats, that flew and bit mercilessly just at sunset, rendering evening rums in the cockpit a thing of the halcyon past. Then rigging the screens and slathering ourselves with mosquito repellant in time for that invasion right around full dark and lasting the night. Fortunately, we still had a few bottles of rum. Ran out of things to talk about. Waited.

We played gin rummy. We polished brass, greased blocks and winches, spliced fraying cordage. Half-heartedly scraped weed off her bottom and got a little of it. Listened to mosquitoes whine in the dusk. Heard occasional and unexplained screams and wailing from the interior in the night. A waft of breeze brought the sound of chanting, drums. A primitive, compelling rhythm.

The next night they were there again, maybe fainter. We listened to them instead of the radio, speculated on them.

A few days later, in a still, hot morning, a Haitian sloop of some sixty feet came in and warped onto the wall astern of us. No engine; they ran anchors out on their two dinghies, used them to kedge her to the wall and lay her on, two aboard with long poles for the fine work at the end. Eight or ten men aboard, as I recall. Great boat-handling. Made me embarrassed to be stuck waiting for engine parts.

We watched the guys on the sloop most of the day, tidying up, sending a man into the town, chatting along in a French-sounding Creole. Jack had a go at talking with them while I was fixing lunch, but couldn't get through. Near evening the water truck came down with the crewman they'd sent, followed by a delegation of gawkers from the town. They watched as the trucker topped off her tanks, and as we bought what he had left. They chatted and commented.

The water didn't smell good, but the man on the truck said it was sweet water, mon, truly sweet. We did laundry with some of it, siphoning it out of the tanks to save the batteries. This delighted the gathering, all of whom seemed to find two white sailors washing clothes to be entirely comical. When we were finished and had the wet stuff hanging all over the rigging, they left in twos and threes. Just before the gnats arrived.

Well, that night all but one or two of the Haitians went ashore, down the road to the town. One of them, a short, scrawny old fellow, wore a battered top hat and a tailcoat, strutted, leading the way. A few hours later the drums started, louder than they'd been either of the previous nights. This time the chanting was not the low, humming sound we'd heard before, but higher pitched, more insistent, and accompanied by howling and screams.

I've got to look, Jack told me. I've got to know.

Jeez, Jack.

I'll be careful.

He burned the end of a rum cork and darkened

his face. Took a knife.

Watch till there's no one on the sloop's deck, he said. Then tap the ladder twice.

He hovered just below the opened forward hatch. I watched aft toward the sloop. There was only one man on deck, smoking. After a while his cigarette hissed as it hit the water, and he ducked below. I tapped. Jack was gone before I could turn around to look for him.

So I listened to the drums. Shouts. Shrieks of what might have been laughter, but if so it was of the most diabolical sort. About two hours of that as I tidied and tested the wet laundry and eyed the Haitian sloop for movement or any sort of change. Nothing. Finally I had an extra dollop of rum and slather of repellant—we were running out—and lay in my bunk.

I woke, still in the dark, to the silence of the drums. I used the little moonlight to check Jack's bunk. Not there. Had another look at the sloop. No one stirring. Lit a smoke, kept it cupped. Sat in the cabin and sweated.

There was a pale line of light behind the trees to the east when I heard the crunch of gravel under someone's feet. I tensed, grasped a rigging knife. Felt her shift as someone stepped aboard. Recognized Jack's canvas shoes as he stepped down the companionway ladder. Hardly recognized his face, though, when he was all the way down, grasping the handrails and gasping great breaths of air.

He was covered with blood, his hair thick with it. He smiled through it, though the sort of smile I'd hate to see on anyone's face again.

My mother was Catholic, he said, and laughed a fearsome laugh.

You told me. What happened to you?

She tried to kill me.

You told me that, too. What happened tonight?

She didn't kill me. They saved me from her. They danced and called up a demon and the demon killed her and they spread her blood all over my body and now she can't ever kill me again, never, not ever.

Jeez, Jack.

Not Jeez. They called him Jambo.

I heard more crunching of shell, the broken rhythm of several men nearing. Are they coming for you, Jack?

Who?

The men who're coming.

Why would they come for me?

Jeez, Jack.

But the footsteps went by, went to the Haitian sloop, there were greetings, creaks and groans as she shifted to the weight of her crew returning. We stood facing each other like that, he by the companionway, I by the table, neither of us moving, I because I couldn't.

I have to wash, he said at last.

Yes. Jeez, Jack.

I'd better do it on the foredeck.

Yes.

With the bucket.

Yes.

He moved toward me then, and I stepped aside, let him pass. He got a towel out of the head and passed me again, went out on deck. I listened to his splashing and the thump of the bucket. Washing himself took a very long time.

The Caicos Banks

Finally the mail boat arrived with the engine parts. It took us three more days in that awful place to rebuild the engine. When we left at last it was like going to heaven. But near sunset the first day out the southeast filled with columns of cloud rising all the way from the surface of the sea to the very top of the sky, brilliant orange and reds modulating into purples darkening to grays and black at their apex, a wall between us and our course. I'd once seen a painting by an expressionist trying to render visually the opening chords of a Rachmaninoff concerto and had been impressed by the work. This in its brilliance made a mockery of it.

Soon after dark it blew fifty knots, hurled eight-foot waves into our faces. We furled down and rigged a sea anchor. Even with that the storm was wild enough that in the morning we found the headstay fitting hanging on its last, badly-bent bolt.

By the next afternoon we were bucking the east wind and chop of the Caicos Bank, making only a knot or two under power, sailing rig furled and tucked, her frayed and rusting shrouds slack, a jib halyard jury-rigged to a mooring cleat all that supported her mainmast forward. Under the clear blue-white of midday, the world all around us was a disk of emerald water but for a low brown smudge to the northeast, the island of South Caicos.

Jack stood in the bows, periodically glassing the smudge, an arm hooked through the slack headstay and jury-rigged jib halyard, binoculars neck-slung and loose in his hands. His hair was still short if somewhat ragged, even after two weeks on the boat. He looked heroic, of course, as always, and neat.

I have never looked at all heroic, and at that point I certainly wasn't neat. My hair was a tangled bush, my blue sweatshirt filthy with grease and unidentifiable chunks of bilge muck, my bare legs smeared with the same stuff. I sat at the tiller with half an eye on the compass, the rest of my attention directed down the open hatch to the engine room at my feet, watching for the spray to start again as the water in there rose to the level of the flywheel.

Like me, the boat was a mess. Things below were worse even than on deck, especially in the engine room. She'd got shaken up so badly in the storm that all the wood chips and shavings and sawdust that had been in her from the day she'd been built were afloat, so the water stayed aft and all attempts to clear the limber holes had been to no avail. She was leaking badly through the stuffing box. Whenever the water level got high enough the flywheel would spray it up onto the generator. Her hand pump had lost its diaphragm, so her only pump was electric. And with the generator failing, she wouldn't have power to go on with the pumping. The only way to stop the leak was to turn off the engine and hank down the stuffing box. But she couldn't sail, because the headstay fitting was gone and we were headed upwind.

Jack came aft, his long, craggy hero's face revealing nothing.

That's it, he told me. About five degrees to port. I could see the roofs. Cockburn Harbour.

Jack handed me the binoculars. I scanned, saw the village. Couldn't get much of a picture of it, because after a moment or two the flywheel started spraying and I had to start the pump running again.

The town was beautiful at a distance of two miles. Up under its shores, as the glorious emeralds of the Caicos Banks darkened to browns, it looked tawdry, a slum but for the government house and the green-roofed Admiral's Arms Hotel. Only one boat lay on the hotel's dock, a sixty-odd foot motorsailer, a ketch with a bowsprit. Jack quickly, gracefully as always, rigged the fenders and cleared the mooring lines. An easy docking, under the lee of a breakwater and the little easterly above it just enough to keep her off.

A big, round, blond man, deeply tanned and wearing only a pair of shorts, scurried off the motorsailer, spouting an enthusiastic flow of instructions in heavily-accented English. Despite the flurry he created we warped her on without a bump. Once his lines were coiled, Jack stepped lightly back onto the dock. He was introducing himself to the big man, chatting and smiling, while I stared glassily into the pilothouse of the motorsailer.

Seated there, on what might be called the dashboard, behind the propped-open windshield, reclining with one long bare leg extended and the other raised seductively at the knee, was a girl with free silver-gold hair, watching Jack with pale eyes set in a face so perfect that it seemed to radiate a golden light, dispelling the shadows in which she rested. Her eyes shifted to me for an instant. That glance stirred up a stew of fears and losses and longings in a mixture I'd never felt before. To this day I don't know whether I've ever sorted out all that I felt in that moment. I'm sure my tanned face turned as red as a Michigan tourist's.

Her eyes quickly returned to Jack, of course. I clambered wearily below to find a wrench with which to tighten the sorry, worn out stuffing box.

Cockburn Harbour

I noted the docking in the log at three in the afternoon, but I don't remember the date exactly. The autumn of fifty-five, October for sure, as we had more or less celebrated Columbus Day — Discovery Day to them — on Inagua.

We could leave her here and fly back, I said later, as we were rigging awnings against the sun.

Go back to what?

We went up to the hotel for showers, bought some ice. The showers were slightly brackish but the ice was clean enough. I reserved us a table for dinner, then we went back to the boat and sat in the cockpit and drank iced rum, Vat 19.

Did you see the girl? I asked.

No. Thorssen's daughter. Nineteen. Elke. They're Danish. He didn't look at me when he said it, the sharp-cut, narrow hero's face to the south, squinted blue eyes on the horizon.

She's really something to see, I muttered. Anyone else aboard?

Two sons, fifteen and seventeen. Erik and Leif. Forget which is which.

We dropped the subject. I was grateful to, both because I didn't want to think about the girl and because I had to think about how to get the boat fixed enough to get on to St. Thomas. The headstay fitting was the main thing. We could go without the engine, of course, maybe even without electricity for the pump. But we couldn't go without a solid headstay fitting.

The sun was getting low, the light going copper over the silver-green of the Bank. The rum filled the tiredness, slacked all my sheets. Even Jack seemed to be relaxing. The cool wafts of the Trade wind softened as they came in over the breakwater. The boat moved softly under us, barely noticeable after the heaving we'd been through on the Atlantic and the chop that had pounded her crossing the Bank. We went quiet, listening to the wavelets under the dock, the occasional slap of the awning above our heads, the rustling of palms and shrubs from the hill above.

Another? Jack asked, standing to go below.

Before I could answer, the quiet was broken by a harsh sound of metal on metal aboard the motorsailer and the even harsher voice of Thorssen, a loud smack, a high-pitched feminine wail. Then two other male voices, raised and angry, and scuffling. Then the female voice raised, too. Neither of us could help looking that way.

A blond, tanned boy, a slimmer version of Thorssen, tromped forward of the pilothouse, bent to the deck to open a hatch. At the same time I caught a glimpse of tanned leg and much long blond hair flying from somewhere aft onto the dock, which in an instant became the girl, in cut-off jeans and white dress shirt with the tails flapping, running up to the hotel. Thorssen's harsh voice followed her, telling her to come back. She didn't.

Jack and I looked at each other. He raised one eyebrow — something I've never been able to do — turned and went below. I kept my eyes down there with him then, but listened closely to the motorsailer. I heard a thunk, presumably as the forward hatch dropped back into place, clunky footsteps, presumably as the boy went aft, and then muffled argument, presumably between the boy and Thorssen. Some clatter of eating utensils. Jack brought up fresh rums and we lighted our Rothmans.

Well, I whispered.

He sat staring after her for several seconds, long enough for me to watch a lock of his hair sway back and forth in the wind. He seemed to have gotten lost somewhere in himself. He shuddered slightly before he spoke.

So now I've seen the girl, he said. Cheers.

Near the end of that round the sun plunked under the horizon in its unceremonious tropical way, leaving thin twilight almost instantly. Lights appeared on the veranda of the hotel. It was time to go up to dinner. We both glanced into the cockpit of the motorsailer as we passed. No sign of the boys, but Thorssen sat staring out at where the sun had been. He didn't look up or respond to my nod and false half-smile. In the low light I could just read her name on the transom: *Lazy Drummer,* and her port of call, just Panama.

As we climbed the coquina rock steps up the hill I reeled to the sudden evening scents of bougainvillea, and maybe gardenia, which couldn't reach the boat on the easterly breeze. I'd had a drop or two of rum, mind you, but the feeling was, I'd guess, excessively, I'd guess, romantic. She was there on the terrace in one of the deck chairs, her tightly-clasped knees pulled up to her forehead, the very picture of the picture of, I'd guess, despair. I'd guess, I'd guess, I'd guess. As I mentioned, I'd had a drop or two.

Jack, bold Jack, stepped over and spoke to her, too quietly for me to hear. She didn't budge.

Give me a minute, Jack whispered, close to my ear. You go on in.

Well, there it was. I nodded, as I recall, or perhaps just bowed my head, and walked into the Admirals Arms Inn. Not at all steadily. Straight to the bar.

Jack didn't come in for dinner for damn near an hour. At least when he came he was alone.

Well, that was the start of a period of that odd sort of relationship between friends such that you're not exactly friends anymore. Jack and I sat pleasantly enough over coffee on the hotel terrace the next morning, divided the chores, discussed the problems of getting off to sea again, the problems of the passage to St. Thomas ahead of us. But he made no mention of Elke or what had happened the night before, and I wouldn't ask. No more bringing up the past to explain the self, to describe the sort of friend your friend had in front of him. No more mention or feeling of camaraderie.

From up there on the terrace we could look down on the dock at *Femme Fatale* and *Lazy Drummer*, on which vessel Thorssen fiddled with one thing or another, while the boys putted off in their dinghy to dive for lobster near Six Hills Cays. No sign of Elke. We could also look out to the southeast, from which direction the Trades blew steadily, and in which direction we would have to sail our sorry charge. We lingered there though, as long as we could, just happy to be off the hot boat and in the shade and the full flow of the breeze.

But we couldn't dally so forever. We'd found out that there was a machine shop connected to the British fishing operation on the island. Jack's first chore was to take the headstay fitting over there, see what the machinist could do with it. Then he was to find a store, see if he could get us some food. All we had were a few cans of vegetables, some soups. My first job was to remove the generator and take it apart, see if it could be saved.

The generator's brushes were gone, gone. I cleaned up the rest of it as best I could, put the brushes aside in hopes we could find replacements somewhere ashore. Jack came back late in the afternoon with tinned butter, ham, chicken and mushrooms all in cans, a loaf of fresh island bread and a bottle of Vat 19. No headstay fitting.

He's working on it, he told me. He's going to drill it out, give us bigger through-bolts instead of the threaded ones. All he's got is iron, of course.

Did it look as if he might be able to fix the generator? I asked.

Maybe.

I could see that Jack was tired. We called it a day, went up to the hotel for showers, changed into decent clothes. Sat at the bar and drank until dinner. Fried grouper, Bahamian peas and rice. Pauli Girl. I went down to the boat and straight to my bunk. Jack stayed up there for a nightcap, or so he said. I hadn't seen the girl all day, and Jack hadn't said a word about her. It occurred to me that he'd been gone a long time just for one conversation with the machinist and one bag of groceries. I heard him come aboard sometime later. Much later, I thought, though I didn't check the time.

I woke well before him in the morning, went up for coffee and a bun on the terrace. I kept a second log in those days, a private one, more like a diary. I worked on that for an hour or so, sitting there in the cool shade of the veranda with the scent of flowers chased by the sea air.

I saw Elke coming up the steps to the hotel, but she turned to go around it to the town beyond. She was a beauty, all right, not all that tall, not the Nordic ice-queen type, face soft, eyes set wide, a full, sensuous mouth. The proportions of her were wonderful, long limbed and short in the torso. A good mover, coltish.

But enough of that. Jack joined me a bit later for his coffee, bringing the generator up with him. I went back down to the boat, spent the next couple of hours doing what I could to help her along, you know, polishing brass here and there, greasing this and that, checking lines for wear, sewing up a grommet in one of the jibs, that sort of thing. Took a nap. Wrote some more in my log.

When Jack came back this time he had the headstay fitting. No generator. The machinist thinks he knows one of the captains who might have spare brushes for the generator that will fit.

I asked him if he had an idea when.

Tomorrow, maybe, was what they said. Island time.

How much?

Don’t know.

That left us with the problem of money. The owners had left me with some US and had cabled me some in Bahamian at Inagua, but it was going pretty fast up in the hotel and we were paying a daily dockage fee. Still, two more days would be all right unless they charged us an arm and a leg for the generator repair. On the whole it looked like we'd make it.

We got the headstay fitting mounted that evening. The heavier bolts looked as if they'd do the trick. Then we went up for showers. Being short of money, we agreed to do our drinking aboard instead of in the bar. We bought some ice and went back to the boat.

Thorssen was piddling around on the dock, fussing with some sort of electrical gadget. Jack suggested that we invite him for a drink. That was okay with me, so Jack went up and talked to him, listened to him explain his problem with the electrical gadget. After a few minutes of that Jack came back, and a minute or so later Thorssen went aboard the motorsailer.

He'll come after he washes up, Jack told me. We touched up our drinks and waited.

He came in a few minutes, his hands reddened and raw, an old white dress shirt hung over his massive shoulders, unbuttoned to reveal his massive belly. Golden tanned, hair blond almost to white, just like Elke's, though of course thinner and shorter. The weight of him stepping aboard made *Femme Fatale* lurch against her mooring lines.

Ja, thanks, thanks, he boomed, accepting a glass. He sat easily in the cockpit, seeming to use his weight to settle the boat back to quiet. Vat 19 rum. Thanks, thanks. We get Barbancourt all the time in Haiti, bring it up here, to Turks, to the Virgins.

So, are you just cruising? I asked him. Do you charter?

He speared me with icy blue, a warning.

No. We trade. We bring this rum and fruits and vegetables from Haiti and Dominican Republic, also sometimes woodwork. Here and in Turks we get lobster and conch. Other things sometimes in St. Thomas. We trade.

He shot me a smile then, not very convincing. And

you. Are you just cruising?

I told him about our delivery, the owners back in New York wanting the boat in St. Thomas. He nodded, and nodded.

No cargo? he asked.

I laughed and told him no.

A waste to go without cargo.

Jack asked him how he transported the conch and lobster.

We got aboard two big freezers. So long as the generator is running we have very cold.

I went below to see if I could find anything to serve with the rum. I found an old can of peanuts still sealed, popped it. Not elegant, but something. The nuts smelled richly of the inland, somewhere far away. I took them up to the cockpit, offered them to Thorssen. He took the can, poured out a handful and dug in. Jack took two or three. I passed on them, re-charged my rum. I asked him about his boat.

She is Dutch, built before the war, he said, staring at the peanut can. I got her in British Honduras, a trade.

His eyes twitched, then snapped at me from lowered brows. He munched, sipped. The boys are good workers, most of the time. Good at catching the lobsters. Elke cooks and cleans. She is a problem.

How? I asked, blurting. Dumb.

Blue spears again.

She is tired of the boat, I think. Wants to be ashore. Not yet, not yet, she is still too young.

Another round, the peanuts gone.

Ja, I must go. Thanks, thanks. You come aboard *Lazy Drummer* sometime.

We tidied the drink things, closed her up. The

sunset was another of those dull plops into the sea out over the banks. As we were walking up the dock, Elke was on her way down with a grocery bag in her arms. Jack and I said hello to her almost in unison, ready to stop and talk. She looked down at the planks, whispered hello and kept moving. It was an effort not to look back once she'd passed. Harder yet, I'd guess, for Jack.

The next day was a Sunday. Jack went up to the Fisheries, found it locked and abandoned. We did what we could with the boat, this and that, and found the port upper shroud badly frayed. We tried drawing some fresh water, but the batteries were so low the pump wouldn't deliver. There was not one damn thing we could do. I lay in bed then through the heat with nothing to read. Jack went up to the hotel, or somewhere off the dock. I assumed he was with Elke, or trying to be.

On Monday afternoon late we got the generator back. I got it connected, but we didn't have enough power to crank up. On Tuesday Jack borrowed a battery from *Drummer* so we could jump start her. It worked. We went up to the hotel to get away from the engine noise, let her run for several hours. When we went back we tested the water pump, the lights, all that; she was charging, all right. We were elated. We'd be able to go the next day.

All of the *Lazy Drummer*'s crew were there to see us off, four heads of white-blond, skins of gold, paired flashes of ice-blue, all glowing in the sun and casting green shadows. Elke stood behind Thorssen and the boys hardly looking at us. She waved once we were off the dock and I noticed that after the males had left and gone back aboard the motorsailer she still stood there hugging herself, a golden figurine expressing perplexed loss. I watched Jack for a while. He never glanced back.

Turks Island Passage

From Cockburn Harbour you just poke her out due east if you have an engine. The Trades usually are southeasterly, of course, but at that time were pretty much due east and blowing right about twenty knots. Some light, high cloud, seas three or four feet. We drove her into it with the engine and the main close-hauled. It was wonderfully cool, taking that breeze on the nose. Though the movement of the boat under power banging into it like that is not exactly pleasant, it felt like great liberation. In those days the only time I felt safe and whole was at sea under sail. Shore time, even dock time, was painful, confusing. Under way at last, the boat alive and bucking and the spray flying, just minutes away from shutting down the engine and setting a headsail, I was almost wild with joy.

At which point the engine surged, screamed. I felt a thump in the steering and we lost all headway.

What was that? Jack hollered, grabbing a shroud. He was forward, rigging the jib.

Well, I didn't have an answer at the moment. I throttled down to idle, bore off to port and eased the main enough to get some way on. Once she was manageable I opened the hatch to look into the engine room.

The drive shaft had come completely clear of the coupling. It hung in the stuffing box, quivering as the sea flowed over the propeller, banging it occasionally against the rudderpost.

I called Jack aft to steer, crawled down in there, tugged at the shaft trying to get it inboard. No go.

We can't go on with it like that, I said.

Damn. Just damnit.

So we wore her around and headed back in to Cockburn Harbour. As she jibed, that frayed port shroud parted with a snap that sounded like my heart breaking.

Cockburn Harbour

When we got back into the harbor we had to swing her toward *Lazy Drummer,* in fairly close to the wall. That of course brought Thorssen and the boys running onto the dock, shouting and waving, afraid we were going to ram her. Nevertheless, we rounded her up about parallel to the motorsailer, slowing sharply and luffing, and Jack coolly stepped off onto the dock with his bow line and didn't hand it off to anyone. When it was just time to stop I tossed the stern line in a neat coil to Thorssen, who fiercely tugged the last bit of way off her.

When she was snug on her fenders I looked down the hatch. Reached down into the bilge and plucked out a small, distorted, torn piece of brass. It was the key that held the propeller shaft into the coupling. I'd forgotten to slack off the box after I stuffed it, and the strain had broken the key.

That was at one-thirty in the afternoon. Jack headed up to the machinist's with the twisted fragment. I rummaged around in the storage lockers for some wire and bull clamps for the shroud. Found this and that, came up with what was needed. I sat sweating on the starboard settee, frustrated and exhausted, pondering the idea of unlucky days for sailing. Superstitious lot, sailors.

One way or another, I knew I wasn't going to try for it again that day.

We planned to have the last dinner we could afford at the hotel. As it turned out, there was something of a party on the terrace, a group of young English people, members of the VSO or its predecessor. They were from several of the Caicos Islands and Turks, gathered for an annual meeting of some sort. We got in with them, all jokes and laughter. One of the girls was a hearty, blowzy, let us say plump, lass, Lady Caroline Something, half a head taller than I. She was entirely tiddly and after Jack straight away. He made his escape as pleasantly and quickly as he could. Then she deigned to cast a dark and a roving eye at poor little Cap'n Bren, who was in no mood for escape.

Her accent was that drawling sort you hear when the Royals speak. Her hair was Latin-dark and long, her skin that wonderful olive shade that comes from carefully-timed hours in the sun over months and years.

We must eat something, must we not? she murmured, well into the evening.

We should, I agreed, but all the money's gone.

Bosh and bother, we'll put it on the bill.

Whew.

After the conch and grouper and peas and rice and Courage, a beer they patriotically preferred to Pauli Girl, we all moved out onto the terrace, where one of the fellows had a guitar. Bawdy songs mainly, which I didn't know. Lady Caroline the bawdiest of the lot, pantomiming delights as they sang, funny and sexy at once.

The wind was coming up, though, gone south, even a touch west of south. I stepped unsteadily away from the lights (to the tune of *We Know Where You're Going,* naturally) to have a look at the sky. No stars.

We're about to get it, I think, I told the company. Rain, at least.

Bosh and bother and party pooper. I was hooted off the terrace and made my way down the path to the dock. Some big gusts blew sand into my eyes, and thunder rumbled up on the wind. It had the feel.

Both *Femme Fatale* and *Lazy Drummer* were tugging at their lines like leashed hounds on a fresh scent, though the motorsailer moved less, being inshore and so much heavier. The surge was already enough to require some sense of timing to get aboard. Mine wasn't too good, despite the amelioration provided by my dinner on Lady Caroline's bill. I tripped headlong over a lifeline and skinned my shin on the coaming. It was, after all, very dark. While I was writhing in pain and trying to stand up in the cockpit, Jack's head appeared in the companionway.

What is it? he whispered.

Blowing up, I told him. Took a fall.

Shh, with a finger to his lips.

Why? I whispered back. He just shook his head.

Finally on my feet again, I rubbed my shin and shook my head back into the present.

We've got to get the awnings down, I told him, still whispering, and get more lines and fenders rigged. It's going round southwest.

Okay, he whispered back. A minute.

I went forward to start on the awnings, fumbling for the ties in the dark as the canvas whipped and snapped in the wind. I glanced aft at a sound. A pale shape emerged from the companionway, hovered sprite-like at the rail, leapt gracefully as a fawn onto the dock and disappeared instantly.

A moment later Jack was on deck, peering aft into the dark. Then he turned forward and spotted me, came up to lend a hand.

The rain came in a great sheet, no dribbles ahead of it, no time to get foul weather jackets. And it blew, gusts over forty knots, while the boat lurched and bucked against her lines, as hard to ride as a scared mustang. We got everything we could over the side to buffer her from the dock, life jackets, cushions, what have you, hanked down extra mooring lines as hard as we dared. The surge had become a chop, three- and four-footers and breaking. When we could look up, we saw Thorssen and the boys doing the same things for *Drummer*, only by flashlight, held, apparently, by Elke. She'd probably got aboard and woken the others right away, serving both the needs of the boat and her secret at once.

Jack went below, handed me up a waterproof. I sat with the boat in the weather, off and on examining the fenders and lines and making adjustments to minimize the chafing. In between I huddled in what lee I could find, back to the wind, mind spinning. I couldn't help but envy Jack. I'd chased the girls in various ports, of course, but shyly and without much hope. I realized that Jack had to get the girl, had the right to her, the need for her. I had no rights, and no idea of what it was I needed.

It was a night of that sort of thing, and a long one.

The rain ended after what passed for dawn but the wind continued out of the west, then finally, around noon or so, shifted to the northwest. Once there the chop subsided, softened into a surge. It was still blowing over thirty though, showing no signs of diminishing. Jack and I sat in the cabin, drinking coffee he'd brewed and smoking cigarettes.

I've got to sleep, I told him.

Sure.

You get any rest?

Some.

Open her up for a while, will you? It'll probably rain some more this afternoon, and she's soaked.

Sure.

So I found some dry clothes and put them on and pulled the spinnaker out of its bag and rolled up in it in the sail locker with its wonderful smells of canvas and hemp and mahogany and brass going green and whatever else made those old boats smell the way boats are supposed to smell and don't anymore. I heard Jack's voice and Thorssen's once or twice, and some banging and clatter. Apparently *Lazy Drummer* had taken some damage, and Jack was lending a hand. That was okay, there was nothing to do on *Femme Fatale* until the machinist came up with a new key for the shaft, nothing to do until the wind was back into the southeast and the sun had dried the decks and warmed the bones of Cap'n Bren, and then I was asleep and that was another day stuck to the dock.

I woke near sunset, vampire-like, extracted myself from my silken cocoon, moth-like, and staggered aft, drunk-like but not drunk. The boat wasn't lurching anymore, the howling in her rigging had settled to less than a hum, and the sole underfoot was dry and wonderfully clean from its rainwater wash. I brewed coffee and laced it with a half a shot of rum.

Laughter and a hail from the dock, Cap'n Bren Boy Sleepy Head, Duty calls, in high-pitched, upper-class Brit. I palmed my hair to each side and poked my head out the companionway, sniffed the air. The breeze with that north left on it brought all the smells of rain-soaked earth and tropical flowers right down from the land, overwhelming the scents of boat and sea. Jack stood grinning. Elke stood with her eyes squinched and a hand covering her mouth. Lady Caroline struck a pose, hip cocked, jiggly, rubbery flesh, a Junoesque nanny. She was wearing a red French bikini and had a sort of muumuu of a dress pulled up all the way to her neck. They all laughed at the sight of me.

Duty? I asked. That brought guffaws.

A party, Lady Caroline stated, recovering her arch manner. A new nightclub, up the hill. The first to grace South Caicos. Your presence is required.

With which she produced a quick, poker-faced bump and grind. Even I laughed then. I'll dress, I said, and ducked below.

Jack came aboard. They'll feed us, he whispered.

Who will?

Don't know exactly. That British volunteer group, I guess. At this point, who cares?

Anything on the key?

No. Their power went down in the storm. Tomorrow, I suppose.

I dressed, he changed, we rubbed our bristly chins and shrugged. Locked her up and went over to *Drummer*, before which Elke and Lady Caroline stood on the dock chatting. Her Ladyship's muumuu was decorously in place, hanging all the way to her ankles. A quick shift in the breeze, however, revealed that it was slit to the hip on both sides.

Thorssen glared up from *Drummer*'s cockpit.

Oh, *do* come, Captain Thorssen, Lady Caroline pled. There will be *ever* so much food, and *ever* so much fun. Bring the lads as well. *Please* do.

Ja, ja, it is all right. But not Elke. She should not see such a place.

Oh *no*! She simply *must* come! *Everyone* simply *must* be there. She'll be perfectly safe, every *minute*.

Elke just hung her head, waiting. I spotted one of the boys in a corner of the deckhouse near the helm, looking steadily at Lady Caroline. His hand rested on the pommel of one of a row of machetes racked in the strakes aft of the deckhouse. The other boy stood under the coach roof, where, I suddenly noticed, there hung a 12-gauge bang stick they used for killing sharks. Everyone else was looking steadily at Thorssen, who looked steadily at Elke.

You will be a good girl? he asked her roughly. No tricks?

Yes, Papa, she whispered, still looking down.

You promise?

Yes, Papa.

All right. He glared, still looking at Elke, his voice harsh and still threatening. We go.

Thank you, Papa.

Very *good*, Lady Caroline cheered, clapping. Very good indeed. We'll all meet up at the terrace of the hotel then, have a little drinkie before we go. Then with a small wave and even smaller smile, Ta ta.

Elke turned to go with us, but Thorssen shouted her name.

Elke! You wait, go with me and your brothers.

Lady Caroline didn't even try him that time. Jack's face whitened and his fists clenched, but in a second he managed a thin smile and a wave. Elke went aboard, head still down, and we three moved reluctantly up the dock.

What *is* going on with them? Lady Caroline asked, after we were seated and sipping our drinks.

I left that one to Jack, who peered into his glass.

She's only nineteen, he said at last.

Well, yes. But *still*.

We chatted about anything else for the twenty minutes it took the Thorssen party to join us.

It was full dark by then, though a few stars were showing and the Trades were back, due east again. I noticed that Jack made no attempt to walk next to Elke as we picked our way up the hill behind the hotel, dodging puddles, stray dogs and cats and one recalcitrant donkey. He in fact had taken one of Lady Caroline's arms, as I took her other when she offered it, and he chatted her up about London and the stock market and other things I had no idea he even knew about. The Thorssens followed at a slight distance, silently, so far as I could tell.

The new nightclub was a concrete block house lit only by a kerosene lamp, with gritty cement underfoot and no glass in the windows. It was hot with bodies, Gladys, the hotel's bartender, one or two of its busboys and maids, a number of children, three or four of the Brit volunteers who'd been on the terrace the night before. Lady Caroline introduced us to a number of people, black and white, whom we couldn't see. The only way you could tell black from white in there was by the accents. There was a rudimentary stage, on which we could make out the shadows of musicians setting up, moaning about the power's being out.

Where Jimmy with that generator?

He comin' mon, he comin'.

There was a buffet along one wall and a bar along the other. The Thorssens went to the buffet. We got drinks. Everyone but Lady Caroline and I had rum with soft drinks, ice brought from the hotel. She, being English, wanted whiskey with plain water, and I joined her to be polite. Then we went to the buffet and ate conch fritters and bits of lobster in hot sauce off paper plates, standing. A gas engine kicked in somewhere behind the building, lights came wavering on, and a guitar started tuning. The drummer bashed at his kit, someone shouted testing, testing over a squealing microphone, and a general cheer went up. Next thing I knew it was Rock Around the Clock and Lady Caroline and I were miming a jitterbug with hands full of paper plates and whiskey glasses.

Well, you know, like that, for a couple of hours and several whiskeys with water. The highlight for me was *Yellow Bird,* danced on my toes while Her Ladyship found some way to snuggle down to roughly my level. She nibbled on my ear and licked my neck. I saw Jack, and one or two of the Brit volunteers, ask Elke to dance, but after a glance at her father she hung her head and shook it each time.

Anyway, later it was all slap and tickle in Lady Caroline's dark bedroom farther up the hill, quite lively and, as it turned out, rather warm and touching. Then a few hours later it was dawn, she moaned, my stomach ground itself up, and when I tried to kiss her goodbye, she whispered, No, sorry, no. Dreadful sickies, love.

Begone. You were wonderful, but begone.

So I dressed and went quietly. Halfway to the hotel I bent double with stomach cramps. Diarrhea in the hotel john, sweats right through my shirt. Down the dock to the boat, cramps again, diarrhea again, cold sweats, then hot, then shaking with cold. Wrapped freezing in the spinnaker.

You drank the water, Jack said, bending over me sometime later.

So did Her Ladyship, I croaked. She's sick, too.

You've got dysentery, Cap'n Bren.

How bad is that?

Several days at least, if we can get you some medicine. You might even die if we can't. Let me cable the owners for another couple of hundred, arrange for credit at the hotel and see Lady Caroline about some medicine. Okay?

He left.

Mid-morning of the next day I was burning inside, from the hellhole of my raw rectum through the fiery twistings of my abdomen to the clamped tongs across my soaked temples. I held myself motionless in the roll of blankets, closing my eyes to the claustrophobic bunk, withdrawing into the cocoon of glowing pain.

With a prolonged growl I shivered hysterically out of the blanket and ran, clutching my middle, to the head. On the seat I buzzed with sudden false relief that blinded me and warmed me and emptied me, of nothing but a little vile water.

Jack, who had been seated at the table writing, threw down his pen, jerked out of the settee and stepped forward, paused at the open door to the head, didn't look in.

Nothing personal, Brendan, but I just can't stand it.

Right. Get out of here.

I heard his footsteps headed aft and then up the companionway and then in the cockpit and then on the deck. I braced myself for the rocking when his jump would however gently shift the delicately balanced arrangement of organs which kept them from grinding. When that was over I opened my eyes, rose and pointlessly flushed out the empty fixture. Back in the main cabin I leaned my elbows on the table, thrust my buttocks into what little cool air flowed down the central isle. Stared at my dirty hands, the grain in the varnished mahogany tabletop. Here's what Harper's great voyage of adventure has come down to: Sweat, shivers and shit.

I slid carefully off the settee, removed the towel from around my waist and used it to wipe my sweat from the table. I stood there testing the condition of my intestines; would it be the bunk first, or the head? The head, definitely. I scurried.

Hours later, sweating in my bunk, I heard the creaking of the ladder under Jack's feet, the tink as his watch struck the housing of the stove. I opened my eyes and saw Jack's face, heard his breath.

I'm awake, I told him.

Saw that auditor from Barclay's Bank up at the hotel. The cable's in at Turks.

Fantastic. How do we get it?

Don't know. It's in your name. You'll have to get over there somehow. There's a plane day after tomorrow, if you can make it.

Lady Caroline and the medicine?

She's got it, but she's still down herself.

Maybe I'll be better tomorrow.

The next day offered no change. I sweated and shivered, couldn't eat, drank water with fear in my heart. Our tank was almost empty, the pump sucking nothing but air when she rolled the least bit to starboard. Toward evening I couldn't get up at all, just lay there. Jack stayed the hell away, and I couldn't blame him. I drifted into fever-visions, stuff from childhood, snakes, huge waves, that sort of thing. A thin white line cutting the blackness, tilted just off the horizontal, and the silhouette of a ship, an old-time pirate ship made of the same white, fell down that line toward me, accelerating, then exploding into blinding white. Over and over again.

It was while the white line was re-forming for the umpteenth time that I woke to feel cool water on my brow, a hand on my shoulder.

Mommy, I croaked, the pirate ship keeps falling on me.

Poor old Bren, you are rather a mess, aren't you?

It wasn't my mother's voice, but Lady Caroline's. She sponged me in water she'd brought down from the hotel, rolled me out of the filthy blanket and onto the other bunk, then held my head up and gave me the little white pills. Forced me to drink more water, then even more. Then she took off her shirt and bra and lay down and held me, whispering.

You'll be all right soon, very soon, rest and you'll soon be all right, poor dear boy.

She was still there in the morning, standing at the stove boiling eggs and frying bread, wearing nothing but her cut-off jeans. She'd lost some weight from her own bout with the amoeba and looked the better for it. Hadn't lost anything in the chest.

She made me take more of the pills, then served the food, just water to drink. I was able to sit and I was ravenous. She ate a few bites with me. Jack came aboard, spoke to Her Ladyship first, not even raising an eyebrow to her topless costume.

The jeep leaves for the airstrip in half an hour. Can he go?

Crikey! she squealed, of *course* not. He nearly *died*.

I've got to, I said.

I stood up, took two steps and passed into profound blackness.

I woke in my bunk to the noise of big diesels, their stink and the smell of fish. I lay there wondering what that was all about, wondering how I had got there, naked but for a clean towel draped over me, and wondering how in the world the men who had built *Femme Fatale* had learned to fit the varnished teak and mahogany overhead so perfectly. I shrugged off the last, figured out the second, and had no idea about the first. No one else was aboard. I realized I was neither sweating nor shivering, and that I had no need to go to the head. Wonderful. But why that damned noise? Those awful smells?

I stood, grasped the table, headed aft, still a little shaky, and peered out through the companionway. The noise and the smells were from *Lazy Drummer*. She was surrounded by local fishermen loading her with packages of fresh lobster. The noise came from her engine and her main generator, powering her freezers. She'd be leaving soon.

I closed the hatch and latched the louvered panels. That cut down the noise a little, though it did nothing for the smell.

On the table I found a note from Jack telling me that he'd borrowed my wallet and intended to impersonate me at the bank on Turks. There were several practice runs of my signature after the note, and a postscript from Her Ladyship: I was to take two more pills on waking, with as much water as I could drink from the jug in the sink. The pills were folded into a tissue next to the note. A kiss was impressed on the paper with heavy red lipstick. I did what I was told, opened and ate a can of tuna as I slugged down a quart of water after the pills. Had a cigarette and a swallow of rum. Went back to bed.

Jack didn't come back that evening, nor did Her Ladyship reappear. I lit the kerosene lamp and flipped through an old copy of *Yachting*. *Drummer*'s diesels ran all night, or at least the generator did, making me dream of motoring through a Venice- or Lauderdale-like canal, a narrow, straight waterway with houses and lawns on either side, still water beneath, no way to get lost or damaged. Sunshine, land birds in the trees, a faint cool autumn breeze. That sort of thing.

In the morning I saw that the Thorssen boys were preparing *Drummer's* lines for warping off. I went up onto the dock, took their aft spring, stood ready to hand it aboard once they had her turned.

Whither bound? I asked.

Puerto Plata, Thorssen hollered.

Bon voyage.

Then she was off, Thorssen at the helm, the younger boy coiling lines on the foredeck, the elder in the cockpit taking up the spring I'd passed him. Elke bent to take in the last of the fenders, stood a moment to look at me.

Tell Jack goodbye, she mouthed, or perhaps said; no way to know which over the hammering of the diesel. I nodded to her and waved, and watched for the ten minutes it took *Drummer* to round the point, then the five more minutes it took for the tops of her masts to disappear behind Long Cay. Then I went back aboard *Femme Fatale* and poured a rum and drank it and smoked a Rothmans and missed Elke, even though she wasn't my girl but Jack's.

Jack showed up in the evening, making a grand entrance. A small, gaff-rigged native sloop rounded the point, slipped by the end of the dock at some three or four knots, just close enough for Jack to step nimbly off, turn, shout his thanks and wave. He walked slowly down the dock, eyes scanning the banks. When he stepped aboard his face was grim.

This morning, about ten, I told him. Bound for Puerto Plata, north coast of the Dominican Republic.

He grunted.

She asked me to tell you goodbye.

He grunted again. After a moment asked, Was that all?

Yes. Sorry. They were already underway.

He went below, washed and changed clothes, came back up to the cockpit with a rum in hand, neat. I hadn't gone up for ice. Handed me my wallet.

Hope you don't mind, he said. Came off without a hitch.

How much did we get?

Two hundred American.

That'll do. Dinner in the hotel, then.

Over drinks he told me how he'd traveled, the jeep to the airstrip, the plane to Turks, where the pilot waited for him to get the cash before taking off so he could pay his fare. There was no plane back, so he wandered the docks until he found the little sloop, whose captain accepted five dollars for his passage to South Caicos.

Great guys, those, he mused. Fine sailors. No engine, coral rock for ballast. Smelly old thing, of course, and none too clean, but really rather fast. We timed a chip off the bow once or twice and it came up seven knots each time.

An old preacher stopped me on the dock as we were returning from dinner. He was selling Haitian woodwork for the new Baptist church. I gave him a dollar, not really looking at the wares.

Maybe this be best for you, the old man said, and gave me a hardwood cane carved with a coiled snake.

Looking old, am I? I asked him, amused.

No. Big seas out there, mon. Maybe something going to get broken.

I peered at the serious, dignified face in the dark. His eyes came right through mine, into something beneath or beyond.

Thank you, Reverend, was all I could say.

In the morning we got the fuel truck to come down, paid off the hotel, cleared Customs. That took all but a few dollars of what we had. We were ready to go by noon, except that the water truck hadn't shown up. Jack tried to find it up in the village, but couldn't.

We could haul it down in jugs from the hotel, I suggested.

Sixty gallons? Fifteen trips each? Come on.

We pondered it over lunch on the terrace. I think I've got it, I said after a long silence. Her Ladyship's kindergarten class. Fifteen kids, two trips each, if we can find that many jugs. Give them a few bucks for candy.

So Jack went to the hotel kitchen in search of jugs, and I went up to the village in search of Lady Caroline. She had a school in the house next to her own, two classrooms, one for her kids and one for her roommates', who taught upper grades. I explained my idea. She asked the kids. They apparently took it as a lark. School was out at three. They'd be there.

By three we had the boat ready to go, engine cranked and burbling, the water tank intake open and mounted with a clean funnel. And here they came, fifteen little boys and girls, each with two one-gallon wine jugs full of water, followed by Lady Caroline and Jack, also two jugs each. Her Ladyship led them in a song, Heigh ho, heigh ho. I took each jug in turn and poured. It took quite a while. Jack brought the last two with lids on, stowed them below while I screwed down the cover on the intake. Then I stepped onto the dock, stood as tall as I could and faced Lady Caroline. Handed her five dollars for the kids and thanked her.

She looked me over, down her nose as it were, her mouth pursed. If only you were a head taller and very rich, she said.

How I wish I were. Next life, perhaps.

I wanted to embrace her, but she turned and bent to one of the children, whispering, and when she straightened she said Good sailing, and then Jack had the boat on nothing but the aft spring line so I stepped aboard and put her over hard to port and backed her bow out on the spring and called Jack aboard with the line and throttled forward, Lady Caroline and her fifteen charges waving farewell, and we were truly off to sea at last.

Turks Island Passage

We motored out through the gap, the sun low and diffused by a rain squall well to the west. The light went oddly mysterious, deep red and golden on the varnish and the teak, a green sheath over a profound black reaching down into the sea. By the time we had the main up and were ready to bear off to fill, the sun had dropped below the squall and even Long Cay, so I slipped below and switched on the running lights and the masthead. Jack was ready with the jib by then, so I throttled back, drove her off a touch more, sheeted home.

Very strange, the light, uneasy, portentous. The sails glowed in it, Jack's khaki shirt read pink, nothing was the right color. I switched on the binnacle lamp, vaguely hoping it would help with the odd light, though it wasn't needed quite yet. The brass of the winches and cleats gleamed red, the lines of manila cordage were green or blue depending on the depth of the shadows in which they lay. Jack's tanned hands were a ghostly white as he trimmed and coiled.

The problem of the light soon took care of itself by going to full dark, its portent left un-read. Then there was just the faint glow of the binnacle lamp, the steaming light bouncing off the headsail, the occasional flash of red or green as the running lights forward lit up a splash of spray. A little cloud of exhaust now and then illuminated by the stern light. A yellow glow from the galley as Jack heated up something we'd call dinner.

You learn to steer at night by the sounds of the boat and the wind and the sea, coming to depend on the volume and tempo of a leech fluttering or a halyard frapping, the tone and frequency of blocks and timbers creaking, cordage stretching and contracting, the particular rhythm of the seas bumping the forefoot going to weather or lifting her quarter when you're off the wind. The sound goes with the movement like music with the dance. Under sail, especially at night, this ancient anthem linking sail and sea is intact and glitters in the silver of wave tops and endless starlight.

The engine noise broke that link, disrupted the orchestration, forced it off-key. So when Jack was finished cooking I got him to shut the engine down and turn off all but the running lights and the masthead and binnacle before bringing up dinner. I trimmed her for the change in her motion that caused, and then we ate, plates balanced on our knees, coffee cups tucked into lee corners of the cockpit. I don't remember what we ate but the atmosphere was perfect, with the faint, planet-like presence of the masthead light and the excellent dinner music in the rigging.

Jack, however, was concerned. We'll have enough juice to crank up tomorrow, won't we?

We'll run it for half an hour when we change watches, okay? We'll know then if there's anything wrong. Want me to take the first one?

Sure.

Off Sand Cay

There were stars and planets moving westward on a blue-black velvet sky, and I listened to them. The breeze had fallen to a whisper. For the next hour, or two if I could stay awake that long, there was nothing to do but watch and steer by the compass and keep my mind away from all forms of regret. Watching and steering were easy.

By three in the morning I was fading, having a

hard time with my eyes. I tied down the tiller and went below and lit the kerosene lantern and found Jack in the starboard lower bunk in the main cabin. He lay facing aft on his back, arrow-straight, with his feet together and his arms folded across his chest, like the effigy of a knight on his stone tomb. I stood a yard short of the foot of the bunk and called his name. He opened his eyes, wide, as if shocked.

Good morning, I said, as softly as I could.

Right. Good morning.

He went to the galley and ran some water from the sink, just enough to wet his face. Then without saying anything more he went up to the helm. I started the stove and rigged the percolator and smeared jam on bread. While the pot was heating I logged course and speed and plotted a dead-reckoned position in faint pencil on the chart. Then, not having decided what to do, I went up and felt the air. The wind had dropped even more, bare zephyrs. I went below and found the coffee perked, turned off the stove and poured and served. We sat in the cockpit and sipped and munched and felt the boat drifting and rocking and going nowhere in no wind with the main, belly empty, lazily banging port to starboard, starboard to port.

I guess we should crank up, I muttered.

I turned the key, punched the starter. It groaned a few times, but clearly had no intention of starting.

So it's back to this, Jack said.

Except that the headstay fitting is still okay.

So what do we do?

Sail to St. Thomas, I guess. Or go back to Caicos, but damn, I dread that. I just don't think I can do that.

No, I can't either.

What are you steering?

South, more or less.

I shined the flashlight over what we had for a wake.

Maybe a knot, I told him. Her bottom's thick with grass despite all our scraping at Clarence Town and Inagua.

Damn.

It can't stay this way forever. You know that.

Not forever.

To hell with it. I don't care if the noisy stinking thing won't crank. To hell with it.

I sixed my coffee, went below and lit us cigarettes and took a slug of rum straight out of the bottle. Then I handed Jack up his smoke and blew out the lantern and sat at the chart table and smoked and worried about the electrics and the weather until my smoke was gone. Then forward and into the cocoon of the spinnaker and a little more worry and then a brief dream, just an image really, of Elke dressed as a medieval lady, walking on a green hill with a knight to either side, the three laughing and chatting, old friends. Jack was one of the knights. I suppose I was the other.

Off the Haitian Coast

I woke that time to early daylight and slow rolling motion and the sound of the sails thumping empty. I looked out the companionway to see Jack staring glassily at the compass, arm draped limply over the tiller. He looked at me. We shrugged.

Sea and sky were empty of all but blue and white-gold around the morning sun. I tried cranking the engine. It couldn't even manage a full turn.

That's that, then, Jack said.

His face was harsh with it and as empty as the sea and sky. When he went below I sat in whatever shade the sails provided, waiting for a breeze.

At about three in the afternoon a few zephyrs pulled themselves together a little south of east, giving us two or three knots on a decent course. Half an hour later there was a smudge of faint gray dead ahead, and by four it became the top of a mountain.

In sight of that mountain we lay in calms or chased zephyrs for the next two days. The land rose a thousand fathoms above, the sea some two thousand below. It felt like being suspended between the planet and the sky and seemed that if only the boat were lighter it would rise in the heavy air and float on that rather than on the water.

We were nearing the edge of the time zone, so it was twilight before six o'clock and dark not long thereafter. We could see the lights of Puerto Plata dead ahead by the time we finished dinner.

I've heard a lot of bad stuff about Puerto Plata, I told him. Sadistic cops, prisons, bribes required, arbitrary Customs fees, all that. We've got what, eight bucks between us?

Seven. He stared at the compass.

I know she's in there, Jack. I know how it feels. . .

You don't, he snapped.

And we're low on cigarettes. . .

That doesn't matter. We can't go in. I know that. You know that. Let's just get on with it.

I tried to think of something comforting to say and

couldn't. I worked on it for nearly a minute. No go.

Okay, I said, we'll go in.

I walked forward on the weather side, looped an elbow through that buggered port upper shroud and closed my eyes until the lantern light was out of them. There was little wind on the surface, but at the level of the mountaintops small clouds were racing, wispy shadows in the starlight, streaming toward the land. Weather was on the way, certainly.

So we put her over onto starboard tack. I went to my bunk for a couple of hours of uneasy sleep.

The breeze was sweet when I got up, the old bucket had a small bone in her teeth and chewed on it like a proud puppy. Her rig was humming as she made three or four knots. It felt like real sailing after all that calm. Jack figured we'd done an average of three knots toward the northeast over his two hours at the tiller. Nice.

It stayed like that through my watch except that the course steadily deteriorated as the wind shifted northward, so that by dawn I was back down to north by east. The wind picked up as it shifted. By eight or so it was blowing eighteen to twenty and the seas were up to four feet and close together. She wanted a reef, maybe even the smaller jib, but I was too weary to do it and Jack was tired too. I let it go like that for an hour or so, then hollered Jack up so we could reef the main.

That done, we traded off and I went below. At one point I crawled into the narrow compartment forward to look at the underside of the iron through-bolts. They seemed to be holding all right, though were thick with rust even under the grease on them. I went back up and told Jack about them. He nodded with no expression, his eye alternately on the sails and the compass.

How are you holding up? I asked him, dreading the answer.

Great! he shouted, and grinned. Is this not just great sailing?

On that surprising and delightful note I headed for my bunk, feeling as light and fragile as an autumn leaf, as brown and withered.

But in the sea and the gusty breeze the old sloop had begun working, loosening her joints and fittings so that she had been given voices. There was an anguished donkey staked out by the mast, mice skittering in the deck beams. I was worried about the donkey. I got up to examine the blocks of teak forming the mast step. I saw no evidence of its shifting, nor of any donkey suffering thirst or loneliness. I kept hearing what seemed to be humans somewhere in her bowels, speaking at random through the drains. I returned to my bunk wondering what they were trying to tell me, wishing they would either speak distinctly or shut up.

I'm sorry, I can't understand you, I told them. I'll try again later, but now I must sleep.

There were a few muffled protests from the galley sink I just ignored.

Off Puerto Plata

Night time, my next watch. The sloop was plodding along under jib and reefed main at some three or four knots in the lulls, five or so in the gusts. The seas were up and all the tacking and the reefing and the lack of a solid block of sleep had together imposed a burden of exhaustion I couldn't continue to ignore.

The barometer had to be falling; I had that familiar sense of apprehension and dread that accompanied a drop in pressure. I thought I saw lights occasionally in the corners of my eyes, but when I scanned for them there was nothing. I huddled again, rested my head again, rested my eyes again, just for a moment.

A massive cloud structure was building up, a big sea and a strong wind sure to come with it. In the periodic squalls it got over twenty-five knots, some bigger gusts. Just steering was getting tough. I put the kettle on the lighted burner and went forward to Jack's bunk, spoke his name and touched him lightly on the shoulder.

Sorry to wake you. Kettle's on.

I went back to the galley, turned off the burner, poured hot water over powdered cocoa in the cups and stirred. We'd run out of coffee. Jack rolled slowly out of the bunk, put on a tee shirt and shoes. How's the weather?

About the same, I told him, or maybe easing off a little.

Go to bed.

Yeah. Hey Jack, do the drains talk to you?

Yeah. And there's a donkey suffering in there somewhere.

Scares hell out of me sometimes.

Go to bed.

I made my note in the log and then did just that.

The next morning I saw a sail in close, heading east from where I thought Puerto Plata to be. I watched it for some time. We had a steady eighteen to twenty knots of wind and a biggish sea running, but it was clear and we were doing fairly well on port tack, close to southeast. I was able to see only the top half of the sail on the crests, and I'd lose that in the troughs. Several miles away, but I expected her to be closing faster if she were on starboard and making a course ninety degrees from ours. If she were on port she'd have to tack offshore sometime.

But after an hour of gaining on her very little and seeing her bearing as increasingly off to the east, it was clear that she either had an angle of breeze we didn't or she was motoring. When Jack heaved himself into the cockpit I pointed her out to him. Without a word he ducked back below, came up with the binoculars.

He watched her for a long time, standing with an arm crooked into the weather shrouds. That put him five or six feet higher than I stood at the helm. After ten or so minutes of that he came aft.

It's *Lazy Drummer,* he said, handing me the glasses and taking hold of the end of the tiller. I'm sure of it.

So I went forward to look. If not *Drummer* it was a motorsailer much like her. She was under reefed main alone and bucking hard into it, making something near to due east. I thought I could make out a human shape at the helm in the shadow of her deckhouse, but I couldn't be sure. Certainly no one on deck or in the cockpit. No Elke. I went aft.

You must be right, I told him. Either *Drummer* or her sister. She's plowing into it under power, the main just to steady her. She's headed right about east.

I thought she was going back to Caicos.

That's what they said. She isn't. At least not today.

He said they trade in the Virgins sometimes.

Yes. I remember.

Something caught my eye a moment later, another

vessel close in to shore. Lost it in a trough. Went forward again with the glasses.

It was a powerboat painted in a patchwork of colors, perhaps a Chris Craft, maybe thirty-five feet long, judging from the size of the two men on her foredeck. They were fussing with a tarpaulin, some kind of gear under it, having a tough time in the big sea. She would rise on a crest, slew every which way near the top, then show off her dirty bottom before slamming down into the trough. The skipper clearly was pushing her hard.

Once the foredeck crew had the cover off, I could see that it was a gun mounted there, a fifty caliber machine gun. I went aft and traded the binoculars for the helm.

They're manning it, Jack shouted. Cripes, they're bearing it onto us!

Come aft! Tack! Tack!

We tacked. A burst kicked up water all around us, the chattering report coming faint and later. I bore away, stern to her. We could hear the next burst whine over the masthead.

Tough shooting in this sea, Jack commented.

Yeah, but why shoot at us at all? They think we're the *Drummer*.

He stood and put the glasses back on her. She's turned. She's going after *Drummer*. Oh God . . .

We hardened on again, starboard tack now. Not that we could fight anyone, but maybe we could save someone after the fighting. Elke . . .

We could hear bursts of fire, see the casings flash in the sun as they flew. Then a wave broke just as it crested under the gunboat. She arched upward, bow aimed straight at the sky. Hovered there for a long moment, as if she meant to fly.

Then fell backward into the sea. Rolled once. Then one more time, showing her keel like the back of a whale.

One Dominican gunboat less, Jack said dryly.

Then he hustled forward and put the glasses on *Drummer*.

She's still going. Don't see any damage.

Thank God.

Lazy Drummer, found and for some reason driven out of Puerto Plata. So, even with neither of us saying it, the chase was on. Not that we could catch her, having to tack up while she was going almost straight into it with the engine. Still, the chase was on.

We sailed into a bit of a lift and I stuck with it as long as I dared, to where with the binoculars we could make out small buildings not far up from the beach. That had brought *Drummer* hull up, even from the cockpit. Tacking felt as if we were abandoning the game. But as we clawed offshore we sailed back into a better lay and at least didn't lose sight of her altogether.

Toward evening she was hull down, though, and I could see Jack's heart sink as the last scrap of sail went under the horizon. After dark we took a big header and tacked, and saw after half an hour or so what we took to be her masthead light. It bobbed around out there for another hour and then that was gone, too.

As I steered through the night I drifted along on the edge of sleep's coast, with the context of a dream always there when I crossed to that soft shore. But in the dream the machine gun stuttered and bullets tore the mainsail and it was us, not the gunboat that went down. In the morning I got out the binoculars and focused them on the mainsail. There were three holes in it up high.

None had hit a seam. Easy to fix when we got the chance.

From there on the passage was essentially uneventful. Big swells in the Mona Passage but long soft ones, the Trades filled back in at some twelve to fifteen knots, never swinging outside an arc between east and southeast. An unbelievably beautiful sunset, with Bach on the radio, a Dutch station hopping to us from Bon Aire. We lucked into a land breeze in the lee of Puerto Rico for a few hours. Dolphins, of course, bottlenoses frolicking in the swells. And oh, we saw a pod of pilot whales and had to dodge some shipping off San Juan. Five or so more days, as I recall, one of them Thanksgiving, with a dinner of our last canned creamed corn. Having run out of rum and especially cigarettes was hard for the first day or two, but being so tired and having nothing appetizing left aboard to eat, we simply desiccated, moved closer to the purely ethereal.

The Virgin Islands

The only fuss was near the end. Jack insisted we look in at Charlotte Amalie, St. John's, even the West End of Tortola and Christiansted, to look for *Lazy Drummer* before we went into the Lagoon. It took an extra day and a half at least. We sailed the edges of each of those ports, Charlotte Amalie by night. By the end of all that I was left a zombie. As I recall we ate nothing in that whole time. *Drummer* was nowhere to be found.

St. Thomas

We left *Femme Fatale* on a mooring, as clean as we could get her without running water. Packed our gear. I debated whether or not to take the cane I'd bought from the preacher on the dock in South Caicos, then tucked it between the straps of my duffle. Got a lift in with an old couple in an outboard dinghy. Their little cutter was waiting for engine parts. No talking past that, with the buzz of the engine and the exhaustion. Still, as I looked back at *Femme Fatale* lying in the Lagoon where I'd been charged to leave her, I felt a considerable sense of accomplishment. It had not been an easy passage, had it?

We'd been smelling land for days, of course, the first, sweet, loamy scent of it off Puerto Rico, the flinty, rocky smells of the west end of St. Thomas, the scent of tropical flowers in the harbor of St. John's. Filled you with longing for something you knew you didn't want. Clambering onto the dock there at the Lagoon it was the sharp-edged brown smell of creosote and then the metallic of anti-fouling paint and the ozone of the mechanic's shop, gasoline and diesel and solvents, all harsh on the nostrils and pressing on the temples, making everything somehow too bright. The un-giving solidity of earth underfoot disconcerted the body still bracing itself for the movement and liveliness of the boat and the sea.

We found the office at the yard, with a young, big, blond guy in tee shirt and dirty khakis behind a desk. I explained who we were, told him about *Femme Fatale*. He called Customs for us, cleared her over the phone. Then I described all her problems. He agreed to haul her, check out her electrics, do something about the key and the stuffing box, the iron bolts in her headstay fitting, the jury-rigged shroud. I called the owner, told him we were in, what I'd arranged with the yard. He told me to go the Hotel 1829; he'd arrange credit and send a money order.

No one was going to drive to Charlotte Amalie that day, but an old diesel fishing boat was leaving and would take us. We grabbed our duffels, helped the lean, weathered fisherman with his lines and puttered off in the stink toward the big city.

Not far from Buck and Capella Islands we saw her, *Lazy Drummer,* motoring east, almost within hail. Jack begged the fisherman at the helm to turn after her, even threatened.

No mon, not that boat. That one evil boat. We go Charlotte Amalie.

What do you mean, evil? I asked him.

I hear things. About shooting. Yelling and fighting.

When was this? I asked him. Where?

Early yesterday, mon. Near the Brasses. My chum inside, on the reef. He run for the Lagoon, mon. He say was two boats, then just that one, running down the nor'west.

Jack went stiff and walked aft watching *Drummer* recede, standing at attention with clenched fists. I dug the binoculars out of my duffel, put them on her, saw Thorssen and one of the boys. She had a cluster of holes near her tumblehome aft, and some odd, dark stains on her port rail. I handed the glasses to Jack.

Look at her quarter, I told him.

He looked for a while, focusing.

Buckshot. And that's blood on the rail.

Could be fish, I offered.

Sure.

Could be the other way around, that she was attacked.

Sure.

He handed me the glasses, then slumped down to half-sit on the gunwale. I've got to get her off that boat. Away from that fat bastard.

I know. I just don't know how.

Where do you think she's headed?

Maybe St. John's. It's mostly private, I think. They'll have to clean her up before they go anywhere very public.

Charlotte Amalie

We got to the Hotel 1829 in rotten shape and dead broke, having given the fisherman a five and spent the other two dollars on the short taxi ride. It's a lovely place, up fairly high and overlooking the harbor, old coquina rock, wrought iron gates overgrown with vines leading to a shaded central courtyard. The bar was dim and cool with ceiling fans. No one was in there. I yelled hello a couple of times, and a fellow in a chef's hat and apron appeared from what I suppose was the kitchen, on the other side of the courtyard.

He had a pleasant face, dark hair and a big, black moustache, which split as he smiled.

Captain Harper, I presume, he said, in a slight German accent. I'm Theodore Kussnacht. Welcome to St. Thomas.

At which point I knew we would be all right for money. We were led to our room, again cool, with a ceiling fan. He asked us to go easy on the water in the shower, and we took turns trying to do that, with little success. Back down in the bar in relatively clean shore clothes we drank a beer with Kussnacht, who gave us the wire from the owner and directions to the bank where our money was waiting. I would have been happy to sit where I was, drinking beer until cocktail hour, then switching to martinis, then having a leisurely dinner, a brandy and a night and another day of sleep. Jack was not about to let that happen, however, so we were out again into the heat and down the hill toward the bank before the beer had gone from cold to cool.

He wanted to be paid off right there in the bank's lobby. There was plenty of money. I laid out the amount the yardman had said it would cost to haul *Femme* and then split the rest with him even.

So now what? I asked him.

I'll poke around, see if I can find a boat to follow them.

Okay. Then what?

I'll find them. I'll get her off. I'll get her away.

I had a moment's grace, didn't ask him how.

Okay. I'm going back to the hotel and the bar and dinner and sleep. Join me when you're ready.

He looked at me sharply, that cragged face showing something, hurt, disappointment, maybe the sudden understanding that I wasn't one of his grunts. He nodded, turned on a heel and left. I watched his military gait, squared shoulders and straight back, until he turned a cobblestoned corner toward the harbor and was gone. She's your girl, I silently told his back. It's your quest, your prize. Maybe I'll help, but you can't just assume I will.

Made me feel a traitor just to think it.

So I found a cab and rode back up to the hotel. I thought I'd spend the rest of the afternoon drinking, but I went to the room first, wanting to stash the boat money and enough for a plane fare back to Miami. I didn't think I could actually spend that much in an evening, but who knew? I did that, saw the bed, undressed and fell into it and was gone.

It was a few hours later when Jack woke me. I rolled out bracing myself for the pitch and roll that didn't come.

Have you eaten? he asked me.

I told him I hadn't, and asked the time. It was almost eight, still time for dinner. He hadn't eaten either. He said he'd go down to the bar, reserve a table, meet me there.

I took another short shower, pulled myself together and went down. The place wasn't crowded but there were people there, some in coat and tie, some even scruffier than we. A couple of pretty girls in pedal pushers and heels, a couple of Coast Guard officers in short-sleeved whites. We had martinis, got called to a table and ate fillet mignon with the best Béarnaise I've ever tasted. Kussnacht was, of course, Swiss.

Through all this Jack seemed unusually quiet. I realized it was due mainly to the presence of the Coast Guard. Not one word through dinner about his plan to find *Lazy Drummer* and rescue Elke, nothing at all on the subject until we took a pair of H. Upmanns out onto the veranda on the second floor adjacent to our room, settled ourselves into a pair of rockers and lit up.

There's a guy with a seaplane, does tours. He'll take me in the morning. You really think they were going to St. John's?

That direction. They'd have to go somewhere to hide, clean up. Of course, beyond there are all those British, French and Dutch Islands, St. Martin, Anguilla. I've never been to them, so I can't say.

Mind if I take the large-scale chart and your binoculars?

Help yourself. If you find them, what?

I don't know. I probably won't be able to get her off with the plane. Maybe I'll try to join on. It'll have to be by ear.

A huge cruise ship made her way into the harbor below us, lit up like a floating city. What a way to do the trip, eh? She docked around the curve to the left, smooth as fresh varnish.

When the cigars were stubs Jack got up and headed for bed. I stayed for a while. I considered returning to the bar to see what was what with the two girls in their pedal pushers, but I drifted off, and when I woke up a while later, the world was silent but for the Trades whispering in palm fronds. The cruise ship was darkened, the hotel asleep. I went in and undressed and got into my bunk and tossed and turned for a full twenty seconds before sleeping. When I woke in the morning, Jack, his kit, the chart and my binoculars were gone.

St. Thomas

I took the next day easy, bought a fresh shirt and a copy of *Lord Jim*, read till late afternoon. Took a cab out to the Lagoon to run some clothes through the laundromat there and get an idea of what was being done to *Femme Fatale*. She was just coming up the railway when I arrived. I saw they'd propped her nicely and that the donkey engine on the winch was very slow indeed, so I stuffed the washer with my stinking wardrobe and dug back into Conrad. Felt like Marlow, trapped forever in his endless skein of quotes upon semi-quotes.

When she was up and chocked I went over to look. She seemed to sag, bedraggled and fat, grass three and four feet long drooping from her keel. The prop looked all right through the barnacles. They rigged a ladder up to her rail. The yard boss and I went up together. I showed him the stuffing box and the shaft key and the iron bolts in the headstay fitting, pointed out the broken shroud. He said it wasn't too bad except for the key. Using iron in there had chewed up the coupling. Might be fixed, might have to be replaced. I gave him money, got a receipt.

When I got back to the hotel in the evening, there was no Jack and no message from him. I called *Femme Fatale's* owner, told him what the yardman had said, asked him if he wanted me to stay. He said he didn't, I was discharged with thanks. I counted money. I could stay another day at most. I called the airlines.

aboard *Adagio*
Ft. Lauderdale

I flew back from St. Thomas, having left a letter for Jack telling him a couple of places in Ft. Lauderdale where he might find me. Flying back was the damnedest thing. You see everything, everywhere you've been. The glittering Silver Banks, the green of Hispaniola, Turks and the Caicos like amber beads set in emerald satin. In just a few short hours you cover in reverse the whole story of that long beat to weather, which for us had taken weeks and weeks. The flight is a synopsis written backwards. Strange experience, almost making a joke of it, mocking what had theretofore seemed a significant accomplishment.

The plane put me down in Miami, I caught a Greyhound up to Lauderdale and called an old sailing chum, Stan Mallory, who had a yacht delivery and maintenance service. He put me up for the night and then called around in the morning to find me a boat. By noon I was working again, helping to refit a big ketch-rigged motorsailer, *Adagio,* ostensibly for charter in the Bahamas. I could live aboard. I would see that she stayed safe and happy while varnishing the brightwork and spars, replacing some running rigging. Ho hum, but it would do for a while. She was in that yard near the mouth of the river, can't remember the name. I think it's gone now, the real estate got too valuable.

I worked on her alone for the first week or so, the yard boss checking in now and then. Stan sent a kid to help on Saturdays. Slow business, but I taught him how to sand the railings so he'd have something to do on deck once he'd hauled me up a mast. It was a huge project; the deckhouse would be needing a new coat way before I'd finished with the spars. Not a really pleasant berth, either, the noise and stink from the yard a constant from early morning to sunset. After about two months of that, with little time to try to find a boat that was actually going anywhere, I was fairly disgusted with it and not very happy.

A Sunday evening —I remember because the day had been quiet— a while after sunset on a hard day of it alone, I saw a figure I thought I knew making its way through the yard mess to the docks. There wasn't quite light enough to see his features at that distance, but the posture, the movement, was familiar. He came out my dock, saw me sitting on the box aft of the deckhouse, and waved. He was toting a small duffel.

Found you, then, he said.

So you have, Jack.

Had to return your chart and binoculars.

Come aboard.

It was early in January so there was no need for screens and cool enough to want to be inside after dark. We went below, I to cook and he to bathe and change.

I lit the cabin lamps, their light soft and warm on the mahogany and teak. Jack came aft from the head. I could see that the clothes he wore were clean, but torn and stained. Even in that light his face was pale and emaciated and badly bruised around the left cheek. There was a bandage taped to the back of his head. When he sat on the starboard settee where he could turn and face me as I galley-puttered, he used both arms to lower himself, and grunted.

Mallory told you where to find me? I asked.

Yes. Gave me a lift to the bridge.

Fly back?

Yes. Out of Turks and then Nassau.

Turks?

Yes. Got a smoke?

I pulled out my Luckies and then dug for ice, chipped, poured rums. I went on cooking, though I was curious unto distraction. I don't remember what I cooked; seaman's fare of some kind. We sat to eat, the food smelling good, I do remember that, the meal served on plates and silverware monogrammed with the burgee of the Watch Hill Yacht Club. We stuck with rum to drink.

Jack offered to do the washing up but I could see that he was dead beat, barely able to rise. I cleared away, ran water on the mess in the sink, then hacked up another bowlful of ice and brought that and the bottle to the table. Topped off both our glasses.

You know you've got to tell me, Jack.

He nodded to acknowledge that he did, leaned back into the cushions and, wincing, got his legs up onto the settee. Sipped. Smoked. Then he started.

The seaplane buzzed the Brasses, dipped looking for wreckage. Something maybe, dark over the reef. Then east to St. John's, then the West End on Tortola, Norman and Peter Island, Road Town, Virgin Gorda, any of the little ones between where she might have tucked in. He glassed every boat he saw that had a sail up or any sort of tall masts, docked or anchored or underway. They went out over Anegada Reef and that was where they found her, anchored up under the lee of the island, no other boats nearby.

Through the binoculars he could see Thorssen in the dinghy aft to port, working on the shotgun damage. One of the boys was ashore, couldn't see what he was doing. He said his heart broke when he saw Elke peer out from under the wheelhouse, shielding her eyes against the sun, looking at the plane. He almost asked the pilot to put her down on the banks, but thought better of it. Instead he signed him to turn around, head back, no hope to get her off with the seaplane in that chop and no way to trust the pilot if it came to that.

He got off the plane in Spanish Town on Virgin Gorda and hiked the six or seven hard miles to the top of Virgin Peak. There he camped, glassing the sea for hours, hoping she'd come back westward. He watched through the night, but saw no lights at sea other than some big shipping out in the Atlantic. The next afternoon, wet and tired and hungry, he made his way back to the village.

He looked, but as the pilot had warned him, there wasn't much going on in Spanish Town. He couldn't get a boat to take him out to Anegada. Instead he got a lift on a native sloop back to Road Town, hired onto a sports fisherman there as a general flunky, serving drinks and baiting hooks. They fished the reef once or twice, often in clear sight of Anegada, the island itself, but he never saw *Lazy Drummer* or anything like her.

After two weeks of that he figured she was lost, he'd have to find her by plane again. To do that, he'd have to make more money than he could on the boat, so he took an inter-island ferry back to St. Thomas. There he started with the 1829 (where, incidentally, he collected my letter), asking for a job as a bartender. Kussnacht didn't have enough clientele to warrant hiring him, sent him over to Bluebeard's Castle, with a kindly and unearned reference. He got the job.

He rented a cheap room up the hill that had a good view of most of the harbor. He slept little, spending his mornings walking the docks, taking a cab out to the Lagoon, to the various other little coves where *Drummer* might settle herself. He'd ask about her everywhere. Have you seen a sixty-five foot Dutch motorsailer with huge freezers in the cockpit, a fat Dane and his three kids on it? One skipper, of a small, filthy craft not much more than a self-powered barge for hauling diesel fuel to the smaller islands, thought maybe he'd seen a boat like that south of Vieques, maybe headed for Christiansted. His heart leapt when he met an old man on a lovely Herreshoff New York 40, who said he had met Thorssen and seen the boat two weeks before, in San Juan.

Odd duck, but charming enough, the old fellow told him. Kept the girl out of sight most of the time. Said they were leaking from the centerboard trunk.

Which news elated and upset him at once. He was glad she was that close, but worried the old bucket would sink and drown her. He flew the next morning to San Juan, searched the docks. He found a girl selling plantains and avocados and mangoes from a cart who knew a little English and told him they'd been loading with so much fruit there was nothing left that day for herself to sell. How long ago was that? She counted out eight of her fingers. Did they say where they were going? She shook her head. Jack thanked her, bought a mango.

So you figured that because of the fruit they were headed back to the Caicos? I asked.

That's what I guessed. There or just over to St. Thomas, but I'd been watching closely all that week. I'm sure I would have known.

He banged on the ice a bit, plunked a chunk in his glass, poured rum over it.

All that time it was as if I wasn't I at all, you know? It was a kind of limbo. I watched my life, saw it becoming nothing but that of a bartender obsessed with a girl, a lost girl at that. A cracked bartender in a luxury hotel who spent all his off hours wandering around the docks, asking sailors and fruit vendors the same question over and over. A sad, crazy time, for sure.

He continued his visits to the docks, no longer searching for *Lazy Drummer* but now to find a boat to Caicos. Meanwhile, he was doing fairly well at bartending, a falsely cheery soul who could make mixing a martini appear to be a feat possible only for a magician. Smiles, jokes, big tips. His other life: it irked him.

One night a group of five people came in, two of them very attractive women, one in her mid-twenties, the other about thirty. The younger one had boyishly short dark hair, a narrow face with strong cheekbones, very slim. The other was taller and on the voluptuous side, short blonde hair, though not as extreme a cut as the dark one. Of the three men, one appeared to be in his fifties, bulky and bald with a gray fringe, wearing sunglasses and a silk blazer slung across his shoulders. He and another, who looked like a sailor, hard and brown, thirties, medium sized, listened listlessly to the exuberant lecturing of a short, dark, wiry guy, whose English was strongly accented. The two women spoke quietly to each other in French.

They took a table near the end of the bar. Jack listened in when he could, the first interesting people ever to come into the place. As it happened Jack had good French, even if it had failed him with the Haitians at Inagua. I had only fractured Cuban Spanish, from two years in high school and too much time in bars in Tampa and Key West.

He couldn't get all of it, of course, hustling up and down the bar, dancing for tips, he called it. There was talk between the women about movies. The sailor-type was silent, just nodded occasionally, agreeing with the little fellow, now clearly also French. The older guy spoke occasionally in French, with, Jack thought, an Italian accent, though he couldn't be sure.

The short guy was talking about diving.

After a few rounds — the little guy wasn't drinking, just soda and lime — they went in to dinner. Ordered red wine for the table. Jack hoped one or more of them would return to the bar when they'd finished, but none of them did. At closing he checked their bill to see if they had charged it to a room. They hadn't.

He spotted the two women in town next morning on his way down from his place up the hill. They were shopping casually in the cobblestoned market square, wearing straw hats, light summer dresses, sandals, sunglasses. He pretended to shop too, but there wasn't much shopping in Charlotte Amalie then. He went down to the docks, knowing there wasn't anywhere else for them to go.

A broad-beamed, eighty-odd foot schooner he hadn't seen the day before lay docked out near the end, flying the tricolor. He strolled out, looked her over. Forward of the deckhouse air tanks were stacked in a row near a great wheeled pump and a generator and long, coiled black hoses. No one on deck, the hatches locked. He went aft to read her transom: *Plus Profond,* Cannes. The Deepest. He ambled back up to the seawall.

A wizened old fisherman he had come to know in his weeks of dock-questing sat cross-legged on the planks, his gnarled hands, more gray than the dense black of the rest of him, working with twine on a small net spread out over his knees. He chatted with the old man, asked about the fishing, what the net was for, offered him a cigarette. They smoked in silence for a while, the old fellow leaving the net alone to pay full attention to the smoke. After a while he followed Jack's gaze, fixed on the big dive boat.

She the one you be lookin' for? he asked.

No. Just interested. When did she come in? Jack asked him.

Yesterday late. Down from Martinique, I believe.

How many people aboard?

Seven, when she come in. But some kinda row. Two boys from down there, they get off, want to go back home.

Where are the rest of them?

I see all but the Cop'n, mon, they go up onto the hard. I think he go up real early like.

That's how he told it, doing the Biwi accent and all. Anyway, the opportunity was clear; she needed crew.

Finding the women again was easy, up in the market. Each now carried a big straw basket and extra straw hats. The baskets were filled with fruit. They walked toward the hotel, chatting in French. Jack followed. It was coming up on eleven in the morning.

He was dressed in his khakis, deck shoes, figured

he looked nautical enough. They went into the 1829, through the lobby to the dining room. The Maybe-Italian and the wiry Frenchman had a table and were waiting for them, dallying over coffee. Jack took a table near them, ordered coffee and croissants, listened. In French, the blonde said she wanted to take a room in the hotel, then in English asked the old guy if they could. He said nothing. The dark girl and the little guy sat, seeming embarrassed, fussing with their cups. The old guy finally said okay. Then the little guy changed the subject, brought them back to French.

Do you think the captain would be able to find good crew here? Such a problem, using native sailors from the islands. Never want to go anywhere.

That was, of course, Jack's cue. He apologized for breaking in, said he couldn't help overhearing that they needed crew. I guess his French was good enough, as they asked him to sit with them. He pulled his chair over and started pouring them charm instead of booze.

It worked, of course, I noted, chuckling.

He smiled sourly.

So you joined her. Whither bound?

Jacques, the little Frenchman, wanted to set a deep-dive record in the passage off Mona Island and have it filmed. Gian-Carlo, the older guy, a film producer, wanted to try some easier, prettier stuff first. He's the one with the money. We're out of ice.

So we are. A moment. What about the women?

Mimi, the little dark French one, Jacques's mistress and publicity agent. Fran, an American, Gian-Carlo's mistress and student filmmaker.

Oh. Like that, was it?

Mostly. Not entirely. Jacques really is a serious diver, one or two depth records. Otherwise, yes, amateur fun and games.

I poured cold water out of the bowl and chopped some ice back into it. Jack lit another smoke, groaned.

How bad are you hurt?

Couple of ribs. Not pissing blood.

Mimi? I asked. Fran?

Not like that. Elke. The Thorssen troika.

You found them!

Yeah, he said bitterly. And lost them again.

As it happened he hit it off okay with the skipper, a taciturn Yankee from Maine who had taken her over from the delivery crew in Martinique. They signed on two more guys, natives of St. Thomas, calypso musicians who hoped to make it eventually to the big-time in Nassau or Miami.

They went out to dive on the Anageda Reef first, but it was December and blowing the water into an opaque mess. The skipper was relieved to get the schooner out of there, away from the coral heads. Jack extolled the beauties of the Caicos Banks, the safety of Cockburn Harbour and the comforts of the Admiral's Arms. A piece of cake, downwind for two days, three at most. Great sailing he said they had, the wind steady and strong well south of east. Jack cooked and steered and invented fruity rum drinks. Piloted them into the cut. Laid mooring lines and fenders, secured her to the dock, leaving her transom a fathom clear of *Lazy Drummer's* stubby bowsprit.

Wind rattled a halyard on a boat nearby and

whined briefly in *Adagio*'s rigging. She shifted slightly, and I could feel her kiss her fenders. Jack sat in profile to me, the lamplight emphasizing the crags of hard cheekbones and iron set of thin lips. He stared at the barometer mounted on the bulkhead forward as if it would tell him something more than it was meant to.

Lost them *again!* he shouted, and shivered.

Then, quietly, Sorry. It's just . . . .

I said nothing, waited, staying still as a hunter in the bush. It took him a minute, maybe a bit more.

As they were docking Thorssen leapt around helping with the lines. Jack called out his name and smiled and chatted and made a big thing of an old friend. How have things been? How are the boys? Introduced him to everyone aboard *Plus Profond*. Kept his eyes from scanning for Elke. He didn't even see her for the next three days, as *Plus Profond* spent almost that time at anchor out on the Banks. He found it maddening, naturally. He didn't even know for sure she was aboard *Drummer* or on the island at all. He chafed as he charmed, worked the lines and the air pumps and the galley.

The Trades steadied in the southeast, the skies held cloudless and full of sun in the day, were canopied with stars after dark. Cool enough in the evening to want a jacket or sweater, hot enough in the day to swim and appreciate the cool of the gold-chased emerald water. The diving party spent hours with their snorkels and tanks and weights, Gian-Carlo with his cameras. Jacques so excited he never tired, enthusing volubly whenever there wasn't an air hose or snorkel in his mouth. The women wore French bikinis, which were still considered shocking in the States. He continually dreamed of seeing Elke in one.

He thought about trying to enlist the Yankee skipper somehow, to use him as an ally. He thought about warning him about Thorssen, the whiff of danger. But he held it all in, worried to distraction that *Drummer* would leave while he was stuck out on the Banks, often in sight of her spars, powerless to stop her.

Finally the women wanted freshwater showers and the men wanted fresh ice for their drinks. They had also perhaps begun to tire of lobster and grouper as the exclusive main courses, wonderful as they were. So they went back to the dock at the Admiral's Arms the afternoon of the third day, took two rooms in the hotel, and at last left Jack free to get on with his plan.

Jack poured rum over his ice. I could see him trying not to cough. I got up from the settee and went aft to the companionway, poked my head out to look at the weather. I could feel the wet in the wind. It would rain soon. I pulled the hatch shut.

So what was your plan? I asked, walking forward, glancing at the portholes and the lovely old-fashioned skylight, all closed.

He shifted head and eyes, clutched at sore ribs. Examined the tip of his Lucky.

To find Elke and talk to her alone, get some details as to how I could get her off and away. To keep glad-handing Thorssen, charm him into trusting me, taking me on. To enlist local help if needed, especially from Lady Caroline. That was as far ahead as I could think at the time.

Parts of it worked, more or less. *Lazy Drummer*'s main generator was funking out, so Thorssen had a gas-powered spare up on the dock and in pieces, trying to get it to go. Jack helped. In an hour they were able to hook it up to one of the freezers, shift the contents of the other into it, disconnect the main diesel and go to work on it. This got Jack aboard, though only into the engine room, never into the main cabin. While he was down there, tugging wrenches and nicking knuckles, he took in everything he could, electrics, belts, fuel lines, saltwater intake, cables running aft for the steering. He would know how to disable her in a hurry if it ever came to it.

Toward evening, with the gas generator growling away and stinking and the diesel spread out in pieces below, Thorssen said to leave it, and hollered forward that he wanted his dinner and that they'd have a guest. Elke answered. He'd heard her voice.

My heart, he said, clogged my throat with nothing but fear. What if she . . . .

But it was all right. Although all she could say when she saw him, bent as he was over buckets and washing up with Thorssen there beside him on the dock, was Mr. Morgan, without smiling, and all he could say was Hello, Elke, without smiling, he knew it was all right, from her eyes. The boys came back with the dinghy and their load of a half-dozen lobsters.

The four of them ate, plates on their knees in the cockpit, iced tea, no rum, no Elke. It was quickly over, with no conversation over the generator. Jack offered to help with the dishwashing, but Thorssen wouldn't have it. It was full night by then, and Thorssen yawned ostentatiously. Jack took the hint and his leave, shouting that he would go up to the bar for a nightcap.

He had a drink there, then took another outside onto the veranda, in sight of the dock and *Drummer*'s cockpit. He nursed the drink through two cigarettes, watching. Elke didn't appear.

After another quarter hour he left his glass and strolled through the little garden to the east and around the building, southeast along the rocky cliff, a place where they had met before. Nothing. It was too late to call on Lady Caroline, so he went back to the terrace, collected his glass and went back into the bar for one more.

He gave it up after that one, said goodnight to Gladys and the skipper of *Plus Profond,* headed down the walk toward the dock. The bougainvillea rustled and whispered in the Trades, the lights from the hotel shimmered in their leaves. He thought he heard his name in the whispering. He stopped.

Then she was there, wrapped in his arms, pulling him down among the dark plantings. They huddled together, twisting into an invisible shadow, he on his back on the sharp shale of old coral, she on his chest, whispering, whispering.

Whispering terrible things.

Jack lit a smoke and took a deep drag and a long swallow of rum as preamble.

In Puerto Plata they gave her to the Customs officers as a bribe, who used her in turn as long as *Drummer* was in port. At places like St. John's they dressed her like Monroe or Mansfield and paraded her, drawing in the crews of yachts without women aboard. Then, when they knew which boats were going where and when and with how many aboard and how well armed, they would rendezvous and show Elke in a bikini or even nude. Just before the fighting one of the boys would tie her to her bunk and lock the cabin. Then they'd board the boat, kill all aboard and take valuables and cash and weapons and then scuttle her.

No wonder they keep a rein on her. Lord, do you really believe that?

Of course, he glared at me. Don't you?

I couldn't answer. He continued to glare. I slugged some rum and got up and went aft to the galley, puttered with the dirty dishes for a time. Disbelief was my first reaction, the information too awful to take in.

It's true, he said after a while.

Okay, I granted, but was still slow to accept. Then why don't they do anything when they're at South Caicos?

Same reason they don't do anything at Puerto Plata. They need places that aren't popular yachting centers, out of the way. In Puerto Plata they can sell off loot, guns and the like, because they have — well, had — the officials in their pocket. At South Caicos, hell, the only law is a couple of chocolate soldiers in striped trousers, one old Customs man and an annual visit from the Ministry of Fisheries. But even there some of the native sailors have heard something, avoid them like plague. The main thing, though, is that rich yachts hardly ever call in at either place.

So the trading in fruit and lobster is a front?

Right. And Elke is mostly hidden when all they're up to is trading in fruit and lobster.

By the way, did she ever tell you what happened in Puerto Plata to send the gunboat after them?

Yeah. Some ugly fat guy tried kidnapping her on

the dock. Leif saw it happen, beat the crap out of him. Turned out he was the commissioner of police. They ran for it.

There in the cover of the hibiscus she told him that Thorssen would never let him sail with them, not anyone other than the family. He would have to get her off by night, somehow to the twice-weekly morning plane. They'd never make it on the French boat, *Drummer* would follow, take her off and kill everyone else.

There were other problems. Thorssen kept her passport locked in a compartment under the chart table with the logs and documents. Locked with a combination only Thorssen knew. And even if she had it and they made it to the plane and to Nassau, the radiotelephone system sometimes worked, so Thorssen could call ahead and have her held or even returned, as she was still a minor.

Nevertheless she had to get free of them. He had to find a way. He asked how long she thought they would stay there. She told him perhaps another week. And that there was talk of going to West End on Tortola, where Thorssen said there was a good place to careen the boat and repair the centerboard trunk.

They lay still and silent as *Plus Profond's* captain made his unsteady way past them and down to the dock. They stayed for another half an hour or so, he said, not talking. Then she went down (circuitously, not on the walkway until near the bottom) and he went up to the veranda to watch the dock and her return to the boat. He saw her step aboard, but stayed up there in the quiet for another hour before going down to *Plus Profond* himself. He slept on deck, wrapped in the furl of the jib.

In the morning he cooked breakfast and cleaned the galley and then polished brass until noon. The two women aboard sunned in their bikinis on the foredeck, Jacques and Gian-Carlo went off in the dinghy with snorkels and fins and spears. The skipper went up to the bar. Mid-morning, Thorssen started the gas generator and disappeared again below, presumably into the engine room. Erik and Leif took off in the dinghy, presumably after lobster. No sign of Elke.

When his brass was gleaming, Jack headed up to the town himself. The germ of an idea was working; something to do with Lady Caroline and the occasional visits of private planes.

A flash and a close blast of thunder. The first drops of rain, big heavy ones, on the deck above. Jack's voice came up and alive, whether just to sound over the noise of the rain or because memories of plans and action stimulated him I couldn't say.

So anyway, I rigged it with Lady Caroline that she would be willing to drive us in the VSO jeep out to the airstrip when the time came. Bless her. That night I went again to the bar, talked with the owner of the hotel. He expected Tommy — remember Tommy, the bush pilot? — anyway, he expected Tommy to fly in Friday night with a charter party, some investors in something or other who had reserved rooms in the hotel for the weekend. That was on Wednesday. Pass the bottle, would you?

He poured, not bothering with the last of the ice swimming in the bowl.

See the plot? It almost worked, too.

He took a swallow. The problem was her damned

passport. Tommy, at the bar late Friday night, thought it would be cool, a lark. He told me his room number, said to wake him when we were ready. I told him it would have to wait until Saturday night, or rather, Sunday morning before dawn. He said that would be okay, his party wasn't leaving until midday Monday.

I'd explained it to Elke. The only hard part would be to get at her passport. I suggested that we just leave it, that Tommy could fly us all the way to a strip he used west of Lauderdale, no Customs. But she wouldn't have it.

Another lightning stroke, so near we heard it snap-crack just before the huge bang of thunder. Jack sat with his glass halfway to his mouth and the other hand on the bottle. I flinched, deaf and blind for an instant. Then the thunder rumbled off to the east and the rain came in a sheet, pressure-washing the world. It lasted like that for two or three minutes, then settled into a gentle, steady drip. The wind had passed on with the squall, left us with only the soft sound of the rain. Jack took a sip.

So I went over to give Thorssen a hand in the engine room Saturday afternoon, as soon as I heard his gas generator kick in. I figured that in the course of the work down there I could slip forward with the big bolt cutters from *Plus Profond,* snap the lock and rejoin him before he noticed anything. Elke had packed a small kit and was ready but for the passport. I carried the bolt cutters openly, as if I'd just been using them on the other boat. Hailed him from the dock.

He stopped then to light a Lucky. Shook the match, watching it closely, shaking his head in time with it. Took a deep drag.

The two boys were in the dinghy, still tied off *Drummer's* transom. They were up and out of the boat and charging me the moment I spoke, yelling You can't take her! You can't take her! Erik had the dinghy's anchor and was swinging it like a mace on a length of its line. Leif had an oar, carried it like a staff. I parried the anchor with the bolt cutters, blocked a thrust from the oar with my other arm. Had to turn my back on the boat to do it. When I did, Thorssen was on me with a length of heavy chain. That's when I got this. He pointed to the bandage on the back of his head.

At least I think so. I went down. He started beating me around the back and sides with the chain. I rolled and grabbed the end of it and held on, but the boys started kicking in my ribs. All the time they were yelling and cursing me, calling me a thief and a kidnapper.

I pretty much went under at that point, still clinging to the chain. Jacques and the skipper of *Plus Profond* came running, pulled the boys off me, screamed at Thorssen to stop, sent one of the Biwis up to get the cops. Last thing I saw for a while was Thorssen throwing his end of the chain at me. Hit me in the cheek.

He rubbed his ribs, then, remembering what I guess was the worst of the pain. Drank again.

Who told them? he asked no one. Were we overheard, or did Tommy or Caroline actually tell them?

Or Elke herself? I wondered aloud.

No! he shouted. Not possible!
Sorry, Jack. Of course not.

They questioned him about the charges. He denied everything. They sat him in a chair in the corner of their office, radioed Turks for a plane.

The plane took him to Turks, where he was put in jail. A very nasty jail, smelling foul in the heat, the mosquitoes a torture day and night, no-see-'ums at every maddening sunset. He was there for a week, peas and rice and water, no further medical attention. At the end of the week he was given his kit, sent over from *Plus Profond* and including his pay for the last month and my chart and binoculars, and was deported, out on the waiting flight to Nassau. From there he got a flight on Mackey Airlines to Ft. Lauderdale.

Not actually deported, he insisted, not officially. Charges were dropped when *Lazy Drummer* sailed. Sent off under a cloud would be the better description. I can go back there, though probably not to a very warm welcome.

Ft. Lauderdale

What a charming town Lauderdale once was. It was in the throes of greedy construction then, with Las Olas Boulevard losing its elegance to new stuff near the causeway over the Intracoastal. Lovely yachts still moored along the river, though, and the marinas out on the beach side were still fine, of course. Especially in winter, the Trades alternating with the mild northers, the sun all asparkle on stucco and flashing through the tropical plantings and the vestiges of the Everglades lining the river. But I was tired of life in that boatyard, where the only charming element was a patch of swamp across the river.

Jack stayed with me aboard *Adagio,* helped me some with the varnish and brass. We talked little. He was constantly on edge.

We've got to get after her, he said, so often I was getting edgy myself. Is this boat ever going anywhere?

A few days later, a Monday afternoon, calm with a slight overcast perfect for varnish, I was nearly down the mizzen suspended from a halyard, almost within reach of the deck, the varnish above gleaming, the sanded wood waiting beneath. It was the final coat on the spar. All that was left was one more thin coat where the sun had dulled the coamings and the hatch covers. The yard manager came down saying there was a phone call for me, *Adagio's* owner.

I left the rest of the mast to Jack — he was tall enough to reach it by standing on a halyard winch — and followed the manager up to his office. He was shorter than I but thick, maybe forty-five or so, an almost somber man always wearing a dirty white yachting cap, the sort most of us wore, like a Naval officer's but with the spring out of the crown. My own was a Yalie type, with a short, almost vertical brim, salt-stained but clean. Only old men from Michigan on vacation at the beaches wear those yachting caps anymore. When did sailors trade them in for ball caps?

Anyway, on the phone the owner asked if the boat was ready and I told him it was. He said to move her to the dock on the canal behind his new Ft. Lauderdale house and he'd be down on Saturday. I said okay yes sir, we'd have her there when he arrived. I asked if he were planning a cruise and he said not soon. He might, however, want her moved later to a berth at the Ft. Lauderdale Yacht Club, he wasn't sure.

When I told him, Jack wryly asked what had happened to the charters in the Bahamas.

The mizzen done, we hustled the coamings and hatch covers. The varnish would be dry the next afternoon.

I took a cab to the owner's house to look over the dock, all that. The house was a huge, sprawling slump brick with lots of glass blocks and tile roofing. I had the cab wait while I walked around it on freshly-sodded St. Augustine to the water side for a look at the dock. It was all right, extending out into the canal for about ten feet, ranging some hundred feet along the seawall. A stone mermaid topped every piling. There were no mooring cleats. The canal was a hundred feet across from an as yet un-dredged swamp. *Adagio* was eighty-six from bowsprit to davits. It would be something of a trick to get her turned around bow out.

The yardman stopped me as I got back, just before they were quitting for the day. I was to call T. Stan Mallory.

I've got you a new berth if you want it, Stan told me. Alden yawl, fifty-five footer. Skipper and crew to tend her until late March, then deliver her to Cos Cob, run her for the summer racing season. I told him what you wanted for pay, and that you would pick your own crew. You can live aboard, both here and in Connecticut. She's at Bahia Mar. Named *Capriole.*

I told him we could start late the next day, once we'd moved the motorsailer. I would go over to Bahia

Mar and have a look at her straightaway.

Bahia Mar was a classy marina even then. I enjoyed the scent of the salt air coming across from the beach and the dock smells, boat smells, the colored lights along the piers just coming on, last hint of fire in the sunset over the 'glades.

Capriole wasn't a mess, but not Bristol fashion either. She'd just been delivered down the Trades from Argentina, had been tidied for the docking, but her sails had been roughly furled, bights of her main sheet used for gaskets, a jib still on the stay and tied also with a sheet. Her brass was dull and the teak decks had gone gray.

She had a centerboard in a framed trunk well aft and cleverly concealed under a teak counter which marked off the galley. The cabin smelled musty and damp, had been tidied but not cleaned. The delivery crew were Argentineans. They must have had some weather coming up.

I took the cab back to *Adagio*. Had a rum or two. It scared me just to think about what I knew we were going to do.

I woke in a tepid bath of gray light, the features of the cabin clear but colorless. I rinsed my face in the galley sink and went out on deck barefoot.

The breeze stirred vaguely in my tangled hair and over the swamp to the east barely rustled the tops of the mangroves. Above the trees a line of pale pink spread, silhouetting their tops, suggesting watchers in the leaves. I stared through sleep fog at the pilings of the pier near water level, seeing tiny crabs at work on the barnacles there exposed by the tide, and knew it would be a good day for the work at hand. High slack water wouldn't come until early afternoon.

Adagio was heavy enough that my movement forward along her port rail brought no response from her hull. Beneath her bow the river's current flowed sluggishly, the surface a strange shade of copper in the soft early light. The clock in the deckhouse tinged faintly, four bells. Two hours before the yard's workmen arrived. I smelled coffee and went below.

Lovely morning, Jack said cheerily.

'Tis that, indeed. Perfect for the run into the canal.

Oh, right, we have to move this boat. Forgot about that. Tell me about the new boat.

I hadn't exactly forgotten, but hadn't been thinking about it. Didn't want to think about it quite yet.

She's fine. An Alden yawl. Needs some cleaning up. A bit big for just the two of us, fifty-five feet. Fairly shallow, with a centerboard. She'll do.

What's the deal with the owner?

Just what we wanted. We'll have her to ourselves until we get her to Connecticut in April. Then we'll be her live-aboard racing crew.

Perfect.

Look, Jack, let's leave that till this afternoon, okay? We've got to get this one moved first.

I know. Sure. What's her name?

Pardon?

The new boat. What's her name?

Oh. *Capriole.*

Jack chuckled, then leaned back and bellowed with laughter. *Capriole*? You can't be serious.

Why not? What's it mean?

It means `caper,' he chuckled.

I smiled, but I really didn't find it funny.

So I changed into work clothes, cranked the huge

GM diesel, let it burbble. Stowed all her gear. Jack set to cleaning the galley. By eight-thirty she lay on her fenders in the river's current, what there was of it as the tide rose, one spring line aft. I went up to sign the bills at the yard boss's office. I'd call the owner later, once she was on the new dock.

She was the biggest and heaviest boat I'd run since the Coast Guard cutter, and then there had always been some college boy officer telling me what to do. So I did everything at dead slow, deeply grateful for the calm and the gentle current.

None of it proved any problem. I eased her downriver at low revs, just enough for steerage way. Jack had her fenders aboard and mooring lines coiled down before we entered the Intracoastal.

It was still pretty then, trees, only a few well-kept lawns in front of modern houses, no big hotels or condos yet on the beach side, still quite a few patches of mangrove and swamp. As we passed the yachts docked, but not crowded, at Bahia Mar, Jack stepped into the pilothouse to ask which one was *Capriole*. She was on the outermost finger, so it was easy to spot her.

Is she not absolutely beautiful? he grinned.

I allowed as she was, and smiled back.

Jack paced. I watched the cranes and herons hunting and pecking in the doomed mangroves.

How bad is she? Jack asked. *Capriole*.

Not too bad, I think. Needs a good drying out and a cleaning. Don't know about the engine or the hull, the bottom paint. We'll know some of it tonight, the rest tomorrow.

He went forward to pace some more. A pair of flamingos flew lazily over the swamp, the morning sun hitting their wings at an angle turning them to neon. A flock of small, green parrots zipped through, performed some amazing twists in perfect unison and disappeared. A great blue heron stabbed a fiddler crab and held it up in the air for a few seconds, the crab wiggling. Swallowed it.

I think I'll go over to Nassau on the plane, ask Tommy to take me for a recon.

Good idea, I agreed. Good to have some notion where to go when we go.

Where do you think she might be? he asked.

Can't guess. Where do you think?

Caicos, maybe. Not Puerto Plata, of course. Maybe west. Maybe even Cap Haitian.

Well, even without Puerto Plata on the list, a recon would be a good idea. We won't have forever. The owner wants his boat in Cos Cob by the middle of April.

To hell with the owner.

He'll give us sound hell if we're too late.

To hell with him anyway. He can't do anything to us.

He can ruin me for sure.

More of Jack's pacing. More birds in the mangroves.

How fast can *Capriole* get from here to Caicos? he asked, having paced alongside the pilothouse.

Given normal weather, six or seven days. Faster if we get a manageable cold front once we're clear of the Stream. Hell, you know how those things go.

He paced aft this time, so I didn't have to watch.

We were up to the dock in less than an hour. I backed and filled until she was aimed back out the canal, stirring up clouds of brown muck with the prop, laid her on starboard side to. Not elegant, but we were there.

Rather start the clean-up, or walk a mile to the pay phone for a cab? I asked him.

Where's the phone? he asked.

In front of a bar, I told him.

I'll walk.

So I cleaned her and buttoned her up. Hoisted a last swallow of her owner's rum in her honor, as every one of those fine old wooden buckets deserved their honor, sad to have plunked her in a prison, an artificial canal in front of an ultra-modern mansion, where with her gleaming varnish she would lie for God knows how long mired at her keel in dredged mud instead of sailing free out there where she belonged.

I got our duffels onto the dock and around to the street side of the house, remembered my Haitian cane again. When Jack came with the cab I dropped the boat keys through the mail slot next to the ornate front door. Bahia Mar, I told the driver, and don't hesitate to press on canvas.

Nevertheless, I had him stop at the pay phone in front of the bar and called the owner to tell him she was there. Sort of fellow I've been ever since the Coast Guard.

aboard *Capriole*
Fort Lauderdale

After a shower and shave and dinner up at the restaurant, I called Stan and told him we were aboard *Capriole*. I strolled out the dock then, enjoying the lights and the sea smells, dock smells. Someone was playing a calypso tune on a guitar on one of the boats, several boozy yachtsmen singing along. Laughter, ice clinking in glasses, galley smells off one or two of the smaller boats. All very pleasant, took my mind away from the problem of what we were going to tell the owner. We aren't going to *steal* your boat, just borrow it for a few thousand miles.

I spent the evening taking an inventory of the equipment in the cabins; charts, galley, head, radio, all that. No sextant, however, no almanac or sight tables. But apart from having been soaked and left dirty by her delivery crew she was in almost new condition, all the gear barely used. I'd go over the dirty stuff in the morning, engine room, bilges, bottom paint, rigging.

I picked up a copy of the current *Yachting*, skimmed through. There was an ad for the Bahamas Tourist Board listing the dates of the Miami-Nassau race in February. By then I no longer cared for ocean racing, finding the boats overcrowded after sailing short-handed so often, but it nevertheless struck me it might be an interesting element in our criminal equation.

We've got to concoct a tale. Any ideas?

Jack sat at the chart table, lit a smoke and peered at the big chart of the North Atlantic I'd laid out, folded to show just the west side of it, from Maine to the

Equator.

The obvious thing, I would think, would be simply to go as if headed for Connecticut, and devise excuses for taking so long after we get there.

I got up and washed my face in the galley sink. But how do we explain to the dockmaster that we left in February, when we're not expected up there until mid-April?

Repairs at a yard, say in Miami?

Yeah, maybe. But there's really nothing wrong with her that I've found so far. Maybe something in the engine room. And then we'd have to come up with a phone number in Miami.

Back and forth like that, for most of another hour. Finally, a sleepy agreement that we would play it by ear in the morning. Off to our bunks.

I was up early and at work on the decks without even bothering with coffee. Sail covers, neat coils, brasses polished. Not at all sure I was doing the right thing; if we needed a repairs excuse, her fine appearance would all be to the bad. It was, I suppose, habit as much as anything; make her look Bristol fashion.

That more or less done, I went below, into the hatch aft to the engine room, crawled in. Everything looked fine, no oil in the bilge, no smell of gasoline. I crawled back out, switched on the electrics, went up on deck and ran the bilge blower, cranked her up. Started on less than a full spin. Idled her, engaged forward and then reverse without even a clunk. Went back down and watched the cooling system and the shaft coupling, all that. Smooth and almost shiny. Pristine. Perfect. Barely had to wash my hands.

Jack was up and filling a pot for coffee. I waved

him off and sent him up to the dockmaster's with two cups in hand. Never leave signs of the crew's life aboard. Checked the pumps, one hand-operated and one electric. They spurted merrily, about six ounces of water. Examined and sniffed the bilges; sweet, so sweet, you could tell she lay in seawater, that absolutely unique sweetness of scent only a fine wood boat possesses, a subtle perfume found nowhere else in all the world. Apart from a faint gloss, she was dry.

Jack returned with our coffee. I had a sip, went forward to change into swim trunks. Found a pair of goggles and a weight belt in a locker, took them out on deck. Only a few questions left.

The sun was just beginning to warm the decks. I rigged a knotted line overboard to port, away from the dock, slugged down the last of the coffee, put on the goggles and weight belt. Tied a long line under my arms and told Jack to give me slack, but not too much.

In I went. I have always hated being in the water. Water is supposed to stay out of boats, people to stay in them. But there I was. It was cool and a slightly tannish red from the nearby mangroves, no real current running. I let the weights take me down, all the way to the base of her keel. Felt around the slot for the centerboard, looked at the screw and the rudder. Went up for air.

She's really very clean. A couple of patches of small barnacles, a little algae. Help me out of here.

I stripped off the goggles and the weight belt, handed them up. Climbed the knotted line until I could grasp some fine varnished rail. Jack grabbed an elbow and heaved. I stood dripping. Jack asked How does she strike you?

Nothing at all to worry about so far.

Jack handed me a towel and I went to work with it. We'll have to run her under power for a while to be sure of the engine and shaft.

We spent the next couple of days studying her, and there really was not a single damned thing wrong, though we let on to the dockmaster that there might be this and that. We gradually stocked her, not too much at a time, looked like just enough for a week or so. We spread the tale that we might have to take her to Miami for repairs. We had decided it would be easier for Jack to catch Tommy with the plane in Nassau, so we decided to delay his recon flight until we got there.

On our last day at Bahia Mar, Jack went off on another shopping expedition and was gone all day. He got back just around full dark. I was finishing a frugal dinner aboard, don't remember what. I had just poured a rum and lit a cigarette.

He clambered down the companionway with a big and apparently heavy grocery bag. Clear a space, would you?

I hastily moved china and silver. He plunked down the bag, started rummaging through it. Some essentials, he said. He pulled out two volumes of the celestial navigation tables, and one of the Nautical Almanac for 1956. Then a square, handsomely varnished wooden box with brass fittings.

This is for you. He placed it gently in front of me. I opened it. A beautiful old sextant, a Plath. Yours to keep, he added, with no particular emphasis.

Thank you, Jack. It's a marvel.

While I admired it he pulled out a Colt .45 combat automatic pistol —I recognized it, having trained with it and occasionally carried one in the Coast Guard— two spare magazines and a box of shells. This is for me, he said. Then out came some oil, oilcloth, electrical tape, other stuff. He spent the next twenty minutes fussing with the gun, loading the magazines, snapping one into the pistol itself and chambering a round. He coated everything heavily with oil, wrapped the lot in oilcloth and taped it all up into a tight package.

With the engine spares, I guess, I told him.

Right. He went aft to the engine room, opened the hatch. I could hear him rearranging things in the spares locker. Came out. Closed the hatch. Washed his hands in the galley sink.

I toyed with the sextant, a fine old piece, brass and blued steel, a silver scale, clear mirrors and a full compliment of filters.

This must have cost a pile, I commented.

Not so bad. I went to pawn shops well inland. Plenty of guns, but that was the only sextant I could find. Are those the right books?

Yes.

But for all the beauty of the sextant and its inherent empowerment, the pistol, even wrapped and hidden in the spares locker, brought a new mood aboard. For the first time I realized fully that it was we who were about to become the pirates.

The Gulf Stream

Oh, she was grand, that *Capriole*. The day we left was clear and sparkling, the easterly just what you would call brisk. We hammered her out against the rollers as far as the paired Numbers 2 and 3 buoys, bore off south under a medium jib and full main, a beam reach. She took a bone in her teeth and lay over handsomely and roared southward, the morning sun lighting up her brightwork, her rigging full of song. Jack ran out the taffrail log and showed us at eight knots. The motion was joyous. *Capriole* capered.

We put her up a little closer, anxious to be out of sight of land as soon as we could and still be credible as bound for Miami. On that course an odd wave would occasionally bump her sheer, sending aft fine spray filled with rainbows.

In an hour we could see nothing but the tops of a few tall buildings. At a moment when, even from the spreaders, no shipping was in sight, we lowered the centerboard and close-hauled her, onto a course which would show us the Gun Cay light or, if the Stream were running harder, Bimini. Once we had her trimmed and I got the feel of her to weather, it was clear she wanted the mizzen set. That done her helm was balanced, and Jack pitched the log. Six knots on average for ten solid minutes.

Still early in the day, the sea was a million colors. Later it took on its proper shade, the bluest of translucent indigo seething over an impenetrable black, over 400 fathoms of it, straight down beneath. Sweet *Capriole* seldom pounded, generally cut through the crests and kept her head up in the troughs. A gentle sea, no more than five or six feet up and down. She was happy, and so was I.

Jack was, too. He made us sandwiches, opened beers. Sat with me in the cockpit to eat, chatting easily about the boat, the weather, the general sense of luck and pleasure in it. Lit our cigarettes in the companionway.

Took the helm, got the feel of her quickly. Sang something, I've forgotten what, The Eddystone Light perhaps. I took a noon sight with my lovely old Plath.

When I went below to figure our position, the rather more somber aspect of our voyage struck me in the chest. I would, of course, have to keep two logs. I first wrote up the one that put us at anchor at the Coconut Grove Yacht Club. Then in my private notebook where I thought we actually were. Noted the wind and sea conditions, all that. Checked the barometer. It had fallen a little since morning. That done I went out on deck and looked back to the west. There were indeed clouds building over Florida.

In less than an hour after that it shifted to the southwest, and rose hard, with rain in it. In the span of another ten minutes we had thirty knots of nor'wester hammering us. Had to reef the main, soaked through and shivering, hands like dead toads. Took forty minutes doing it alone in that erratic buck and twist, all the gear so big, so heavy. Even with the reef she moved like a rodeo bronc.

The rain was over before dark and we could see a thin line of old twilight under the black to the west. It stayed wet on deck, of course, salt wet, and our sweaters and oilskins did little to keep out the cold. What had been song in the rigging became a white-noise roar, punctuated with kettledrum bashings on the relentless chop, bass drum thuds through the hull. Cymbal crashes as tops broke over her bow, followed by hissing snares as the water ran aft. Artillery reports as the main luffed and then suddenly reloaded. Tchaikovsky during a very bad rehearsal.

We took short turns at the helm. When steering

you sat in a circumscription of light from the binnacle, like a tortured martyr in the dramatic focus of a dark chiaroscuro, flexing at the hips in a movement threatening to turn into the rocking of an incarcerated autistic.

On our breaks from steering neither of us went below for more than a minute or two for this and that, huddled instead in the lee corner of the cockpit, drifting away to the arms of our beautiful dream girls or fixated on the humming tension of a sheet squeaking over a block or turning a coil of line into a fantastic South American snake.

And always, at the helm or crunched in the lee, the taste of salt, a margarita's rim with only brine in the glass.

The Gulf Stream

Well, we were lucky. Not long after noon the next day we caught a glimpse of something off the starboard bow, then kept seeing it. By then, the wind had gone close to due north. Through the binoculars I could see that it was Great Isaac Light, the top third of it or so, the glassed room glinting now and then above the gracefully tapered, almost medieval tower. We eased her off to leeward and pulled up half the board and she set herself to a fine canter, twisting some but no longer hammering into that nasty sea. In less than an hour we were clear of the light to the north, could see all of it and the little block house and flagpole with the Colonial ensign stretched out red and shivering and the sparse casuarinas, all behind a kind of white film, sea spray atomized into a visible wind.

Northwest Providence Channel

Once fully around the light we bore off to the east, an open, gentle reach toward Great Stirrup. I cooked something at last and laced our coffee with a tot of rum. Jack let me clean up and have a lie down. *Capriole* became a cradle gently rocked by mother sea, and I slipped into the emptiness of infancy.

Somehow Jack managed to let me have two full hours. He had to shout and bang me up, unable to leave the helm in the quartering sea. I relieved him, groggy though I was, but caught her rhythm in a minute. Oh, she was a happy, willing vessel, needing no more than a spoke or two when an oddly angled wave would roll beneath her. Jack warmed the leftover coffee and laced it and handed it up, then a lit cigarette. Oh, how she moved! Awake and warmed and settled into her dance, I let her lead, wave tops sparkled as the sun joined the cotillion, the jib sheet forward of its turns around the winch thrummed atavistic music, and on the occasional lee roll snapped rainbows into the air. I smoked and sipped and sang ditties from Gilbert and Sullivan.

We rounded Great Stirrup just after sunset. Once around Jack cooked, the wonders of a second meal in the same day, a steak, I remember, and a bottle of Chateau Margeaux Jack had picked up on one of his shopping tours and kept secret. The reach was broad after the rounding and we set a mizzen staysail.

Stars by the millions in the norther-washed sky. Now and then I put out binnacle and running lights for a few minutes at a time, steered by the wind in my hair and wondered about the stars. I remember having the thought then that each star was a spirit, a reflection of a living thing, and what we thought we knew about them, about astronomy, was as far from what they are as we are from them. New Age stuff now, but back then it seemed primitive and true.

Nassau

The glow of Nassau was definite by midnight, and shortly thereafter we ran the range lights into the harbor, rounded up and balanced the tide against the wind to lay her on the dock at Yacht Haven, the deck tidied, yellow Q flag on the spreader and the yacht ensign two-thirds up her mizzen. We were awakened at eight in the morning by the cheery hail of the Customs officer, who cleared us with hardly a question, no interest at all in whether there might be a pistol in the engine spares locker.

Through the morning we rigged awnings and signed in with the dockmaster, drank coffee and tested our land legs. After a lunch at the Pilot House Jack took a taxi to the airport to look for Tommy and his plane. He'd packed a kit which included a number of charts, my binoculars, and his pistol.

Which left me with nothing much to do for an unknown period of time. I tidied and cleaned and greased and oiled and polished, took a taxi over the hill for stores. Finished *Youth* and started *The Shadow-Line* for the fifth or sixth time.

The entries in the official log had us lying to in

Miami, making fictitious engine repairs. The Miami-Nassau race would have started early that morning, and the boats would be showing up in Nassau in a few days. I kept wondering if once they were here we would disappear among them or become an apple in a basket of oranges. Most of them would moor at the Nassau Yacht Club, but the dockmaster told me that all the slips at Yacht Haven were reserved for Sunday night. We'd have to anchor off before then, probably across on the Hog Island side. Hog Island, by the way, was what is now called Paradise Island. No buildings on it in those days. Well, maybe a shack or two. There wasn't even a bridge across Nassau Harbor.

I was sitting in the cockpit under the awning enjoying my book and the breeze and the shade when Jack strode down the dock just before noon on the fifth day, the second day of the race.

West Caicos, he said, no hello, how are you. They're anchored off some ruined houses there. Must have had some damage. They're diving.

He took his kit below, stowed things. I finished a fine Conrad paragraph, stood and stretched, looked out over the harbor. A pleasant Sunday morning. Lovely day for a cruise.

We slipped away from the dock under main alone, rigged the big jib once we had steerage east. Clear of the hook at the end of Hog Island we let the board down, set the mizzen, and close-hauled her. The course was good to leave Great Abaco well to leeward. *Capriole* positively bounded over the waves, all taut and trim and balanced with sheer power. Oh, what a boat. What a fine, pure aristocrat of a boat.

Northeast Providence Channel

Off to the north we saw a few sails, all hull down, racing for Nassau from the turn at Great Stirrup. They'd made good time from their Saturday morning start at Miami, those gold-plated leaders, probably *Ticonderoga* in front. The likes of that lot are never to be seen again.

The North Atlantic

The Atlantic rollers squeezed up tall in the night as we passed through Hole in the Wall, the big light at Abaco flashing calm and steady, right there where we wanted and needed it. It was gone well before first light and by Monday's dawn there was nothing of the land to see astern or anywhere. *Capriole* greeted the large soft seas on her starboard bow with the elegant grace of a fashion model. Jack towed the log, and it showed six and a half knots steady.

The log attracted a school of dolphins, not the usual bottlenoses but little pearl gray guys with spotted pink bellies. We sang to them, I from the wheel, Jack way forward in the bows lying prone and waving a hand. Don't know what tunes Jack sang, couldn't hear him from the helm. I sang Gilbert and Sullivan, which seemed not to impress them particularly. Switched to the Ninth Symphony, *Freuden, freuden*. Either Beethoven or Schiller got to them. They stayed with us for nearly an hour.

Once they'd gone I got the time and took the midmorning sun sight, hardly a cloud in the sky. Then I cooked tinned bacon and fresh eggs and fried bread, coffee with a tot of rum. Jack was able to tie the helm and join me below for a civilized breakfast at her gimbaled table. As we ate he asked once when I thought we'd raise West Caicos. I told him that if the weather held, likely Thursday afternoon. He said that would probably be too late, they wouldn't hang on an anchor that long. That was all. The grim tension eased away from him after that and he actually smiled, talked about *Capriole* and her sailing qualities. Well, she was something to smile about all right.

After the meal and cigarettes I cleaned up the galley and lay down until Jack called me just before twelve to take the noon sight. It put us within a mile or so of where my dead reckoning had her, suggesting that we could tack as soon as I'd taken the afternoon sight. I stayed up to steer her, would let Jack sleep till two-thirty or so.

The afternoon sun sight again confirmed my dead reckoning. It was early to tack to get a sure lay on West Caicos, but it seemed wiser than holding out for it.

There was a haze with some heavy cloud over it when it was time for the midmorning sun shot Tuesday, so I couldn't get anything, even with the filters. I managed a timed noon shot, though, and liked it. Just after sunset the light on San Sal flashed faintly, showing we had safe distance to the lee. Obviously we'd picked up a lift, some of the south gone off the Trades. Still, I wanted to take a hitch for a watch, four hours, just in case. When I took the helm back at midnight, we put her on starboard tack.

By morning the sky was clear again and we put her back on port tack. Sun sights were sharp and within five miles of the dead reckoning at noon, within three after the shot at two-thirty. We were a touch east of the course to the light on Providenciales, we would see it well after dark. If it was working.

The reefs between Providenciales and West Caicos Island are dangerous, shallow coral heads, breakers. You can pass them right close up in good daylight and the prevailing wind, but we'd have to stand off them in the dark. I explained this to Jack as Wednesday's sun dropped into the sea. He nodded, grunted once. It's too late, anyway, he muttered. They won't be there.

The Caicos Islands

He was right of course. Thursday morning we hove to off the ruined houses an hour after dawn, wondering what to do.

If they have the engine they'll have gone onto the Banks, I said. If they're sailing without the centerboard, it would have to be downwind, maybe to Inagua.

Jack made sandwiches as we rocked lightly, drifted slowly away from the shore. Opened warmish Pauli Girls. Spread the chart out on our knees in the cockpit.

Might they have tried for Cap Haitien? he asked.

I thought about it. Bit close on if they've lost their board.

So it's Inagua if they're sailing, South Caicos if they're under power.

At a guess. There can't be anything for them at Five Cays and it's pretty far to Georgetown.

We ate and drank and didn't talk for a while. Jack stared at the chart as if gazing into a crystal ball. Finished his sandwich and beer, took the leavings below. Came back with lit cigarettes. Let's try South Caicos, he said.

Okay. I folded the chart and handed it to him, freed the jib sheet and put her helm over. We close-reached to the north northeast, watched the breakers to weather and a curiously pink stretch of beach. It began to shimmer and seemed to be rising. Then a great flock of flamingoes rose in a cloud, turning the sky to pink and the beach to white. A while later we hardened on after rounding Northwest Point. Tacked a few minutes after noon, had to take a hitch to clear the reef off East Caicos at sunset. Docked at the Admiral's Arms just after ten. No other boats there, just the native sloops at anchor near the Fisheries. No one on the dock, no lights at the hotel. Raised the Q and slept hard in the heat.

Cockburn Harbour

In South Caicos in those days the Customs agent didn't come to you, you had to go find him. A small, very black man in his black uniform and dirty white cap with a grand gold Royal insignia, carrying a clipboard in the Customs warehouse, counting crates. He did not want to see me. With barely a word he filled out the form, *Capriole,* sailing yacht of twenty-some tons, in ballast.

I tried. You know Captain Thorssen, of *Lazy Drummer*?

He grunted. I took it for an affirmative, knowing it had to be.

Was she here recently?

Another grunt. Didn't know how to read that one.

When did you last see her?

Nothing at all then. He turned away, scribbling on his clipboard.

I dug casually in my pocket, extracted a five-dollar bill, folded it, then reached for cigarettes. When he turned my way again I offered him a smoke, the bill showing.

He accepted the cigarette and took the money as he did. We lit up. Two days ago she leave. Cleared her for St. Thomas.

Many thanks.

Don't let Mr. Morgan go ashore. They jail him.

For what?

They think of something.

Thank you. We'll leave no later than morning.

Clear you outward bound now, then.

After that I walked out into the blinding sun, sweated through my shirt in less than a minute. Trudged toward the town, to Lady Caroline's house. She was with her class in the building next door. I waved in through the open window, it had no glass — just a plywood shutter folded open and tied with a strand of old cordage — and she spared me half a glance.

After a hot and empty while she put the children to something and stepped out, led me around the side of the building into some shade. She had regained most of the weight she'd lost to the dysentery, wore a sweaty tee shirt and shorts, shower shoes.

Captain Brendan Harper, she drawled. What brings you back to Cockburn Harbour?

The exquisite Lady Caroline, of course.

How long will you be here this time?

Not long. We'll probably leave in the morning. I paused to consider, then decided to tell her. Jack

Morgan's with me.

Her face froze. She knew what was coming. Oh dear, she said. He'd best not step ashore.

That bad, was it?

Quite that bad.

A shout and a screech from inside the classroom. Her eyes twitched. She folded her arms below her breasts. No bra.

Could we have dinner tonight?

No, dear boy. I've discovered your Coastie Guardies, some sort of new installation on the island. So many lovely boys, so little time.

I dreaded raising it, knew she would hate me for it, never forgive me. Still. I had no choice. When Jack tried to get Elke off . . .

She glared at me. Yes?

Who told them?

Go straight to hell. She turned and brushed past me, headed back to the schoolroom.

Did Elke tell them? I called after her.

She stopped. What makes you think that?

It was too late, of course, but I tried again. I know you wouldn't, and Tommy had no reason to.

She turned back, looked at me, not softened at all. Would I not? And did Tommy not have a reason? He fell under her spell too, after all.

Then she turned away again, bent her head. I suppose she must have done, she said softly.

She went inside then, and there was nothing for me to do but walk away. There'd been no good way to do it I know, but I still feel hollowed out when I think of it.

Walking back to the hotel and then down to the

boat I turned my anger onto Jack, his obsession, my reputation as a captain at risk, and now the loss of Lady Caroline. How much more was he going to cost me? What the hell was in it for me? Adventure and helping out a friend didn't seem to be enough just then.

Jack was rigging awnings. Take them down, I told him, We're leaving.

I turned the key in the ignition and went aft to free the stern line. When I started forward to go up on the dock for the bow line and spring, he stood in my way.

Tell me.

I did. We're leaving.

Tell me, he repeated.

You're not allowed ashore. Lady Caroline didn't tell anyone. Tommy didn't tell anyone. Elke told them.

That's a lie.

Okay. Thorssen's psychic. Anyway, we're going.

What about *Drummer*?

She left two days ago, cleared for St. Thomas.

He absorbed that, then went forward to strike the awnings and the Q. I freed all the mooring lines and took them aboard and put her in gear and we left. Not a word between us, but we both knew we weren't going back to Florida.

The North Atlantic

Clear of the Caicos Passage, the course on starboard tack steadily deteriorated as the wind shifted northward, so that by dawn I was back down to north by east. The wind picked up as it shifted. By eight or so it was blowing eighteen to twenty and the seas were up.

She wanted a reef, maybe even the smaller jib, but I was too weary to do it and Jack was tired too. I let it go like that for an hour or so, then hollered Jack up so we could reef the main.

Reefing is tough enough with a full crew in a breeze and a chop like that. With Jack on the helm and free only to handle the mainsheet I had all the rest of it to do, topping lift, halyard, downhauls, nettles, the lot. It took maybe half an hour, and when we were done I was dead beat. Settled her nicely though, with the lapped jib, even if it cost us half a knot. Just as well. I could no more have changed jibs then than I could have danced a hornpipe. Huff puff.

I sat back in the lee side of the cockpit and looked out at the sea to windward. It seemed glazed, frosted. The sun struck it all at an acute angle, the light scattered and realigned and scattered again by the skimming, broken cloud. Silver on slate in the distance, snowy white on blue-black in close, shimmering, roiling, yet contained by a sheen through which only the occasional, exceptionally agitated wave broke, sending airy lost spray adrift on the wind. Line upon line of whitecaps foamed toward us from the northeastern horizon, the wind and cloud and sea making an absolutely linear totality, a pure composition so perfect as to shame all art, all human design.

Six days from South Caicos to St. Thomas, actually we did it in five and a half. There was a small storm the third night, we sailed through it with St. Elmo's fire in the rigging and a Navy carrier group out on maneuvers far to windward. In the morning after that, with the fleet over the horizon astern, as Jack handed up a decent breakfast, he said the first words between us since South

Caicos. We'd sailed together so long words hadn't been necessary for all that time.

Either of them might have had reasons. Tommy wanted her, just like you and everyone else. The Brit bitch wants everything in pants. Envy.

I thought about that, Lady Caroline's hint. Not Lady Caroline, I insisted.

He wisely let that one go, but I guess it was possible, woman scorned, upstaged, all that. Seemed a petty thing for the woman who saved my life. But, damn it, possible.

Tommy, okay, maybe, I said, when he came up later with lit cigarettes.

We were still hard on port tack, soon to see some part of Puerto Rico. I couldn’t be sure, as I hadn't run the sun sights since we left, unwilling to exchange even the few words with him necessary to do that.

Tommy, maybe, but if he really wanted her he could have taken her off with the plane somewhere.

Not if she didn't want to go with him. Not if she loves me.

We picked up the onshore lift off Aricibo the next night in the glow of the city, and in the morning were past San Juan without having to tack. There was a radio station we tuned in, played both Latin and American pop tunes. A very sexy woman's voice announced the call letters every few minutes. I wanted to put in and meet her, court her in Spanish, marry her and have children and live out the rest of my life drinking rum on the beach in the sun.

The Virgin Islands

They weren't in Charlotte Amalie, not in the Lagoon, not at St. John or Spanish Town or Jost van Dyke. Three more days, asking anchored boats for news of her in all those places and more. Cruising was a growing sport in the Virgins then, not so thick with yachts as the Keys or the Bahamas but more each time you went there. I suppose it's as busy as Biscayne Bay by now.

They were, however, at Tobago, in the cove on the west side. We sailed by just inside the seven fathom line, glassing them. There was another boat in there with her, an Island-built sloop, maybe forty feet or a bit less, at a distance looking pretty trim. They were anchored about two hundred yards apart and *Drummer*'s dinghy was another hundred beyond the sloop, beached.

It was less than an hour to sunset, so the light was good for us and terrible for them. Jack asked for the glasses, asked me to steer and slow her without being too obvious. I over-trimmed the main and let the least flutter into the high-clewed jib we were carrying. The big jib was furled and hanked and ready under it. Jack quietly described the details.

Elke's aboard *Drummer*. The boys are on the beach, near the dinghy. Where's Thorssen? There. On the sloop, with two other people, a man and a woman. They're eating something, I think. Drinking for sure.

He quit talking and scanned. And scanned. Then: No aerials on the sloop.

He suddenly ducked below, came up after a while with the big bolt cutters and a pad and pencil. The .45 was tucked in his pants. I had my first clear sighting of the Marine officer since the gunboat had fired on us, and I was not at all sure I liked him.

Okay, Bren, we'll have to do it fast, before the boys get back into the dinghy, which they'll surely do before dark. He sketched quickly the outline of the cove, placed the two boats and the dinghy. We go in, straight for *Drummer.* I'll jump over, take a minute to cut the padlock so Elke can get her passport, then I'll nip the feed lines to the injectors and disable the radio. Make a fast circle, five minutes max, pick us up and we run for it.

I held my course, thinking about it. No antennae on the sloop for sure? I asked.

For sure.

No insulators on the backstay?

He looked through the glasses again. No insulators.

I thought a little more. When I turn her they'll see the transom.

Right. While you're sailing her in I'll tape over the name and hailing port, the numbers forward, too.

I pondered it, visualized it. Fenders, all of them, both sides.

Okay, that too. Fast, though. Soon.

We jibed her over and put her on the wind. I had time then to worry, to think, to doubt. What came to me was that I knew why Jack would never have taken her off in the plane. He could never have trusted Tommy or his pilot in the Virgins. He knew the power of the plane and thought he might have lost her to it, the lure of the freedom it seems to offer to go anywhere, whenever. He couldn't trust Elke or the pilots or the planes. Tommy, maybe, you see. Tommy might have been the fink at Cockburn Harbour, the one time he'd tried trusting the planes.

Whereas Jack knew poor old Cap'n Bren would be the trusty Coast Guardsman to the end, the stalwart grunt who would go where and do whatever Jack wanted. But my commitment was not to Jack, it was to sail. To the sea and wood fitted expertly to wood, to the wind and cotton canvas fitted cleverly to manila cordage, to the perfect beauty of the natural equation, wind, sea, sail, boat, man. He didn't know that. But he was right enough. I would do what he wanted, because I was also what he thought me to be.

And, well, Elke had to be saved, didn't she?

Jack ripped oilcloth into strips, hung over the sides to cover the numbers near her stem, then over the transom to get the name and homeport covered. We were well inside the cove and slowing under the lee of the island as he got the last of her fenders hung. I should have told him to rig the big jib, the air being so light in there. We might have had time enough. But I didn't.

I steered for a point a couple of boat lengths aft of *Drummer*, trimmed some main. Jack went to the port side aft of the shrouds, stepped carefully over the lifeline. Two spare magazines for the pistol peeked out of his rear pants pocket.

I made the turn to starboard, sheeted home the main, luffed the jib. Had a moment to look aft to where the dinghy and the sloop lay.

The boys were in the dinghy trying to crank the engine. Thorssen was waving and shouting something, nicking a shin as he hurried forward to the bow of the sloop. The couple aboard her were standing up but not doing anything, looking alarmed and confused.

The gap was narrowing. Aboard *Drummer*, Elke

stood next to the pilothouse, watching all this with slitted eyes, not moving. She wore only the strategic black triangles of a French bikini, the only time I'd seen one worn before was when Lady Caroline had flashed me on the dock at Caicos, otherwise just in magazines. Elke's looked more like those. She wore a gold chain around her neck, and when she took half a step aft I saw that she had one on her ankle, too.

I let go both sheets to slow her, it was feet, then inches. Jack jumped before the hulls kissed. I couldn't see what he or Elke did next, watching the small gap of water between the boats, making it wider with a touch of jib and half a spoke. Bore off to starboard, filled the main with the light waft of air, eased her off gradually.

The dinghy was underway by then, chugging toward the sloop with both boys aboard. Thorssen jumped up and down and waved at the boys, twisted and looked at me, then at what was happening aboard *Lazy Drummer*. Jack had said five minutes max. It looked to me like we'd have less than three.

I jibed her over, started slowly rounding up. No sign of anyone on *Drummer*'s deck. No hurry, then. Jeez, right, no hurry.

The boys came under the sloop's rail on the far side, so I couldn't see much of what was going on, only that Thorssen was no longer on deck, just his head and an arm showing. In a moment the dinghy appeared around the stern of the sloop, headed my way. Still no sign of Jack or Elke. I trimmed and took a spoke to weather. It would be bad to be early, but worse if the damned dinghy caught me. The little outboard was screaming its head off. I looked back again. With the weight of all three of them in it they were dead slow, not much faster than *Capriole* was moving. A cloud of oil smoke poured out of the exhaust. Thorssen was waving his arms, machete in one hand. One of the boys, Leif or Erik, was loading the spear slings. It was almost comical, three men in a tub playing pirate. Except this time none of us were playing and we were all pirates.

Behind them I could see the couple aboard the sloop weighing anchor, exhaust burbling. A surprise; most of the native boats didn't have engines.

And *still* no sign of Jack or Elke. I tweaked the main, couldn't wait, no way *Capriole* could outrun the dinghy without the big jib and probably some engine as well. There might just have been time to crank up and run for it if I did it then, right then, that instant, and left Jack and Elke to fight it out on their own, save my ship, my life.

My ass.

I had *Capriole*'s stem even with *Drummer*'s transom when I hollered for Jack to hurry. I pinched up to luff out the jib and shoved at the boom to back the main as much as I could. Jack! Now! They're almost on us!

Jack appeared, dragging Elke by an elbow. She had a blue canvas bag in her hand. He threw something overboard, radio parts perhaps. No bolt cutters. He tugged the girl to the rail, told her to jump. She didn't. I nudged the boat up rail to rail, the fenders groaning, stopped her almost dead.

Jack grabbed the girl around the waist, shifted her up over a shoulder and jumped. They fell in a heap on the cabin roof. I trimmed madly, got clear of *Drummer*, yelled to Jack to set the big jib.

He didn't. He got up and hustled aft, drawing the pistol. I looked back. The dinghy was right on our transom, and the boys had their spear slings fully drawn.

I looked forward in time to see Jack take the spear point high in his gut, fire the pistol. I heard a scream and a splash behind me. Jack fell into the cockpit, dropping the gun near my left foot, twisting horribly on the shaft of the spear. Then the pain came, up from the base of my spine, down my right leg, everywhere, everywhere the pain. I reached back and my hand touched the spear stuck in there and I glazed and went black, would have fallen but for my grip on the wheel and my leg propped against the steering box. The mainsheet slipped out of my hand.

When my vision cleared it came with a numbness, the pain having, I suppose, gone too far. I slid slowly down to my knees, picked up the pistol. I looked up to see Elke sitting still on the cabin top, eyes wide but eerily calm. Then Leif leapt onto the deck waving a machete. I shot at him twice. The second one hit him somewhere in the middle and the machete fell to the deck as he tumbled overboard.

Elke sat unmoving, eyes wide but eerily calm.

I pulled myself to my feet by tugging on the wheel. As I rose the slackened mainsheet fouled in the spear shaft stuck in my back and jerked it out of me. I went black again, screamed at myself not to let go. When I could see again the dinghy was amidships. Thorssen was alone in it, brandishing his rigging knife and saying, Elke, Elke, please. You cannot leave me. You cannot. I will kill you.

And Elke sat unmoving, eyes wide but eerily calm, looking at me.

So I bent painfully, got a grip on Jack's pistol and started shooting at Thorssen. None of the rounds went close to him, but one of them crunched the housing on the outboard motor and it

Stopped.

Hissed.

Exploded.

When the smoke cleared there was an oil slick and a burning boat cushion and Thorssen's back floating, blackened, smoking. I threw the pistol overboard and made myself trim the main, find a course out of the cove. The sloop was there ahead of us, engine running and the main close hauled, pinching for Tortola. I couldn't feel my right hand or any of me on the right side, but I trimmed to follow her. It was all very vague. What wasn't numb hurt.

Elke sat on the cabin roof unmoving, eyes wide but eerily calm.

The Virgin Islands

I followed the sloop so that when she reported what she'd seen she'd tell the cops that we were headed southeast when they last saw us. I followed her until it was full dark and only her masthead light showed. We sailed dark, of course. When there was no chance she could see I let *Capriole* fall off to somewhere around north. We needed a bigger headsail, but I knew I couldn't do it. My shoes were slick with the blood Jack and I had lost or were losing, the cockpit sole coated with it. Elke no longer sat, but was curled in a ball around her canvas bag.

Elke, please see to Jack. Please.

Nothing. I steered north.

Elke, can you help me? Please. Please help.

Nothing. I steered north.

I got to drifting off course, no sense of time, slept after a fashion when the numbness got ahead of the pain. Sometime in the night I felt her hand on my cheek, heard her whisper that Jack was beyond any help, she had set the jib and would steer. I couldn't move. She eased my hand from the wheel, hooked it over the steering box.

Just north, then, till morning, I said. Thank you.

The North Atlantic

The pre-dawn gray revealed the horror in the cockpit in a muted way, no color. Much of the blood had dried, had a crusty feel. I stared at Elke's bare foot, the one with the ankle bracelet, coated with dark stuff. Jack lay in the same position I'd last seen him, the spear shaft still aiming at the sky.

I tested limbs. Some numbness everywhere, but only the right leg completely dead. When there was color in the dawn I tried to stand, almost made it. The pain of any sort of motion was only marginally worse than staying still, so I slid forward on my butt, did a sort of monkey move over Jack's feet, made it to the companionway. Tried to rise to go below, but simply couldn't with the dead leg. I looked aft, saw smears of fresh blood along the seat.

Elke, could you patch me up? There's a first aid kit in the head.

Yes. Can you steer?

Yes, I think so.

So I slid back aft and took the wheel from her,

steered north, a broad reach. Elke moved gingerly forward — God, so beautiful even in that horror — and went below.

I steered north.

She came back wearing one of Jack's khaki shirts over the bikini and carrying the first aid kit. Moved aft and around behind me, pulled up my shirttail, then reached around to open my jeans, murmuring softly as she worked. Everything hurt. She hissed when she saw the wound.

What should I use? she asked.

I thought about the spear that had pierced me, the point having been the death of innumerable crustaceans and a great variety of fish, then left to rust in the bilge of the dinghy for hours or days at a time.

Clean it out with cotton and alcohol first.

I thought about the wound the spear had made, obviously having struck a vertebra first, then slashed into meat afterward. Then stuff it with sulfa, I told her, the white powder in the can.

I screamed the first time she touched it with the alcohol, nearly passed out. Steer! she ordered.

I steered north.

It's pretty clean now, she said after a while. How will I keep the sulfa in it?

Put a small pad over it and use the wide tape. Pull it closed with the tape, tight as you can.

She did that, then wadded up more padding and taped it all around my hips. It was all she could do. She packed up the kit and went forward with it.

We've got to put Jack overboard, she said when she came back up. I can't do it alone.

I know.

How?

Now she's balanced she'll steer herself for a bit, at worst round up. I'll do what I can.

I tied the helm amidships and eased the main a little, then went forward. I took his watch, the only one we had, and put it on. Checked his pockets for a wallet, found Elke's passport. The two spare pistol magazines. Tossed those over the side.

The only way I could do anything with Jack's body was to lie down next to him at an angle and ease parts of myself under him. I told myself this wasn't Jack anymore, but I couldn't make myself believe it. I heard myself sobbing as I worked.

Elke tugged, I pushed up from below. The spear struck the cockpit coaming as he rose, hung up. Can you hold him there? I asked her.

Yes.

I pulled myself up off the sole and was doing okay, sitting on the seat next to him and heaving, seemed to be making progress, when a wave came under her at an off angle and turned her upwind. The movement threw me back against the coaming and made Elke let go and Jack pitched forward and that drove the spear out his back. I looked at it, stunned. After a while I reached over and pulled it out the rest of the way and threw that overboard too.

From there on it was easy. Over the lifeline with a splash, floated face down, to my sincere relief. I went aft to the helm and put her back on course, stared aft at the denim shirt and khaki pants and said, We commit thy body to the deep. Looked at Elke. I shouldn't have. She sat unmoving on the cabin top, eyes wide but eerily calm.

I steered north. She found a scrub brush and a bucket and went to work on the bloody teak in the cockpit, then on the deck to port. Took in all the fenders and stowed them. Found the machete and tucked it under the aft chock for the spinnaker pole.

I steered north. I explained to her how to mark the time when I took a sun shot.

By ten-fifteen we were ready, the sun was right where it belonged off the starboard quarter. She took the helm and the pad and pencil and passed me the sextant. It was hard to do sitting, but there wasn't any choice. I figured in some error for it when I worked out the sight.

She made coffee after that and cooked something. After eating I felt the fever come on, fought it until I bagged the noon sight. Then I couldn't anymore. Gave her the new course and helped trim for it, northwest now, for a day or two anyway, the big jib happy most of the time. Couldn't go below. I lay on a cushion on the lee seat of the cockpit. She gave me a blanket and I sweated into it. She said there were dolphins with us. I asked her if they were the little gray ones with pink spotted bellies. She said they were. I was able to sleep after that.

It went more or less that way for the next several days. Sometimes I could manage two sun sights in a day, sometimes just one. Weather steady, fortunately. Apart from the sun sights and sharing the steering, she did everything. Changed my dressings every day, adding sulfa each time until it was all gone. The fever came and went but was getting worse each time it came. I could move, though not well, the leg was still numb and would continue to be for all the rest of my life. But the pain was steadily easing, and I could drag the leg pretty well. When the fever let up I could do this and that. I remembered about the taped-over name and numbers, stripped off what was left of the sea-soaked oilcloth, rubbed leftover adhesive away with gasoline. Rigged a tie-down on the boom. That sort of thing.

The North Atlantic

Seductive even in sleep, a long, tanned arm stretched along the coaming, long, tanned legs crossed, fine golden hair blowing around the face, that face, the sun itself that face, even with her eyes closed she radiated a secret, arcane sensuality. Not a child sleeping by any means. A deep and mysterious woman. I dreamed of a future for us in the States, I'd get a shore job, go to college, we'd marry and have children, all the standard stuff.

Fool.

Perhaps she felt my eyes on her. She woke without moving, just opened her eyes to slits against the sun. Languidly smiled at me.

Please tell me your story, Elke, I asked. I heard a story about you from Jack, but I want to hear it from you.

Her smile disappeared. She turned her head away, moved slowly, gracefully, into a corner of shade. Yes, I did not exactly tell Jack the truth. What did he tell you?

I told her. Sometimes she shook her head as I spoke, sometimes nodded. Terrible things. When I was finished she sat facing me, speaking quietly. She had the faintest of accents, none of that Scandinavian singsong of Thorssen's.

First, I am not nineteen. I am seventeen. And none of that about hijacking boats is true. The damage you saw was from a bang stick Leif shot off accidentally, getting it into the dinghy. Not that about giving me to the Customs men at Puerto Plata either. I made all that up so that Jack would feel sorry for me, would hate my father and brothers enough to fight them if he had to. They did have me dress up, showed me around the docks, but not to set up hijackings. Only to be invited for free drinks and meals. We were very poor.

I moaned with the shame of it. We had killed innocent men and were genuine kidnappers. And Jack had been a statutory rapist. Oh hell. Well, the killing had been, in a way, self-defense, I suppose. And Thorssen had threatened to kill her.

Still.

No, she said, watching me closely. That is not true either. I am sixteen, and I am not the daughter of Niels Thorssen. I'm not even Danish, I am Dutch.

I quit steering for a moment then, rounded up enough to collapse the jib. When I got the course back and the sail pulling again, she continued:

When I was thirteen I was cruising with my family, my father and mother and older brother, down in Central America, Honduras mainly. Thorssen and his boys came aboard us there in a small port, killed everyone else, stole the boat and took me with them. She was not named *Lazy Drummer* then, and was not from Panama. She was *Stella de Hartog,* of Amsterdam.

She hung her head, squeezed her breasts together with her arms. The rest, what I told Jack, was true. They all used me, Niels, Leif, Erik, the Customs men, rich men at yacht clubs. And the Thorssens were pirates. Murderous, evil pirates.

She got up then and went below. Came up with a

lit H. Upmann, bless her. We smoked it together.

So now you think ill of me, she whispered after a while, primarily to herself. I have been used too much. You will not take me to America and take care of me.

I couldn't respond to that, not just then. Too much. Too many contradictions, too many lies, to someone. I steered northwest. After a while I asked her why she'd revealed Jack's plan to get her off in Caicos.

She didn't answer right away, took a deep puff of the cigar and handed it to me. Then she stood suddenly, darted forward and drew the machete out of the pole chock, grinned at me. She turned and danced forward, jumped onto the cabin roof and propped one pointed toe on the boom, leaned back against the mast with cutlass pointed aloft, a classic pinup pose.

Because I am the bloodthirsty Queen of the Pirates! she screamed. I gave all the orders, did most of the killing myself! I turned my father and my brothers into my crew, and they often blanched at my cruelty! I am twenty-one years old, and have plundered the southern seas since I was twelve! Don't you fear me? Then she threw her head back and laughed wildly at the shimmering sky.

A moment later she dropped the pose, came aft to the cockpit, put the machete back under the chock. Stretched out in her most fetching sunbather's pose, eyes wide again and eerily calm, staring at me.

Yes. Now I fear you, I admitted. Truly.

I did, too.

She smiled softly, almost kindly. Shook her head. I was lying again, just for the fun. No. I told them because I knew he'd been a soldier, a Marine. I hoped he would kill them then and there. I knew there was no chance of ever being free unless he killed them all.

Off Great Abaco

Near morning on the day after our conversation we spotted the lighthouse at Hole in the Wall, jibed over to sail more westward. My fever was worsening, shorter and shorter periods with it in abeyance. I had to give her the helm to take the big rollers as we passed through to the Northeast Providence Channel; I just couldn't do it. She handled it perfectly.

The Bahama Banks

From there I set a course to clear Whale Cay, pass Chub and enter the Banks. I was out of it much of the time, unable to eat, shivering in a blanket and foul weathers. There was no question about it, the infection was bad. Steered off and on until were clear of Chub.

I left for a while, went to a golden autumn afternoon where I raked fallen leaves, maple reds and yellow oak. It was cool and there was no wind and the leaves were damp so that the sound of the rake in them was soft.

You slept well, Elke said from the helm. Eerie to hear that soft feminine voice, coming from the circle of light aft of the binnacle.

Yes, I think so.

I have been able to hold the course within one degree the whole time.

That's great. What time is it?

She put Jack's watch to the binnacle light. Twelve-thirty.

We should see the Gun Cay light within an hour.

Do you need a break?

No, I'm fine.

Take one anyway. I'll be good for a while.

All right.

I slid aft and took the wheel. She didn't leave, sat close to me, thigh to thigh, watching the night. I steered 276° and felt the warmth of her thigh through my sweaty blanket and jeans.

What will we do when we get to America? she asked after a while.

I'm not sure. If we try to clear Customs we'll have to have a good story cooked up. It's been over two weeks since we entered at Nassau. And Jack's not with us.

Will they know?

They might. About the fight. They might.

She rubbed the top of my thigh with her palm, gripped it. I'm frightened.

Me too. But I'll figure out something.

She went below and took a while making coffee. I pondered the problem, came up with nothing much. There was a small cove I knew near the south end of Key Biscayne, no docks, one or two anchorages, I think the area around it was a park, no buildings nearby. Surely that's no longer the case, but at the time it seemed relatively remote. We could lock her up and swim in, if I could get into the water and swim, and we could walk away into anonymity. If I could walk.

She came back up with coffee and a lit cigar. Sat with me again, thigh to thigh. I steered 276° but felt something like awe, this woman of such beauty, no one else's girl, not at a great and disdainful distance but touching me, sick and damaged me, it was the touch of a goddess, I struggled not to allow myself to believe it, not to take joy from it. I steered 276° and sipped coffee and smoked, stifling dreams.

There's the light, I told her when I saw it flash. You steered the course perfectly.

The Gulf Stream

In a little under two hours we bumped through the slot between Gun and Cat Cays and were in the Stream. Not a millpond but not bad at all, with the prevailing southeasterly breathing gently into the night. We trimmed her up to aim ten degrees south of the rhumb line to Key Biscayne, which with luck would put us into the bay right at Cape Florida. There may be ways now to know how fast the stream is running, your GPS or something. In those days you had to guess.

An hour or so later I started to sweat again, went weak and tired. She took the coffee cups below, then returned in jeans and a shirt and an oilskin jacket and took the wheel. I lay back down on the seat in my blanket and oilskins and shivered for a while and then slept some more. Not good sleep this time, the worst kind, with Jack clammy and dragging seaweed and clawing himself up from the sea and over the rail in fury time after time wanting his woman back over and over and I couldn't stop him and I couldn't wake up.

The next time I woke it was full light. I forced myself upright and looked ahead. The tops of radio masts, one or two tall buildings. A freighter at anchor, just her funnels showing in the too-bright sun. Government Cut, then, just over the horizon. A good run, but the ten degrees south hadn't been enough for the

Stream.

What time is it? I asked her.

Almost two.

Good Lord. Let me steer.

We hardened her on a little more, gave her a foot or so of centerboard. She liked it. Elke went below and changed back into her bikini, took her spot on the seat opposite my filthy blanket. This time she slept. She'd steered almost nine straight hours.

The rest had done me good. Still weak but, for the moment at least, sweated out. I had a giddy sense of happiness, steering my beautiful boat on a pleasant breeze, with my beautiful girl in a French bikini sunning herself in the cockpit. What could be better in all the world? My boat. My girl.

Neither mine. But I spent the next two hours making believe that they were.

Biscayne Bay

I got through the jibe without waking her, she just shifted herself slightly, raised a knee to brace herself, unconsciously adjusting to the new movement. We slipped by the tiny opening to the cove. I put the glasses on it, saw no other boats in there. Had to rouse her then, did it gently, stroking her cheek, speaking quietly. She came awake softly, smiled. I almost bent down to kiss her before I remembered, not my boat, not my girl.

We have to drop the sails and go in under power, I told her.

She got up without speaking and went forward to the halyards. I rounded up, cranked the engine. She took in the jib and gave it a quick furl on the foredeck, I didn't have to tell her which one first, anything. Then the main, tugging it down along the luff like a pro as I turned to enter the cove at low revs. She had it furled and in stops before the bows tucked into the slot.

No other boats. The cove wasn't a quarter mile long at its widest span, lined with some low trees and vestigial patches of mangrove. No wind in there, we'd have mosquitoes like mad in an hour or two. Probably why there were no other boats. Couldn't see any houses or buildings through the trees, but an occasional car passed just beyond them on a road we couldn't see.

We anchored near the middle of the cove. She wanted to go right away. I told her we should wait until after dark, better not to be seen by anyone on land until we were well away from the boat. She seemed to see the point, though she was clearly anxious to go.

It was hot there, almost no breeze could get across the island from the sea. She rigged an awning over the cockpit, went below and made sandwiches. The fever was coming on me again but I managed to get one down. Rum and water with it. A short smoke and I was out.

I realized I had missed the mosquito onslaught when I woke. Not aware of much else, the fever back at high pitch, buzzing. Didn't want to move. It was full dark, no idea what time. Faint wavelets pattered, there was a little breeze, some shadowy movement in the lights from the city. A little tapping sound in the rigging; she had forgotten to tie off one of the halyards. I whispered her name, as much in wonder as in hope of an answer. I knew she was gone.

I woke again near dawn. Mosquitoes then, sure enough. I made myself get up, go below, look for her.

Then I looked for what she'd taken away with her.

Her things, of course. Jack's watch. All the money in my wallet and Jack's. Not the two hundred I'd slipped in the envelope with the ship's papers. A waterproof jacket. Two life jackets. My rigging knife. All my hopes and dreams.

I slept and sweated and drank rum through the day and much of the night. Late in the dark I got myself moving, collected my log and Jack's log and our passports and his wallet and mine with the Florida driver's license and the owner's card in it, a change of clothes and shoes, all bundled in taped oilcloth. I passed out once or twice, could hardly handle things, dripping sweat on everything. I got a life jacket on me, had to sleep for a while. Tugged the life ring out of its lashings aft, tied my bundle to it. Remembered the snake-carved Haitian cane I'd bought from the preacher in Caicos. Tossed the bundle over and went in after it holding the cane, big splash, swam towing the floating bundle.

Key Biscayne

Slept on the stinking mangrove beach uncovered by the ebb tide. Got up and changed clothes and hid the ring and life jacket and took my bundle through the brush up onto the narrow road. There were houses not far away, mostly under construction. I limped north, grateful for my cane. If anyone asked I'd tell them it was an oar. Where someone asked what an oar was I planned to live the rest of my life.

Curled up and slept again on the ground. Woke and dragged and crawled and limped some more. A while after dawn a pickup truck came along, headed my way. I stuck out a thumb.

You all right, mister? the guy asked, seeing the sweat and the dragged dead leg.

Not too good, I admitted. You going to Miami?

He took me to a hospital somewhere near Coral Gables. I told them I'd had an accident on a roofing job a week before, the fever just having started a couple of days ago. I was there for two days. After that I was okay, except, of course, for the leg. As soon as I was out I tried to call Mallory, but he was off on a delivery to Marblehead. So I called the owner and told one of the owner's secretaries where he could find his boat. The faithful Coast Guardsman once again.

The race is over, the winner and a few of the others are at the dock and rigging the boats for the ramp and the waiting trailers, most still on their way in. The winner is a small girl, about nine or ten, with free silver-gold hair, pale eyes set in a face so perfect that it seems to radiate a golden light. She goes about her chores calmly, quick of movement, completely focused, moving with easy grace. The boy in the boat behind hers is sullen, his movements angry, awkward. The two do not speak, do not even look at one another.

The old man grips his cane and uses it to lift himself from the green bench and walks in a slow and uneven gait toward the sidewalk at the edge of the park.

Wind, water, sail, boat, boy. Even after all that happened, the purity of it.

BRANGAENE

Brangaene

Mexico Beach, 2005

This surf whispers of myth, of memory both distant and near, of that which has been true for as long as sea has met sand. It is for old men to assess and recount what they have heard from the surf and other such eminent messengers, and sometimes they will hear from them a truth older than the one they remember.

These two old men sit in the late sun, listening to the whispers of the surf and savoring the last of the day's warmth. They watch the breeze ruffling the patch of sea oats stretched in a narrow band between the veranda and the beach. One smokes a cigarette. The other, the larger of the two, pulls the brim of his straw hat down to shade pale eyes. His white guayabera is buttoned at the cuffs. They sip their first ones of the day, bourbon on ice.

I love this coast, Lee James Ford says. Last stretch

to be ruined in all the Floridas. His accent is soft, southern, the voice still melodious. For him it seems the surf is gentle music.

The smaller man nods, opens his khaki shirt another notch, presents his narrow chest to the brightness. He hears the surf's whispers as an exhortation to memory.

Did I ever tell you about sailing down to the Exumas in 'sixty? he asks. His voice is raspy, the accent neutral.

Not as I recall.

I think I'd like to tell you that one.

Well, Cap'n Bren, tell all, hold nothing back, his friend says. They chuckle together at the old reporter's phrase.

Soon the sun hovers briefly over the horizon. In minutes it goes under, so they raise their glasses westward, sip again. The sky is filled with reds and yellows. Brendan blinks, turns it all to green.

I wasn't the captain that time. Didn't dare, even after five years away. Just a deckhand.

It's time to re-build the drinks. The bourbon bottle is on a small round table between them, flanked by an ice bucket and a carafe of branch water. Brendan does the honors, as it's harder for Lee James because of the wheelchair. The sky darkens rapidly, purples replacing the reds. The surf seems louder, the wind softer. They hear a clattering of pots and pans from inside the house, and a moment later a light appears in a window behind them.

I might not get through it in one evening, Brendan says. Don't even know how far I can get before dinner.

When was this again? Lee James asks.

The spring of 'sixty. I'd just got my BA over in Gainesville, needed a job for the summer. T. Stan Mallory had a Bahamas cruise booked for a month, needed a hand. At fifteen dollars a day and no expenses, it would be a fine start on summer savings. I had a graduate assistantship lined up at Tally in the fall.

The door behind them opens, throwing a harsh light across the veranda. Bren rises slowly and carefully, turns. Lee James's wife Ramona stands for an instant in silhouette then closes the door and comes toward them. In that light she might still be in her thirties —her age when Brendan had first met her— just a little rounder now at seventy. She carries a drink, walks out to them.

What a lovely, soft evening, she says. Her smile is audible, though it is too dark to see it.

Hola, Guapa, Lee James says, reaching up to cover the hand she has placed on his shoulder.

Dinner in ten minutes, she says to both of them. I could hold it a little longer, but not much.

Well, Cap'n Bren was about to tell all, hold nothing back.

No, it can wait, Bren insists. You won't mind if I stay two or three days?

They assure him they would hope he'd stay longer than that. He hobbles a few steps across the veranda, picks up a deck chair and starts to carry it up to the little table for Ramona.

Thanks, she says, but I can't sit. I have to keep an eye on the plátanos maduros.

Plátanos? Wonderful. It's been years, Bren says. And appropriate, too. This yarn is mostly about Cubans.

Dinner will suit it, then, she says with a chuckle. Dorado in sour orange, black beans and rice, the plátanos, the whole Cuban thing.

The sky is now black satin, the Gulf a subtly darker

value. Each startlingly white wave breaks on sand gone gray, the sound of the surf seeming unsynchronized with the streaks of light it causes. The air has cooled so that shifts on the breeze have an edge to them. Ramona withdraws to her kitchen. Brendan holds the door open to let Lee James wheel himself inside, then gathers the drink things onto a tray and follows.

It's a large room, its high ceilings beamed and planked with varnished cypress, its floor of glowing old pine, sparsely furnished in comfortable, tropical wicker. In a dining area an old Spanish trestle table is set for three, two chairs of the same period, space at the head for Lee James's old-fashioned high-backed wicker wheelchair. *Cuando se quiere de veras* plays on the stereo.

Lee James wheels himself to the coffee table where Bren has placed the drinks tray. Ramona brings in the steaming tureen of rice, returns for the plate of fish, asks Bren to bring the chilled bottle of wine. Lee James lights the candles. They sit to dine. Lee James pours; a crisp, flinty white from Chile.

The song ends. In the moments before the next one begins they look at one another in a silence that feels longer than all of the future. Ramona is seventy, Bren is seventy-five, Lee James eighty-one. Time does not stop but rather raises itself as a monolith before them. Then Lee James raises his glass.

To our present, he offers.

To our present, Bren and Ramona echo.

Dinner is grand, the Cuban flavor rich with memories for all three of them. They speak of recipes and wines, fine dining in the past. When it's over, Bren helps to clear and stack, Lee James feeds the dishwasher. Bren and Lee James then go back to the coffee table, light cigars. Ramona takes a puff from Lee James's, says good night.

Well, Cap'n Bren, the yarn, says Lee James after a sip of Havana Club rum. Tell all. Hold nothing back.

Fort Lauderdale, 1960

I first saw Isolda Reyes on a warm spring evening, floating alone in a secret moonlit pool in a tropical jungle heavy with the scent of flowers. The only sound was of water falling in a trickle somewhere near. I stood in shadows, holding my breath, entranced, unable to move. She raised a languid arm, shaped her hand into an elegant taper spreading quiet ripples on the water's surface and moving her an increment closer to the pool's far edge. After a few more such sinuous movements she slithered in a single twist to sit nude on the rim, drawing fingers through her long black hair heavy with water. She stood then and walked slowly away into the foliage. After a few moments, during which I still couldn't move a muscle, a light came on behind the curtains of a window beyond.

That turned the tropical jungle into the garden of one of those small, elegant blocks of apartments on one of those famous Lauderdale canals, revealed the mysterious light to be waterproof underwater bulbs and colored lights hidden in the flowering shrubs, the spring a ceramic fountain, and forced me to admit that she had not been nude but that I'd seen the strings of a tan bikini.

A little waft of the Tradewind ruffled palm fronds. I turned and looked toward the canal, where *Brangaene's* spars and rigging rose above the shrubbery. I'd seen her off and on at Bahia Mar in 'fifty-six. She was a stout, miniature clipper ship under ketch rig. Her teak and glass wheelhouse amidships was not quite tall enough to ruin her lines. She poked a long, platformed bowsprit out over her cutwater, and an outboard motorboat hung in davits over her broad transom, the tips of each end of her some seventy-two feet from each other. A light burned in the wheelhouse as she lay starboard side to the narrow dock parallel to the canal. I hefted my sea bag and walked past the pool and onto the dock.

"Anyone aboard?" I asked quietly.

It wasn't in me to disturb the night with a loud hail. I waited a few moments, then stepped lightly aboard and stuck my head into the wheelhouse and repeated myself. Nothing.

The wheelhouse really was also the main salon, with a considerable area of teak deck, a long settee running across the bulkhead aft and around the port side, a large dining table, binnacle and console, fine, spoked mahogany helm. The entire area was littered with grocery bags. It was clear what my first task would be, so I started on it.

The galley was just forward of the wheelhouse, down a few steps through the companionway to port of the helm. I found a switch and flipped it. The light revealed not a cramped galley at all, but a full, if tight, professional stainless steel kitchen, oven, range, fridge, freezer —all electric— double sink, and plenty of varnished teak lockers and drawers, all with latches. Most of the stores were in tins or jars, some of them things I'd never heard of but which presented no stowage problems. Stan would know what do with them, being a better cook than I. The fridge was full of fruits and vegetables, lunchmeats, eggs, cheeses. The freezer was packed with steaks, a turkey or two, shrimp, chicken. I'd never seen a kitchen so well stocked, let alone a galley. All I had to put in the fridge were Pouilly-Fuisee, Dom Perignon, and Paulaner.

I had the empty paper bags folded and was about to go ashore to find a trash can when I saw Stan coming through the gardens. He had luggage in both hands and slung over his shoulders and was making poor headway despite his athletic frame. I left the pile of bags next to the binnacle and went to help him.

"Hello, Brendan, how've you been keeping?" he said. "There's more, believe it or not."

"I'll get it. Not right for the captain, is it?"

He noticed my limp. It really wasn't too bad then. I'd kept after it with exercises every day over the four years since my injury, but still, I limped and it showed.

"No, there's not much more. I'll bring it to the dock, you put it to one side in the aft cabin. You'll see where."

His British accent had faded slightly in the years since I'd sailed with him. Other than that, at least in the low light on the dock, he seemed not to have changed much. His face was ruddy and his longish fair hair was damp and tousled. He bent to drop the suitcases and shrugged the strapped bags off his powerful shoulders, offered me his rough, seaman's hand. We clasped and smiled.

"Good to see you, Brendan."

"And you, Stan. Really, the limp doesn't limit me much."

"That's good," he said, "but it's best this way." With which he turned and went back for more luggage. I started shifting the pieces he'd left me.

T. Stanford Mallory. Never told me what the T. stood for. He'd gone to one of the better schools in England, Eaton, Harrow, one of those, had read the law at London University for less than a year when the bleak views of the city overwhelmed him and he bolted — that's how he put it — for Europe. He and a chum slung knapsacks and guitars, played and sang on the streets of Amsterdam and Paris, made their way eventually down to Athens. There he joined an ocean-racing ketch bound for Australia. It took him three more boats and as many years, but finally he made it all the way around the world under sail. After crossing the Atlantic a second time he'd fetched up in Lauderdale, where he prospered as a sailing captain, the same sort of work I'd had until four years before. We'd sailed together twice in the 'fifties. He taught me a lot about shorthanded offshore work, mainly that humor, good cooking, and rum were the sure antidotes to exhaustion and fear. No matter how rough it got, he was always cheery, considerate, and immensely able. It was he who taught me to sing to dolphins.

Once we had to deliver a racing sloop from Nassau to City Island New York. We'd spent the night before drinking and carousing and woke late aboard at Yacht Haven. We had lunch for breakfast at the Pilot House, fried grouper, peas and rice, several drafts of Courage. We sailed out into a blustering norther, and I was having a hard time holding on to my stomach in the nasty chop. With only two of us aboard seasickness was a prospect not only miserable and embarrassing, but dangerous as well. He sent me below to drink a club soda and have a lie down. Ten minutes later I exploded with a gigantic fart, followed by belly-deep laughter. I went up a few minutes after that, belched richly, farted again, and as soon as I stopped laughing I was able to take the helm.

"He who belcheth and fartheth puketh not," he said. "You have just had revealed that timeless nautical truth." In 'sixty he would have been about thirty-two or three, just a little older than I.

I lugged the first of the cases below, through the companionway aft of the wheelhouse on the starboard side. In that companionway was the chartroom, chart table, radio, some other electronics, and the entrance to the engine room. Past that, aft, the cabin proved to be truly a "great cabin," in the way of an eighteenth-century frigate's. A grand settee stretched across the stern under a row of windows, not portholes. In front of that a gimbaled table. Forward amidships a tiled woodstove nestled up to the bulkhead. To port was the entrance to the head, which was about the size of the one in my student apartment in Gainesville and far more elegant, having Delft tile throughout and a full-sized bathtub.

I found what seemed to be the obvious corner for the luggage and stacked it there. In a few minutes Stan arrived with the last two cases, arranged the lot to his satisfaction in the cabin, then motioned me to join him in the chartroom, where he opened a small-scale chart of Florida and the Bahamas and explained our sailing orders.

"Fellow named Wagner owns the boat, but she's chartered by our passenger and boss, Señor Marco Reyes, formerly of Tampa and Havana, now of Miami. He won't join us until Nassau. His wife, Señora Isolda Reyes, will be our sole passenger from here to Nassau. Our course will round Great Isaac, take the Northwest Providence Channel to Great Stirrup Light, and thence down to New

Providence. Can't sail her upwind across the Banks from Gun Cay, as she draws something over eleven feet with her centerboard down. And believe me," he grinned, "we do indeed want to sail her whenever we can. High tide is less than an hour away, so Señora Reyes should be joining the ship presently."

He then gave me a tour of the engine room, its huge bank of batteries, enormous Mercedes diesel, a large diesel generator. The wiring was a maze, sorted out more or less by an industrial-grade switchbox.

"I've got it all figured out except for the autopilot. Afraid we'll have to steer her all the way."

Back up in the chartroom, he pointed out the Exumas. "Oh, right, I forgot to mention that after Señor Reyes joins us in Nassau, we will cruise the Exuma Cays, Highbourne Cay to Staniel. We will do so very cautiously, what with her deep draft."

"Yes, I should think so."

He led me forward, up to the wheelhouse then down to the galley, where he complimented me on the stowage, then forward again to my stateroom. No kidding, she had two staterooms with upper and lower berths, louvered teak sliding doors beneath the classic skylight. There were four pipe berths forward of that — rough crew's quarters — painted planking instead of varnished teak. Sail bins then, and finally the chain locker.

We went out on deck. The breeze was up a little, laden with its mixture of sea and gardenia, the cool a blessing. Stan showed me the clever electric foot switch for the anchor winch, the various sheets and halyards, topping lifts and downhauls, all that. I could see that setting and furling her big mainsail would be something of a problem where the boom extended over the wheelhouse. Nothing I couldn't manage, though.

"Rather a large boat for just the two of us, I suppose," Stan admitted. "But Señor Reyes didn't want to sign a large crew."

"Stan, do you know what her name means?" I asked. "I've always been a bit superstitious about that, you know."

"Oh, yes. *Brangaene* was a character in an opera, I think. A witch specializing in love potions or something such. Owner seems to have had her built to be a floating aphrodisiac."

He glanced at his watch, looked at the tide line along the concrete sea wall. Raised his nose to the wind, fair hair aflutter.

"Time to crank her up," he said. "Brendan, if you would do the honors with the power cords and then leave her on her spring lines . . . ."

That was how he gave orders, though if it were for something unpleasant or dangerous he might include "Hate to trouble you" or "If you wouldn't mind too awfully." It was one of the reasons I always enjoyed sailing with him. That night, however, I couldn't hear the humor that used to be behind it.

The big diesel started with the clangor of a warning bell, followed by a leonine roar and a cloud of black smoke, with echoes bouncing from the buildings all up and down the canal. In a moment or two the roar settled into a low growl. I was bent over coiling the heavy electrical cord on the dock when I felt someone behind me and glanced over my shoulder.

She stood on the rim of the wall, looking into the wheel-house. She was dressed now in a billowing dark silken shirt and white bell-bottomed trousers and held a large leather purse. She seemed uncertain as to what to do next. Suddenly she smiled toward the wheelhouse and flipped her wrist twice in an almost secret greeting. She stepped cautiously onto the dock and crossed it in what seemed self-conscious insouciance. Stan appeared, took her purse and handed her aboard. I pressed on with my coils, freed bow and stern lines, got all that aboard. Looked a question into the wheelhouse. Stan went to the wheel and nodded. I rigged her to turn on her last spring line and with a deft spin of the wheel Stan put her in gear and we were off the dock, motoring sedately, if noisily, out the long canal.

I took in her fenders as she drove slowly down the middle of the narrow waterway, found stowage for them and the made coils and power cords. Turned a bird dog nose to the salt air joy of the night. It had been four years since I had buttoned up that fine yawl *Capriole,* five years of that other life so far from the sea. It felt like arriving home.

Mexico Beach, 2005

Brendan looks around the spacious room, its wood aglow in the low lamplight. Lee James sits with his head leaned back against the wicker of his chair, eyes closed, spotted hands wrapped gently around his snifter of rum. The surf resumes its commentary on the slope of the beach and the state of the breeze and the tide.

Bedtime? Bren asks.

Lee James is slow to respond. When he does, it's with an almost imperceptible shake of his head.

Now, you never did tell me about this *Capriole,* did you?

Lee James asks. Or has it slipped away while my mind slept?

Bren considers. No, I guess I didn't. Told that one to my nephew and his boy last summer. Pretty good yarn it was, though. Pirates, maiden in distress, tropical islands, blood and betrayals. Left me with this damned limp. Killed my crewman, a friend. I don't have enough time left to tell that one again.

Lee James's mouth twitches in what Bren takes to be an attempt to hide disappointment. They sip.

Perhaps another time this old newspaperman will worm it out of you, Lee James says. He'd been a stringer for the Miami Herald, a reporter on the Tallahassee Democrat, and for a time an editor of one or the other of the Tampa papers.

All right. Now, in the yarn you still haven't actually met her. I presume the woman in the pool and the woman who stepped aboard with a tentative wave and smile were one and the same and was Señora Isolda Reyes.

Yes. I met her briefly after we cleared the 17th Street drawbridge. Stan signaled me into the wheelhouse, asked me to make drinks, rum and soda with lime, as I recall, on ice. When I brought them up from the galley she was there and he introduced me.

What was your impression of her?

Brendan closes his eyes, tries to look out over forty-five years. He listens as best he can to her throaty voice, tries to sniff her Chanel, watch her slim left hand with its long, highly-polished nails settle softly on the varnished mahogany of the console as *Brangaene* takes the first of the Atlantic rollers, tries to see again the cluster of diamonds on the third of those fingers scattering the red of the binnacle light.

She was beautiful, but I can't say if I know that from the pool or the dock or a thousand sights of her later. She was polite, not condescending. You could hear the Spanish in her English, but not much of it. At that point I would say that my main impression of her was that she was elegant and expensive.

Lee James produces a long mm, sips. Bren lights a cigarette, watches the smoke rise and then disappear into the flow between the open window and the blades of the slow ceiling fan.

When was all this again? Lee James asks.

Late May or early June of 'sixty.

Mm again, another sip. All right, then, back to the yarn and the expensive Doña Isolda.

The Gulf Stream — Nassau, 1960

After we finished our drinks Isolda withdrew to the great cabin aft. Stan sent me out to set the main to steady her. I noticed that the engine noise wasn't much, on deck and away from the buildings and the bridge. She had the biggest main I'd ever handled, and the wheelhouse presented the expected obstacle to getting it set, but the sail had been properly furled, the lines properly led, the blocks and winches well-placed and recently oiled. It took me perhaps seven or eight minutes to get it up and trimmed and the halyard coiled. After that Stan sent me to my bunk for a couple of hours, just, I would say, in the nick of time. I'd dozed a little on the bus from Gainesville, but other than that I hadn't slept in over twenty hours.

He roused me gently an instant after I'd fallen asleep — well, the promised two hours after, though it felt like an instant — and pointed me toward the head. Relieved and with face rinsed, I went up to the wheelhouse and took the helm. He went aft into the chartroom to catch up his log, check his dead reckoning against the Loran. When he came up he announced that, as usual, the bloody Loran wasn't working, so I was to hold the course given, trim the main as needed. Then he left her to me and went to his bunk.

As soon as I had the feel of her I stuck my head out to windward, was happy with the set of the main, and saw that the eastern horizon was turning pale. No shipping in sight. I turned off the lights once the new day came on bright enough. Discovered that while the engine wasn't particularly loud it made the deck of the wheelhouse vibrate, a lulling foot massage. There was a fold-out stool for the helmsman, which I tried once or twice, but it was too high for me and hurt my back, so I gave it up and kept to my feet. After about three hours of that Stan stuck his head through the companionway, eyes bleary, but hair wetted down and reasonably neat. He came up, looked around the empty horizon, took in the set of the main and the course on the compass.

"A moment with the log," he said.

He returned in a few minutes. "Still no Loran. Not to worry, we've crossed the Stream a dozen times without that or any other bloody electronic doodad. Should be seeing Bimini or Great Isaac soon."

I gave him the helm, went down to the galley and brewed a small pot of strong Cuban coffee, visited the head. Mixed his with milk, stuck my head and a hand with his cup in it out through the companionway. "Rum?" I asked.

"Grand idea, old boy. How thoughtful." So I laced his coffee with Havana Club, handed it up. Took a good slug of it myself, straight from the bottle. Tidied a little, went to my bunk.

Two or three hours later I was awakened by a vision. The hand of Isolda Reyes, glittering diamonds on smooth fingers tipped with polished nails, laid gently on my shoulder. I stared at it for some seconds, then turned my head to look into tawny eyes set above glossy lips, the face exquisite in every shape and shade, framed by hair so black its highlights were blue.

"Good morning," she said softly.

— Buenos días, I said from my private fog bank.

—¿Quiere Ustéd desayuno?

— Sí, por favor. Pero tengo que cosinar.

— No, está listo.

It took me a moment to sort that out, but it seemed she had already cooked breakfast and I was invited.

—Muchas gracias. Un momento, por favor, I muttered, and moved. She removed her hand and straightened and smiled small. I saw that she wore a white bikini designed to reveal much cleavage. I twisted myself out of the bunk, ran fingers through my hair. By then she was gone.

I pondered this strange conversation while I washed my face and hands. I was sure it went that way, in Spanish, but wasn't dead sure she had started it in English. I just knew that it felt entirely natural to speak to her in Spanish, and she showed no surprise at the switch, if there had indeed been a switch. I'd just been living and breathing in that language through a four-year major in it, after all.

Breakfast was Cuban, of course, fruit and pan tostadas, café con leche. They'd laid it out on the table in the wheelhouse. Stan sat on the folding stool, from which he could reach for tidbits while steering. Isolda sat on the long section of the settee aft, legs crossed and on display. I took the short settee to port, where I couldn't see them. There was no way, however, to avoid the sight of those breasts. I ate quickly and very little, took coffee and an ashtray to the console and relieved Stan at the helm, where I could have my back to them.

A bright morning, the wind light to moderate and from near south. Stan had eased the main to hold the same easterly course. Smudges on the horizon were, I knew, the string of islands that include Bimini. The ship's clock rang three bells, nine-thirty. I steered and sipped coffee and smoked my cigarette. Behind me, Stan and Isolda ate and chatted in low and, it seemed to me, intimate voices. When they were finished, Isolda cleared and made several slow and apparently well-planned trips to the galley. Stan went out on deck, stood at the shrouds and scanned the islands with binoculars. Isolda soon followed him, stood by his side. They talked, though I couldn't make out what was said. He passed her the glasses, put an arm around her shoulders, pointed toward a feature on the shore. After a minute or two of that she returned the glasses, faced him, cocked a hip. They were still very close together. A long moment of that, no talking. Then he glanced at me, stepped back from her, left her there with the binoculars. His face was bright red as he came into the wheelhouse.

"Bimini," he said. He ducked into the chartroom, spent a few minutes there, came back to look over the binnacle. "We can put her off a few degrees now," he said. "Set a jib, see how she sails." He went back out on deck to trim the main and rig a jib. In about ten minutes we had her on a broad reach with the engine off and she was a real ship at last.

Through all that Isolda sat on the deck locker aft of the skylight in a classic bathing beauty pose. I had the impression that she had considered joining me at the helm and had decided against it. Once Stan had everything coiled down and secured he went to her, whispered something, helped her to her feet. He led her aft, past the wheelhouse on the starboard side, avoiding my eyes. She afforded me a brief smile and wave as she passed. There was a considerable expanse of deck back there and a broad, cushioned settee against the aft bulkhead of the wheelhouse. It was an hour before I saw either of them again. When I did it was Stan, redder yet, asking me if she needed a trim to hold her course. I told him she was fine. He went below forward. A little later Isolda came in, went aft to the great cabin without speaking, so quickly I hardly caught a glimpse of her. Smelled her intense flesh, though, felt her heat. Then in a few minutes came the sound of Cuban music from back there, a slow rumba, *Quando se quiere de veras*.

Stan reappeared in fifteen minutes or so, showered, fresh shirt and shorts, complexion back to its usual ruddiness.

"You would like a break by now, I'd think," he said cheerily. "Put your head down for a bit. I'll call you when it's time to round Great Isaac."

So I gave him the helm and went below. Tidied the galley, — Isolda could cook but she couldn't clean, — used the head and went to my bunk. There I re-played what I'd seen and imagined what I hadn't. Listened to the softest strains of another Cuban love song. Fell asleep awash in loneliness.

I awoke an hour later. Stan was alone at the helm. No

more Cuban love songs from the great cabin. *Brangaene* moved gently to the soft rollers on her quarter, the breeze still well south of east. Great Isaac Light stood its lonely post, sharp off the starboard bow.

"We'll be rounding soon," he said. "It will put her fairly close to the wind."

"Right. We'll need some centerboard, I suppose."

"Yes, before we actually put her 'round. We'll have time for some coffee first."

The island was white by then, the sparse casuarinas bravely at attention. I could just hear the surf laughing at the coral rock and sand. Or thought I could. An ant-sized man in a white shirt and dark trousers walked toward the lighthouse from the trees. Never gave us a glance. Not that I could have told at that distance if he had.

Stan came up with the coffee, left one cup for me and took his into the chartroom. In a little while he came back and started taking his bearings over the compass. Then it was time. She yawed when Stan let the centerboard down, bucked in protest. Stan handed me the tail of the lee jib sheet, cranked it in with the winch. I brought her up slowly to the new course. He made fast the sheet and went aft to trim the main. That done, we felt her new motion.

"Lee helm," I told him.

"Mizzen, then."

"Want to trade?"

"No, carry on." He went out and set the mizzen, making her happy, anxious to dance with the seas.

"Cook or steer?" he asked.

"You choose," I said.

He left me with her and went to the galley. She sailed well, enjoyed the closer reach, though steering her from behind glass, no wind in the hair, her various voices muted, would take some getting used to. I'd never sailed such a big boat — small ship, really — and found it strange, abstracted, her responses to the helm pondered afterthoughts. Still, she sailed well.

Beer and sandwiches. Isolda didn't want lunch, kept to her cabin. *Brangaene* frolicked in her lugubrious way, like those dancing elephants in tutus. Making eight knots, she was a pretty hot pachyderm. I wasn't in love with her as I had been with *Capriole,* but it was still a romp of an afternoon's sailing. Stan took a turn at the helm, so I went out on deck, tweaked a sheet here and a halyard there, felt the warm air and playful sprays she occasionally squirted aft. Watched her bowsprit plunge and rise, the big jib tugging at its tip. Followed the shifting of strain from sheets to sails to spars and stays and shrouds, all of that magical apparatus busily converting the wind into motion. The perfectly joined teak decking held my feet in the grip of an old friend, the varnished mahogany handrail brushed my fingers with feline lightness.

Oh, how I'd missed sailing and the sea.

The sun was low when we rounded the Berrys and had to take in the jib and the mizzen, flatten the main and put her under power. Isolda joined us for cocktails, slacks and billowy shirt again, a bit subdued, I think, by the motion. I fixed a light supper, which we ate in the wheelhouse as it went dark. In a few hours we picked up the glow of Nassau, and in the wee hours threaded her in on the range lights and laid her gently on the outer dock at the Harbour Club. Hoisted the quarantine flag. Stan and I went about the necessary chores, coiling and furling and adjusting lines and fenders, all that. Isolda stood near the stern, hugging herself as if she were cold, staring out over the harbor as if she wanted to go back to sea. When we had everything shipshape Stan sent me below to pour rums while he caught up the logbook.

Isolda joined us in the wheelhouse, reluctantly it seemed to me, and we clinked glasses, toasted having made a smooth passage. Conversation beyond that was desultory, neither of them ever looking at me or at each other. I took what seemed to be the hint and excused myself.

It was stifling in my stateroom, not too hot but still and stale. I went forward, propped open the fo'c'sle hatch, opened the wings of the skylight. A little air moved through, making the space bearable. I lay down in my skivvies, sipped my rum. Considered a last smoke of the day, but there wasn't enough fresh air for it. When I closed my eyes my body remembered the motion of the boat at sea and missed it. I listened to the Q flag flapping, heard murmurs of speech from the wheelhouse.

I'd slept for an hour or two I think, and I think a footstep on the deck above was what woke me. Whispers:

She: *I can't bear it. Oh God, I must move into the hotel in the morning. Oh God.*

He: *I know.*

A faint rustling of cloth. Silence for a time.

She: *He is not a bad man, but he will never accept this.*

He: *I know.*

More silence.

She: *Why would he want to go to this Staniel Cay?*

He: *Lovely spot. Wonderful diving.*

She: *I don't think so. He doesn't even like to swim, and he's not very well.*

Another pause.

He: *There's an airstrip at Staniel.*

Soft footsteps. They were still whispering but moving away from the skylight, so I couldn't make out anything else.

Yes, why Staniel? I tiptoed to the head, went back to bed. Why Staniel indeed? The rest of it was clear enough.

As I drifted just offshore from sleep though, it seemed less and less clear. Why was I allowed to overhear that conversation at all? Variations on that question kept me half-awake for quite a while.

The morning shone bright. I started coffee, went quietly up on deck. A few people were doing things on their boats, sports fishermen mainly. The wind had gone back to the east, as if it had turned south for two days just to help our passage. I didn't know where Stan and Isolda were, but I assumed in the great cabin, as I'd never heard Stan come forward in the night. When the coffee was ready I took a cup and cigarettes forward on deck, stretched the sorry back and legs with a hand on a shroud and eyes on the two native sloops racing downwind from the Banks far to the east. I sipped and smoked, waiting. I heard six bells from the ship's clock, so it was still pretty early.

I stood there enjoying the cool morning breeze and pondering the sad truth that sometimes the best and only way to love well is to keep one's distance, which was a variation on what I was in fact doing there in Nassau that morning, carefully not looking aft. The arrival of the Customs officer shut that down.

"Good morning, sah. Bahamian Customs."

I turned to see him, white officer's cap, white shirt with black and gold shoulder bars, gold badge, black trousers. Clipboard under an elbow.

"Good morning," I answered, heartily as I could. "Please step aboard."

I ushered him into the wheelhouse, asked him to have a seat. The ship's clock gave me eight tings through which to assemble a mind.

"You are the captain, sah?" he asked.

"No sir, just a deckhand."

"I will have to speak with the captain."

"Of course. I'll find him."

I went forward to Stan's cabin. Things were neat enough in there, bunk made, guitar case laid out on it. No Stan. I called his name, said "Customs," rummaged in my kit for my passport and wallet, went aft again. Stuck my head out through the companionway.

"He'll be here presently," I said. "Would you care for coffee?"

"No thank you," he said, sternly, I thought. The clipboard was on the table. He tapped a rhythm on it with his pen.

I heard the engine room hatch lock working. It was across from the chart table and just forward of the door to the great cabin, which I hadn't heard. Stan climbed up from there, in shorts and a tee shirt, barefoot, wiping his hands on a dirty rag.

"Good morning," he said to the Customs man. "Engine room. Didn't hear you. Sorry."

"You are the captain, sah?"

"Yes. T. Stanford Mallory." He offered his hand. The officer ignored it.

"Oh, right," Stan said, "greasy mess. Sorry."

"May I see the ship's papers, Captain Mallory? And all the passports?"

"Yes, of course. A moment, please."

I offered him my passport. He nodded, didn't look at it. Stan went to the chartroom, rustled papers, knocked on the door to the great cabin.

"Mrs. Reyes? Customs are here. Would you bring up your passport, please?" This in an elevated and very British tone. Then he came up with the ship's papers and his own passport. Customs perused the packet, *Brangaene*'s registration, the charter contracts, radio license. Then Stan's passport, captain's license.

"Very interesting, Captain Mallory. American vessel, British master, Panamanian master's license, in Bahamian waters. Very international. Do you have an American green card?"

"Yes. I can find it for you."

"No need, sah."

At which point he turned to my passport, made some notes. "You were here before, then? Nineteen fifty-six."

"Yes. The Miami-Nassau race."

"Winning boat?"

"No, unfortunately."

This was a small set of lies. I was there on *Capriole* at the time of the race but not in it, and was a few days ahead of the racing boats. But that too is another story. I just hoped he wouldn't notice the discrepancy in the dates.

Just then we heard the latch on the great cabin door, and Isolda appeared. Tight white pants and another billowing, silky blouse, red this time, flag red. Flamenco, bullfight red. She said good morning to all of us, handed the officer her passport. He looked at her longer than was entirely polite, then looked at her American passport, every one of its many visas.

"You travel a great deal, Mrs. Reyes. Switzerland, Spain, France, Italy. And all these to South America. Are you in business?"

"No. My husband travels on business. I often go with him."

He looked at her some more, then at her picture in the passport. Pondered. Shrugged. Wrote on the clipboard. There seemed to be a lot to write. We waited in silence. Finally he stamped a sheet, stamped our passports, handed Stan a form, all filled out.

"Welcome to the Bahamas. I hope you enjoy your visit. This visa is good for three months. Please leave this receipt with Customs when you leave, or if that is impossible, mail it from your first foreign port."

Almost audible sighs of relief all around. We thanked him. Stan saw him back up to the dock. Isolda returned to her cabin. I dug out the Bahamian ensign, took it up. Lowered the yellow Q flag, rigged the ensign, the Union Jack in the upper corner, a red field with a crest. I paused to read the motto wrapped in Latin around its central emblem: "Expel the pirates, restore commerce." The flag is different now, since their independence, but I don't think they ever got that job done, just gave it up. Having once been a sort of pirate myself, I considered that just as well. Anyway, I ran it up to the starboard spreader and made it fast. The American yacht ensign was already flying at the stern.

Stan stuck his head out the fo'c'sle hatch. "Give me a hand with these, will you?"

What he was poking up at me was a roll of canvas wrapped around a short spar. The awnings. We muscled them out one by one. I laid them on the teak. They were marked "head," "main," and "mizzen." Handed up two smaller packages. The wind scoops. I took them. He followed them up.

We unrolled the canvas onto the booms, fixed them with halyards and secured the yards with quick knots to the stanchions.

When we'd finished with the awnings and were working on the wind scoop over the aft hatch, he started talking. "There's something of a problem," he said. "I just noticed when the Customs wallah was here that my green card is about to expire."

"What's that mean?"

"It means I'll have to fly back to Miami today. Try to get a hearing tomorrow."

"Really necessary?"

"Oh yes. Chuck me out of the country if I don't."

"Damn. When will you get back?"

"Tomorrow night, given luck. Might take a day or two more."

"Have you told Isolda?"

"Yes. She'll explain it to her husband. It's only a day or so in the hotel for them. Plenty of fun to be had in Nassau. Stay with the boat, do the dailies in the engine room, top off her tanks. Your pay continues, of course. Oh, and do the laundry, would you? Linens especially."

We went forward, rigged the wind scoop in the hatch over the sail lockers. While we were at that he had something else to ask me.

"Do you know that song she's always playing on the tape machine?" He hummed the chorus, *Quando se quiere de veras..*

"Sure. It's famous."

"Could you write down the lyrics for me? Translate

it?"

"Sure."

"Before I go?"

"Sure."

"Thanks. I'll fix breakfast while you're at it."

So that was next. Below, with the shade of the awnings and the wind scoops drawing bucketsful of the Trades through her, *Brangaene* was several degrees cooler and smelled deliciously of teak and hemp and canvas. In my stateroom I took out my log, opened it to a blank page near the back, and wrote:

Cuando se quiere de veras,
Como te quiero a ti,
Es imposible, mi cielo,
Tan separados vivir.

"When one loves truly,
As I love you,
It is impossible, my Heaven,
To live thus separated."

And all the rest of it. I made a note that "Heaven" here means, more or less, "darling." Well, it's not very smooth in English anyway. I tore out the page, folded it, and put it on his bunk next to the guitar case.

"I'll have to coach you a bit on the pronunciation," I told him when I went to the galley. "The chorus is the main thing, the melody you remember."

"Right. Thanks awfully. Take these up, will you?"

Plates, napkins, silver. Another trip with cups, glasses, a pitcher of orange juice. I realized we'd been running through a long morning on empty.

She was in a white sheath this time, with a white purse and a pair of matching high-heeled shoes on the settee next to her. Make-up perfect, and enough Chanel to make me forget entirely the smell of frying bacon. A stunning picture, but she was nervous, eyes darting, fingers plucking absently at her napkin. I poured her a glass of juice. She thanked me without stopping her eyes or her fingers.

Breakfast was like that throughout, little slices of chopped conversation, no meetings of eyes. When it was over I cleared the table, set to cleaning the galley. Stan went forward, took a shower. When he came aft again he was in whites and deck shoes, had a kit packed.

"I'll see her to the British Colonial. She has the number for the dockmaster here. If she asks you for anything, please do it, will you?"

"Of course."

"I'll go on to the airport. Be back as soon as I can."

"All right," I said, "I'll keep the old bucket safe. Top the tanks, all the rest."

I went up to see them off, told her to call me anytime, handed her two cases onto the dock, offered to carry them, Stan said no, slung his kit on his shoulder and took them both. On the dock she slipped gracefully into her shoes and off they went. She walked well in high heels, swayed from the waist down. Quite a sight. *Mucha mujer.* I watched her until she was out of sight.

Alone felt good. I had a cigarette and another cup of coffee in the wheelhouse, enjoying the breeze and the shade, the quiet movement of the boat, the flapping of the awnings, the wind scoops, the flags. But something seemed wrong. I was pretty sure Stan had been lying about the green card, wasn't going to Miami at all.

Probably just planning to stay the night with Isolda in the hotel. But then, why that about doing what she asked if she called? Just to keep me with the boat? Probably. Devious lot, the Brits. Probably all there was to it. But with the husband to arrive that very day?

Oh well, there was much to be done, so when the cigarette had burned down to the filter I cast off from the settee and got myself underway. Laundry first. Stan had left his bagged in a pillowcase in his stateroom. I did the same with mine, hauled them both to the galley, collected used napkins and tablecloths and dishtowels. Found detergent. Took all of it up to the wheelhouse. Then had to go aft to the great cabin for Isolda's. No laundry there, not a stitch but the linens. Why had she taken her laundry to the hotel, with the husband due to arrive that very day? Well, maybe they had same-day service.

I hauled the lot up onto the deck and then to the dock and then to the machines in the utility room of the hotel. The machines, though quite new, were beginning to rust, and the dark little room smelled of mildew and chlorine. Everything seemed to be working, however. I pumped in coins, got the machines sloshing and creaking. Went back out into the sun.

The main pier was at least a hundred yards long, with several finger piers forming boat slips, sixty or more of them. Most were empty. One pretty little sea-going ketch. A badly-neglected yawl of thirty-eight feet or so, buttoned up, decks gone gray, varnish peeling beyond redemption. A few sharp, active sports fishermen, maybe twenty-five to thirty feet. *Brangaene* dwarfed them all, lying out on the fuel dock at the end. It was clear that the Harbour Club wasn't making much from its docking facilities. It was a hot walk from there to the Yacht

Haven, shopping, the town, not pleasant for the frugal sailor. Perhaps the hotel and dining room were doing better, but there was no one at the pool or in the lower lobby. A heavy-set, sunburned man climbed slowly up the ladder to the bridge of his sports fisherman, cranked up her diesels, revved them up and down a few times, sending a cloud of black smoke out over the dock. He idled down, pulled out a rag and a bottle of something and started wiping down the chrome. I didn't see anyone else until the end, where the dock master sat in his elevated office doing paperwork. I hailed him. He stood, a very large and very black man in khakis, and lumbered down the steps.

"Hello," I said, "I'm on *Brangaene*. Skipper told me to top off her tanks. She won't take much diesel, I'm pretty sure. Can we do that today?"

"We can do it now, if you like. Water too?"

"Yes, she'll probably take a good bit of water."

"Open the cocks. I'll hand you the hoses and start the pumps."

I went to the chartroom, found the keys, back on deck I found the cocks. She took thirty gallons of diesel, fifty of water. He added the cost to the dockage bill — some outrageous amount — and returned to his air-conditioned post. Clearly didn't want to stand around talking in the sun.

So I did this and that until it was time to put the wash in the dryers. Changed into whites, put on deck shoes. Once I'd moved the stuff and got the machines running I went into the hotel and up the spiral staircase, listened a moment to the fountain at its base, strode into the bar. It was elegant and empty. I sat on a stool and enjoyed the artificial chill. A bartender appeared at last and poured me a rum and soda.

"When does the season start?" I asked him.

"November, maybe. Sure ended in April."

He didn't want to chat either. I finished the one, went back to the laundry room. It felt stifling and wet after the air-conditioning. I folded everything fairly neatly, trying not to sweat into my clean whites. Went back to the boat. Stripped to shorts before making the bunks, hanging the towels, all that. Then I stretched out on the settee in the wheelhouse with José María Gironella's *Los Cípreses Creen en Díos*, in Spanish, and took a nap.

Big, loud rollers were breaking way too close, I was trying to pinch her out away from them, they would tear her apart, she's hauled as close to the wind as she'll go, sheets humming, leeches like playing cards clothespinned into bicycle spokes, the spray from her bows is rain falling skyward, go, sweet ship, just a little more, just a little more, fine, sweet vessel, cleave to this wind, answer to my every half-a-spoke paid to every twist of wave or turn of wind, how can there be surf here, docked in Nassau Harbor?

The surf was not surf, of course, but the amplified ringing of the dockmaster's telephone. I sat slowly upright with a hitch in my hip, donned sunglasses, looked out onto the dock, up to the elevated office. No one was there or anywhere in sight. Still somewhat or somewhere at sea, I stumbled up there, found a phone box near the fuel pumps, pulled the phone out of it. The ringing stopped, so I spoke into it.

"Nassau Harbour Club Dock."

"Brendan Harper of *Brangaene*, please," she said.

— Sí, él habla.

— Aquí está Isolda.

— Sí. Hola, Señora.

Continuing in Spanish, she told me that her husband would be delayed, perhaps for several days. Would it be possible for me to join her for dinner, perhaps dancing afterward? Of course, at your service, Señora. With much pleasure. At five in the afternoon? At the British Colonial? Of course, at five at the hotel. But I'm afraid I won't be able to dance, because of my limp. Of course you will. It is a very small limp. No one will notice. Oh, and will you please bring the larger of my two remaining suitcases? Surely. Gracias.

Filled then with hope and fear, I was thirteen again, anticipating Miss Pauline Bruner's Seventh Grade Cotillion, I think I may have owned a suit then, but was sure I didn't have one anymore. In my kit aboard were just some wash-and-wear whites and — jeez, what a wrinkled mess it had to be — the old blue blazer with the St. Petersburg Yacht Club crest. I knew I didn't have a tie, maybe Stan had packed one and left it.

And dancing? Me? Miss Pauline Bruner. I practiced a few steps in the wheelhouse, maybe the limp wouldn't be too bad if I stayed up on my toes, off my heels, bent one ankle a bit more than the other, the rumba was basically a waltz with a pause on the fourth beat, right? One, two, three, pause, one, two, three, pause. That sort of thing until six bells, then to work on it all. At four-thirty I presented myself at the Harbour Club's desk in whites, polished loafers with dark socks, blue blazer still damp from sponging, and a club tie nicked out of Stan's locker. Had them call a cab for me. Practiced not limping as I carried her suitcase to the front desk of the British Colonial and asked for Mrs. Isolda Reyes.

"She asks that you go up, sah. Two thirty-seven."

A Hispanic guy in his thirties, wearing a white Palm Beach suit and holding a Panama, rushed to catch the elevator and just made it. There were four of us in there, he, an older British couple laden with straw hats and baskets nattering about their lunch, and I. I felt the Hispanic fellow's eyes on my back all the way. He stayed with the elevator when I got out, but I knew he wanted to see which way I turned. I figured that he did. So what? I found the number and knocked. The door opened immediately.

— Hola, Brendan.

— Hola, Señora.

— Entre, por favor.

— Gracias, Señora.

— Me llame Isolda, por favor. Especialmente esta noche.

— Sí, Isolda.

So we were officially on a first-name basis.

I saw that the room was big, the living room of a suite, but I can't tell you much more about it. She was as always perfect, but in her little black dress, hair up in a Flamenco dancer's bun, all that cleavage . . . sorry, can't tell you much about the room.

Well, I know you could follow it all in Spanish, if I still had fluent Spanish. But I don't anymore, and it would get to be an awkward mess anyway, back and forth to waiters and cabbies and so on in English, back to Spanish with her, all that. So just note that we spoke only Spanish to one another, okay?

She took the suitcase from me and carried it into the bedroom. The weight of it didn't hamper her stride at all, still a transfixing sight. When she came back she walked up to me with an envelope in her hand.

"First thing," she said, "is for you to take this. It is an advance in cash for the charter, against your expenses."

I'd been wondering how she would handle that. Should have known that it would be perfectly. She knew I was unlikely to have enough for more than a dinner at a conch stall and a drink or two at a bar on a back street over the hill. I thanked her and slipped the envelope into a breast pocket.

"Next, if you will wait a moment, I will get my things and we will give ourselves martinis in the lounge."

I said that would be fine, but the truth was that having her out of my sight for even an instant would be an agony.

Her absence was mercifully brief. We went down to the lounge, which wasn't crowded at all. Dim. Soft, vaguely Caribbean music. The Hispanic guy in the white suit was sitting at the far end of the bar drinking Hatuí. We took a booth.

"These Exuma Islands. They are beautiful, no?"

"They are indeed beautiful. Especially the colors in the water, which is so clear you can see every pebble on its bottom."

"I look forward to it."

"And I."

A waiter came and we ordered, or rather she asked me to order, two Beefeater martinis, dry, very cold, one olive only.

"How is it that you speak Spanish so well?" she asked.

"I studied it in school, and lived near Ybor City in Tampa. Then after the service I studied Spanish Literature at the University of Florida. I just took my degree. But I don't think I speak it very well, really."

"No, you speak well. Perhaps with the formality of school, and with the accent of Sevilla. No, south of Sevilla. Not always, though. Sometimes it sounds almost Castilian."

"Different teachers at different times, I think."

"Surely. But only that reveals that you are not Spanish."

Well, it was that sort of thing until the waiter came with the chilled glasses and the shaker. He poured. We said Salud and all the rest of it. Sipped and ate olives, murmuring approval. I pulled out a tattered box of Rothmans. She handed me a silver case full of Dunhills and a matching silver lighter. I lit hers, dealt with my own. We smoked and sipped.

"I hear no Cuban accent in your Spanish," I said.

"You would not. It is very slight, very seldom."

I was going to ask her why that was, but she interrupted before I could. "What did your parents expect of you?" she asked.

I looked at her, bereft of understanding, from an entirely empty place. What I saw was a face so perfect you couldn't dream it, with a slight question in it but nevertheless placid in its pure beauty. Did she ask that because she wanted to hear an answer? Or because she wanted me to ask the same question of her? Or to move our conversation to a higher level of intimacy? Or just to make me look at her and be shocked again by the power of her perfection? I couldn't know, so I gave her my straightest answer.

"To be a credit to them, I suppose. And yours?"

She took a puff of her Dunhill, blew smoke to the side while holding my eyes. "To be out of their way. And then to marry, forming an alliance to their advantage."

She said this while holding my eyes in hers. I tried staying with them, managed it just long enough to let her know she'd won me.

We finished the martinis. One more, please. Of course, can't fly on one wing. The guy in the white suit started another beer. Two couples came in together, young, New York from the accents, the men in suits I'd never be able to afford, women in dresses you wouldn't find on racks anywhere. One of the stiffly-waved blondes caught a glimpse of Isolda and maneuvered the group to a table at the other end of the room. Our drinks came, just as cold and perfect as the last pair.

"Can you tell me about Cuba?" I asked. She sipped, had me light another cigarette for her. Gave me her eyes again. They were suddenly harder than before.

"Have you ever been there?"

"Once, the winter of 'fifty-three. The race from St. Petersburg to Havana. Two days only."

"Yes. Old Cuba. It ended on New Year's Day, nineteen fifty-nine. A few days later we were allowed to leave, but without currency, only what we could carry in one suitcase each. We were all searched at the airport. Many were arrested. So now I can't tell you anything about Cuba."

"Did you live in Havana?"

"No. We had a cattle ranch. My father kept a suite at the Nacional. We would use it sometimes for shopping, or when flying in or out."

"Where did you go to school?"

"At a convent not far from the ranch. Later at a convent in Málaga. Then in Switzerland. You are asking too many questions."

Well, that was true enough. Embarrassed, I sipped and smoked, looked around the room. The Americans were tuning up. The Brits too, but not so volubly. White Suit was twirling his glass, considering another. A blond, crew-cut athlete in a white guayabera with the sleeves rolled up stuck his head in, scanned the place, took a seat at the other end of the bar.

I guess she didn't like watching me drift. "What you want to know about is my marriage," she said.

That of course brought my attention right back where it belonged. I nodded.

"Marco is from Tampa. He handled investments for my father, cattle, land, all the business of the ranch. His father and my father were old friends in Cuba. When Marco was old enough and had finished his courses in business in the States, he came to the ranch to study its operation. The first time he came I was seven. When we were married I was eighteen. We lived in Miami. I visited my parents when he went down there for business."

"I see."

"Do you? Yes, it's clear, isn't it? But you also want to know about the money."

I nodded again.

"It was very sudden, the success of the Fidelistas. No one in Havana or Miami or New York believed it was possible. But those living out in the countryside, like my father, thought it was possible, so he made Marco invest in things in the States, Mexico, other places. This he did. And each time we visited, we carried valuable things back, small things. Despite this much was left behind, much was lost. But Marco had invested well, so when my parents had to leave they could live well. Except for the sadness."

"Where do they live?"

"Not far from Miami."

Last sip.

"Enough," she said. Take me to dinner, please. Can we walk?"

"Can we stand up?"

We tried it, laughing. Though out of practice from my sailing days, I could still easily handle tee martoonis. Apparently it was harder for her. She got up gracefully enough, but clung two-handed to my elbow and rested that elegant head on my shoulder.

"Not the dining room here," she said. "It is dull and stuffy. Take me to the White Gates."

"Will we need a cab?"

"No. It is only a short walk. Walking will clear my head."

Another Hispanic in a white suit stood near the desk, then moved almost into our path. Older than the other, actually wearing his Panama. He hardly gave Isolda a glance, which struck me as so unusual as to be odd. He looked me up and down though, catching my eyes and burning them with his own dark, mean ones, set in a face unforgettable in its ingrained anger. Then he suddenly looked behind us, those eyes shifting in alarm. I wanted to turn, couldn't with Isolda's head on my shoulder. What had he seen?

We marched on to the entrance, where an understanding doorman smiled and showed us out into the evening. She kept an arm locked into mine to negotiate the long, wide stairs down to the street, but lightly, not clinging anymore, holding a steady course at an easy pace. Bay Street was still busy with shoppers at the straw market, lights were coming on as the day waned. When we got to the street she let go, took on the insouciant stride I'd seen in Lauderdale, but without the self-consciousness.

The restaurant was in an early Colonial building with a walled courtyard. Behind the wall trees and shrubs cast shadows on stone tables, their umbrellas folded. The headwaiter welcomed her by name. She introduced him as André. He bowed to me. After a glance inside at the elegant but busy dining room, she said she would rather sit outside. I was happy with that, roughly dressed as I was and in hope of some privacy. A white tablecloth came, was spread with a flourish, and rapidly set with linen napkins, heavy silver, candles in chimneys. She asked for Pouilly Fuiseé, a particular one, and conch seviche, and grouper in a sauce I'd never heard of. It all sounded fine to me.

And it was. The conch was peppered but not too hot, wine in it perhaps, or a gentle, herbal vinegar. The grouper had been out on the reef earlier that same day, and swam now in a wonderful sauce reminiscent of Béarnaise. The smoky finish of the wine matched it all exactly. Other diners passed by on their way in or out, but no other outdoor tables were taken. Birds chirped and whistled as they settled in the trees and shrubs around us, and we could hear steel drums on the light breeze, from somewhere on the beach or the street. I looked at Isolda as often as I could, she speaking of restaurants and recipes, the paella of Valencia, the lamb of León, the oysters of Apalachicola. It seemed in the circumstances to be the only way to speak of love.

That done, she ordered cognac and Cuban cigars, reminding me that the Bahamas weren't affected by the embargo.

"Are there planes from Havana?" I asked.

She looked startled by the question, even frightened.

A waiter brought a selection of Havanas in a box. She selected a small one, as did I. The waiter lit them for us. Once hers was going she watched as mine was lit. She puffed, exhaled, holding my eyes. It's wonderful to watch a beautiful young woman smoke a cigar.

"Yes, once or twice a week," she told me. "I think it is mainly cargo. Very few passengers, because there are no tourists anymore. Officials, I suppose. Some businessmen, perhaps."

Always when she spoke of Cuba there was the bitterness she tried to conceal, and a wistfulness she could not. And often, fear. Of Castro, somehow? Her husband? Weren't they both far enough away? We smoked and sipped. The waiter came and asked if we wanted anything else. She shook her head, so I asked for the bill.

"Where shall we go to dance?" she asked.

"I have no idea. I have never been dancing here."

"I have heard of a place called Charlie-Charlie's. Do you know of it?"

"I have heard of it. I think it is authentically Bahamian, but perhaps a rough place."

"Good. I want a rough place, with loud, wild music. I want to dance wildly, with abandon."

That did not sound good to me, but I wasn't going to object. How the hell was I to dance wildly, with abandon? Either she hadn't thought of that or she just didn't care. So it was with some trepidation that I paid the check, asked the waiter if he knew where Charlie-Charlie's was, and if we'd need a cab to get there. Yes and yes, and he would call one for us.

We wandered the courtyard for a while, leisurely making our way toward the street. Her arm folded into mine again, and her head dropped back onto my shoulder. Near the wall a few steps led down to the sidewalk. There she turned to me and reached around me with both arms. "Embrace me, Brendan," she whispered, putting her head on my chest.

This I did, asking myself if I dared to believe what was happening. Could this rich, expensive, perfect beauty want poor, gimpy, scruffy, scrawny little Brendan Harper, not even a captain anymore? Did she truly see through the sorry surface to the deep intelligence and noble heart within? No, no, she is just a little drunk and lonely. Yes, yes, of course she does, she is the goddess who knows and sees all, sees the greatness in me, her love will make the world see the magnificence within, I will accomplish great deeds . . . .

Over her head across the street I saw movement, a flicker as a pair of headlights swept the corner. A man in a dark clothing averted his eyes, raised a hand to his face but too late, it was the older White Suit from the lobby, now dressed in dark clothing.

The pair of headlights which had swept him proved to belong to our cab. We got in, and off we went to Charlie-Charlie's. In the cab she sat behind the driver, leaning on the far door, as far from me as she could get. I made a stab at conversation, something banal, got no response. Gave it up, tried to watch the passing scene. Nothing there either, as we had moved away from city lights and into dark territory. From celestial heights in the arms of the goddess, I was sinking rapidly into bleak despair.

What was that evil-looking bugger doing on that

particular street corner? At that exact moment?

Charlie-Charlie's. Forms milling in front of a dimly-lighted entrance, Bahamian giants, male, in shiny shirts open to the waist, the skin revealed. Tight, dark trousers on them, bulging at the crotch. They made way for us, briefly silenced as the light gave them a clear picture of Isolda. One of them looked at me in amazement. I gave him a small smile and a wink. Subdued patois after that, incomprehensible.

Inside it was as loud as promised, with an electrified band, drums and guitars and a steel-drum kit, the players four more Bahamian giants in bright satin shirts. The place was crowded with dark women in bright dresses, pale women in bright dresses, pale men in sportcoats, suits, Hawaiian shirts, dark men dressed in shirts open to the waist and tight dark trousers, just like the giants. Raucous laughter, shouting, the smell of beer and sweat and spilled rum. And in a corner at the bar sat the athlete in the white guayabera rolled-up at the sleeves, his cold, pale eyes staring at us out from under his blond brush cut.

Isolda didn't even look for a table or a place for her purse, which she simply handed off to me as she spun herself out into the melee on the dance floor. What choice had I but to follow? It wasn't in me to dance with her. All I could do was shuffle around a little, keep her in sight. The band caught on to her first, upped the intensity of the rhythm. Then other dancers got it, gave her room. Her purse was small enough to jam into a jacket pocket, which let me shuffle around a little more freely.

She raised her arms slowly and gracefully, never slowing her body. The movement raised her breasts, exposing even more cleavage. With both hands behind her head, hips grinding, spinning and spinning, she invited all males into her, into that perfect body. As she completed a turn I could see that she was pulling pins from her hair, which she finally shook loose, spreading her arms. Near the bandstand she bent at the knees and laid the pins on the riser, giving the players' eyes full access to her cleavage. Then she rose and faced toward me again and gave me a small and self-satisfied smile, jiggled her sweat-damp, glistening breasts. By then I had given up any attempt to continue shuffling, just stood there barely able to keep my jaw from hanging open.

Suddenly she stopped, just gave it up. Walked slowly to me, asked for her purse. "Please find us a table and order rums," she said, and walked away, presumably to the ladies' room.

I did as ordered, sat and sipped rum and soda and watched the hall to the restrooms. It was crowded with drunks waiting, mostly men. One of them was young White Suit from the hotel lounge, now in a dark blue pinstripe. He wasn't looking at me, but was scanning the room, the bar, glancing occasionally down the hall behind him. Needless to say I wasn't liking any of it. Coincidence was over as an option. We were there, two of those guys were there, the third one had been outside the restaurant, there was no reason for them to have any interest in me, only in Isolda, or, more likely, in Señora Reyes, wife of Don Marco Reyes. Castro's? Reyes's own? Someone else's? Jeez.

She made her way back through the jammed hallway. I stood, wanting to warn her about White Suit-now-Pinstripe, but she didn't notice me. She paused as Pinstripe spoke to her. She nodded and her lips formed a sí. Then noticed me and walked up to me.

"Let us go, please," she said. Didn't look at me when she said it. Didn't sit or glance at her drink.

We left. Outside the big guys were still at it, reluctantly let us pass. A classic Jaguar sedan idled at the curb. "This car," she said. "Quickly, please."

I opened the rear door. She slid quickly across the seat. I jumped in. The tires squealed before I could get the door closed. The older White Suit was driving. Brush-cut suddenly appeared in the windshield, dodged out of the way of the car, turned and ran. The Jag was already doing sixty at least.

I looked at Isolda. Her hair was still loose, her head was down, I couldn't see anything of her face. I started to ask, but she shook her head without lifting it.

We were out in the countryside, still moving very fast. Older White Suit-now-Dark Shirt pulled the car off onto a side road, turned it around, turned off the lights, let the quiet engine idle. We waited.

"Nothing," he said after a few minutes.

"Good. Brendan, this is Juan Mí. He works for my husband."

—Mucho gusto, I said, though I wasn't particularly happy to meet him.

"His associate is Paco. You have recognized Paco, no? We will go now back to Nassau," she said. "We will leave you at the Harbour Club. There is a suitcase on the seat next to Juan Mí. Please hide it somewhere on the boat."

—Sí Señora, I said.

"The blond man in the guayabera is a bad man. He carries a pistol and is a skilled fighter. You should try to avoid him."

—Sí Señora.

"He does not work alone, there are others. They will

be watching the hotel. This is the only way I could think of to get the suitcase onto the boat."

Well, that explained some things. I was too lost and confused to ask about any of the important ones. We were moving again, Juan Mí driving more sedately. I sat back and pondered, then dared a question. "Are you sure they won't be watching the Harbour Club?"

Juan Mí answered. "It is impossible to be sure."

"Then may I make a suggestion?"

"What?"

"Let me off at Yacht Haven instead. I'll hire a boat to take me to *Brangaene* from the bay side, not have to walk out on the dock. In case another bad man is there."

Silence for a time.

"Juan Mí?" she said.

"If you trust him," Juan Mí said slowly, "it would be safer."

She turned and looked at me. It was the first time since dinner that she had. It was dark, so I couldn't read her expression, but felt an earnestness from her, or perhaps just desperation. She was probably trying to decide if her seduction of poor little gimpy Brendan Harper had been successful.

"I can trust him," she said.

She was probably right. I wouldn't kill or die for the damned suitcase, but surely I could get it onto the boat. I didn't know if I would kill or die for her. I know I wanted more than anything to believe in the good moments of the evening, but had to believe in this sad part too if I was to come out of it intact.

So they let me out a block inland from Yacht Haven. I lugged the suitcase quickly to Bay Street and across to the dock. Beneath the Pilot House a little conch boat had just finished unloading. Her skipper was alone, clearing her filthy cockpit, looking for the tails of his halyards between her floorboards. I hailed him.

"My friends took the dinghy and left me ashore," I told him. "Could I ask you to give me a lift out to our boat?"

"Where she lie, mon?"

"On an anchor, a bit east of the Harbour Club."

"That upwind, mon."

"I know. I can hand the sheets for you when we tack, and put twenty dollars toward your stores homeward bound."

"You got it, mon. Step aboard."

I handed him the case and climbed into her, hauled her main halyards, shoved her off the dock. When he'd backed her out far enough I set the jib and trimmed, coiled. The lines were filthy, though of good three-strand manila. She stank of old conch, her bilge soaked my shiny loafers, but close-hauled on starboard tack she held to the breeze and made good way against wind and tide. I sniffed the salt air ahead of her and felt cleaner than I had for the last three hours.

"I'm Brendan Harper," I told him. "May I ask your name, Captain?"

"Cop'n Moxey, sah. From Hall's Pond Cay."

We shook hands. "Good to meet you," I said. "We'll be sailing down your way soon, I think."

"Hope to see you there. Exuma Cays beautiful, mon."

"So they are."

Soon we were out far enough to see the Harbour Club dock. I laughed and gave him the good news. "Oh look. They've moved her onto the dock. Just one tack should do it. Goes well to windward, your boat."

"She do that, mon, indeed. Which one you belong to?"

"The big ketch on the outside. Just slip in close by her port side. I'll hop over when you tack out."

"That boat, she was there when I sailed in."

Which seemed the perfect time to reach for my wallet, pull out the twenty and hand it to him. If he had more to say about that, he didn't.

"Thank you, sah. Time to put the helm alee."

So I cleared my jib sheets and loosed and hauled as if it were a championship regatta. In less than five minutes we were alongside her.

"Great sailing with you, Captain Moxey," I said.

"A pleasure, mon. Free the jib sheet now, please."

I did that, pitched the case onto *Brangaene*'s deck just aft of the wheelhouse windows, grabbed a rail and clung there with the other hand on a lifeline and a knee on the teak. Gave the sloop a light kick with the other foot. Captain Moxey pulled her out of irons and trimmed away on starboard tack before I'd rolled the rest of me aboard.

I lay without moving, quieting my breath, my nose down on the pungent oiled teak. Awnings fluttered, wavelets splashed. Then someone aboard her struck wood on wood and grunted softly. I stayed frozen. A light clicked on below, shone up through the skylight, painted an oblong pattern of shadows on the underside of the awning.

Silently, silently, I gathered my knees under me, crawled forward one sloth's pace at a time. Not a sound, not a sound. Looked cautiously through the slot where the skylight was propped open. Shadows wavered from one of the staterooms. Latches clicked. Silently, silently, I fished my rigging knife out of a pocket, opened it with not a sound, not one sound. Listened so intently my pulse joined the orchestra of awnings, flags, wavelets, the creaks of floorboards and whispers of cloth from below. Only one guy. Surely only one.

Pure sloth again, aft to the starboard side door to the wheelhouse. There I plastered myself to the varnished mahogany aft of the windows. Breathed. Blinked, almost recoiled when the light in there snapped on. Peeked. Clinked the damned knife on the damned glass, which meant that there was nothing for it but to attack with the advantage of surprise. Sprang for the door.

"Oh, hullo, Brendan," Stan said. "Wondering where you were."

He settled himself on the settee, guitar in hand, peered at the page torn from my logbook on the table in front of him as he reached for his glass. "Pour yourself a rum, then give me a hand with this tune, will you? *Can-do say query day bare-ass,* right?"

Mexico Beach, 2005

Lee James chuckles. Nicely done, Cap'n Bren, he says. Yawns broadly. I'm afraid we'll have to leave it there for tonight. I've had about all of this chair I can take in a day.

Give you a hand?

No, the place is all rigged for it. He bends to gather things onto the drinks tray.

At least let me do that, Bren says.

Lee James continues feebly reaching for ashtrays,

matches, napkins. He's having a hard time of it and it angers him, makes him even more awkward. Finally he sits back in his chair, closes his eyes and mutters damnit damnit damnit. Sighs Aw what the hell, barely audibly. And then, Well all right. Thanks.

Brendan sips the last of the rum in his snifter while Lee James pulls back his chair, turns it, wheels to a nearby light switch. Grandchildren tomorrow, he says.

Yes. Ramona told me. When are they due?

After lunch, I think. Could be earlier. He pauses, considers. Only one grandchild, actually, our son's daughter Juanita. Two great grandchildren, one ours, one my brother's.

Great grandchildren. Amazing. How old?

Elena is about four, as I recall. She's ours. Tyler is a bit younger. They're close cousins.

I expect you'll enjoy that.

I will when they're not squalling. He turns his chair around the rest of the way, aims it down the hall. I believe you'll find everything you'll need up there, he says, flicking his head up toward the staircase. Have a good night.

Bren says thanks and good night to the back of the retreating chair, overwhelmed for an instant by a clash of conflicting emotions. His mind is crowded with pictures of his oldest friend, this one the most recent, gray head lolling as spotted, wrinkled hands drive away in lieu of once-strong legs; the earliest on the bridge of the Coast Guard cutter, Lee James as XO in charge of the bridge, a calm, slim young officer, Bren still a teen-ager, taking his first trick at the cutter's helm; in Tallahassee, reporting on the scoundrels in government and real estate who were systematically ruining the coasts and the bays, Bren at the time in graduate school. Seeing Lee James so old and frail brings fear, sadness, wonder and gratitude all at once. He doubts that the phrase lucky to be alive would have any meaning for him if this friend were gone.

When his paralysis has passed he rises cautiously, winces as the bad leg straightens to take the load. It's getting worse, of course, the old spinal wound having had all these years to grind on his flesh and bone, he's fought it all this time with exercise and vanity, but now the deterioration of age stabs him where he's weakest. Need a cane most of the time these days, damnit, but at least I'm not stuck in a chair like poor ol' Lee James.

Bren takes care of the drinks tray, switches off lights and the ceiling fan, climbs the stairs slowly, painfully clinging to the cypress sapling banister. Pauses in the bathroom, does what's needed, finds his pills and swallows them. Then goes to his room. It overlooks the Gulf, has its own little balcony. He slides open the glass door, breathes in the delicious scents of sea and sand, silvered cypress planking, flowers somewhere, carried on a light waft from the land. The surf is languorous, sleepy itself, settled in for the night. He leaves the door open, undresses and lies in the bed, smells sweet sheets, arranges pillows around the bad leg, the failing hip. Waits for the pills to mask the pain of it. In a little while they've done that.

He awakens lost at sea, confused, unsure of where or when he is. Hears muted surf and panics, feels for wind, for the boat's motion. Rolls carefully onto his back, looks out to heavy fog. It's all right. I'm here. It's now.

He rises piece by piece, trying to protect the vulnerable parts of his spine, avoiding any twist of the perfidious leg. Takes a full minute to stand upright, clinging to whatever comes to hand. Hobbles to the open sliding door. He can hear the surf trying to tell him something, but can't see it through the fog. He looks up to the sky, where the fog moves on the wind in viscous clumps, thinning here and there to reveal an anemic blue. He steps out onto the little balcony and bathes in the cool damp air, noting that he hurts less than usual this morning and that there is joy afloat on the blank sea of his mind. Only for a moment can this last. He straightens himself, marches inside and starts the routines of the morning.

Groomed and dressed for the day, he descends the glowing stairway, goes to the kitchen. Lee James and Ramona are already sharing the newspaper over café con leche.

Buenos días, Ramona says. Has dormido bien?

Buenos días. Sí, muy bíen. Y tú? Good morning, Lee James.

Good morning, Captain Harper, Lee James says heartily. And yes, I too slept well. He folds his newspaper, puts it aside. Join us.

He sits, takes coffee.

Lee James tells me that your yarn concerns Marco and Isolda Reyes, Ramona says. From Tampa?

Marco was from Tampa. Isolda was Cuban.

She ponders this. But she came to Tampa after Castro, didn't she?

I don't really know. Somewhere in the States. She had an American passport in 'sixty.

She mutters, Isolda Reyes, Isolda Reyes. I believe may cousin Julia knew an Isolda Reyes in Tampa. A little later, aloud, Yes. I'm sure my cousin Julia spoke of an Isolda Reyes many years ago. I haven't called her in a long time. I should. Today. Another pause. Then, No. Juanita is bringing the grandchildren — the great grandchildren — today. I will call her tomorrow.

Breakfast over, Bren and Lee James take espressos out onto the veranda. The wind has gone into the northeast, so they sit in a lee. Bren lights his first cigarette of the day. Together they watch as the fog thins, showing them sand, surf, the outline of the distant pier.

The fog will burn off completely in an hour or so, Lee James says. The girls will have a fine beach day.

Should be fun for you.

Unless they take to squalling. Now, I presume you tidied your clothes and hid the suitcase?

Bren finds himself confused again, realizes he has been having some little trouble lately remembering when he is at any given moment. Oh, right, he says, Nassau in 'sixty. Yes, I did what I could with my clothes. The shoes were pretty much a ruin. I hid the suitcase in the sail locker forward, in the bottom of the spinnaker bag, all that under everything else. A sailor would find it in a flash, but it would take a lubber a while. And Stan got the hang of the song in an hour or so.

Did you tell him about your night's adventure?

No. I had to tell him about the suitcase, of course, and the envelope for expenses Isolda had given me. Not about the rest of it.

Nassau — The Exumas, 1960

I opened my eyes as a beam of sunlight crossed over them. A fender squealed, a spring line creaked. I lay still, entranced by the perfect joinery and tasteful selection of mahogany and teak in the stateroom, the subtle Florentines hand-carved in borders and moldings, the satin varnish glistening where the sun struck it glowing softly in the shadows. Had the craftsmen who built her ever gone to sea? Did they dream of sailing as they worked? Surely there were hearts and souls as well as hands in that woodwork.

I made myself move, discovered stiff joints and sore muscles. Went forward to the head and showered away all of the hot water. Dressed and went up to the wheelhouse, where I did the series of stretches and exercises that kept the bad back and leg from getting worse. Or at least slowed the decline. Or seemed to. Coffee was in a thermos on the table there, cups laid out, a bowl of grapes. I helped myself.

There seemed to be more activity than usual on the docks that morning, people scrubbing, polishing, making the trek to and from the shore showers, hunching over engine hatches, sorting through dive gear. Stan strolled out of the hotel, pausing to chat with one or two sailors he seemed to know. He had a zippered portfolio tucked under an arm. I tidied up the coffee things, went out on deck to finish my cigarette. He saw me, waved, said another word or two to someone on one of the sport-fishing boats. Headed my way, striding now, not strolling.

"Morning, Brendan. We'll be off in an hour's time. Señor Reyes won't be coming. He'll join us at Staniel Cay. Have to get these awnings down. How are the tanks?"

"Fuel's up. She'll take twenty gallons or more of water."

So we did all that, enjoying the cool freshwater on the decks underfoot, the teamwork as we rolled and stowed the awnings. We had her on her springs with the engine mumbling in less than an hour. Stan withdrew to the chartroom, fiddled with the radio, whatever else. I did some cursory polishing. Isolda was late.

"She'd better get here soon," Stan said, looking at the clock. "It's a good six hours to Highbourne Cay, and not a decent anchorage along the way."

"Yes, but even if it were ten hours we'd get there before dark, wouldn't we?"

"Yes, but much after three the light goes bad for reading the bottom."

"Oh, right. Forgot. It's been too long."

It had been more than five years since I'd had to pilot a boat over coral heads. Hard to see them when the sun is low, even if it's behind you. How much more had I forgotten?

We stewed. Stan paced. I went out on deck to find something else to polish. The clock rang ting-ting, ting, indicating nine-thirty. As if on cue Isolda appeared, a vision in white slacks and a flowing white jacket, huge straw hat. She strode out onto the dock, head high, shoulders back, not a glance to one side or the other. A bellman trotted after her, laden with her suitcases and shopping bags, from which protruded bits of straw objects. I could see silence fall as she made her procession down the dead center of the pier, all eyes following her as she passed sailors and fishermen interrupted in their tasks and conversations. As I've mentioned, she sure could walk. I couldn't take my eyes off her either. Couldn't even move.

Stan stepped out from the wheelhouse as she neared. I went aft to the waist where she would board, so Stan and I stood on either side of the gate opened in the lifelines. She smiled at me, took my hand for the little hop from dock to deck, stumbled into my chest. Stan watched this, as surprised as I was. She ducked quickly into the wheelhouse. Stan and I unburdened the bellman. Stan tipped him. We moved in a flurry then, Stan to the helm, I to clearing the mooring lines. The bellman took the last of the lines so I could jump aboard. Stan backed her down on it, slammed the shift forward. The bellman tossed me the line and we were off. In that moment Isolda appeared on deck in a tiny white bikini, posed with a hand draped over the grab rail on the wheelhouse roof. All eyes were on us, but only the bellman waved.

As we glided rapidly forward I looked back, don't know why. The new line of sight showed the flying bridge of a sports fisherman which had been behind the dock master's office before. On it I saw Juan Mí, with binoculars. He didn't have them focused on us, but on the roof of the hotel. I looked up there and saw another pair of binoculars which definitely were focused on us, in front of a white guayabera with rolled up sleeves. A short-sleeved Hawaiian floral stood next to it, arms with raised palms extended from the sleeves. A white suit under a Panama stood behind them. Paco. I looked back at Juan Mí. A rifle leaned unobtrusively against his hip. But by then we were mid-channel and I couldn't see anything more. Aft, Isolda had gone below. I went back to my coils and fenders.

It wasn't long before Stan waved me into the wheelhouse. He throttled her down, slowing her to three knots. "You'll have to steer now for a time. Runs bloody shallow through here. I'll go out to the bowsprit, signal you by hand, port, starboard. If I wave you back, stop her."

For the next ten or fifteen minutes I kept my eyes glued on Stan, who showed me one hand or the other as he peered intently into the water. Finally he came aft again, pushed the throttle forward until she was back up to eight knots. "We're all right for a while now. Just follow the shoreline at about this distance for the next half-hour or so."

He went to the chartroom then, plotted courses, noted in his log. From the helm I could distinguish some general colors in the water. We were in about two fathoms at that point, and most of it was a pale emerald green. A motley of yellows and browns were off to port. No blue anywhere but in the sky. I'd been there before of course, but had stayed in the deep channels until the Great Bahama Bank, which ran three fathoms deep all the way from the Berrys to Gun Cay and the Stream. This was quite different, and I was glad Stan was the skipper instead of me. He came back up after a few minutes, looked at the shore, the water ahead. "We'll be in the clear shortly," he said. "Then we'll have two hours or so to the Yellow Bank, where we'll have to do a bit more dodging. Are you all right steering?"

"Sure."

"She'll be nothing but a slow engine boat through this, you know. All upwind in shallow water."

"I know. Fifteen bucks a day. Better than scraping the old buckets in a yard."

That was all I would say about it, but I wasn't sure it was really better. Bad men with guns. A capricious goddess, affectionate one moment and an ice queen the next. A mysterious suitcase hidden in a sail locker. My heart wrenched from sky to abyss as many times in a day as I was being paid dollars. I considered asking for a hazardous duty bonus.

Brangaene, with her fine bows, tended to plow into the chop when she was head onto it and motoring. She sailed well, but wasn't much of a powerboat. She would slap waves with her bowsprit, sending spray flying nearly as high as her main spreaders. Isolda came up, still in the white bikini. She stepped out on deck, looked forward to her spot by the skylight, cringed away from a faceful of spray and changed her mind. She went aft behind the wheelhouse where she'd have some protection. Stan made sandwiches. We took turns eating over the sink in the galley. Then he put something on a tray under a saucepan and took it out to Isolda. No idea how she managed to eat anything back there.

We plodded on like that for another hour or so, during which Stan brought in the lunch things, checked his dead reckoning against the chart. "The Yellow Bank starts about here," he said. "I'll give you the signals."

Then he went to the bowsprit again, studied the water and got thoroughly soaked. After a while he waved at me to slow her. I throttled down. He showed me three fingers, so I settled her at three knots. That eased her motion significantly. Then he waved to slow her even more. I set the throttle down to bare steerageway. Isolda, happy with the gentler motion, took up her spot by the skylight. I barely glanced, having to concentrate so hard on the helm and Stan's signals. We weren't more than a few minutes into that phase when the first plane buzzed us.

I don't know planes, hated them at the time, because you knew the people in them considered you silly for sailing. They could get where you were going way before you did. They were noisy and they stank. And they always seemed to pose a danger.

Anyway, I don't know planes, Pipers, Cessnas, whatever. This one had a single engine and was painted red. Isolda shuddered, covered herself with her beach towel as the plane came over us low, then circled and climbed and flew on to the southeast. Stan pointed me to port and I turned her. After a moment he pointed to starboard, then ahead again. Isolda re-settled herself, face down this time to sun her back. We were still on the Yellow Bank dodging coral heads when the next plane came, again from astern. Twin engines this time, white with a red stripe. Scanned us stern to stem, climbed and circled, then came back over us stem to stern. Isolda gathered her towel and came inside, went to her cabin. They flew two tight circles around us, then headed back to Nassau.

After another half-hour or so we'd cleared the Yellow Bank, got her back to pounding through it at eight knots, steering by the compass. Two hours later I started seeing smudges on the horizon. Stan went forward with binoculars, came back and altered the course by a degree or two. He let me off the helm for a few minutes, then called me back from where I'd slumped on the settee.

He went forward again, scanned the shapes of the islands on the horizon, watched them change positions as we moved, slower now and out of the worst of the chop. Hills rose dead ahead, some small coral outcrops appeared. Stan waved me to port, had me settle on due east, throttle down. Then he came aft and took the helm, told me to rig mooring lines and fenders. Apart from having to jump down a couple of feet because of the high tide, it was as easy a docking as any I'd known, all seventy-two feet of her snugged gently onto the new concrete dock, no other boats there, no sign of anyone ashore. With the engine shut down the only sound was the surf, and that but faintly heard from the other side of the high point of coral to windward.

Until the white plane buzzed the island from north to south. It didn't circle this time, just banked off and headed back to Nassau.

"Nowhere to hide, is there?" I said to Stan.

"Quite. Not anymore."

Stan wanted to try to catch the last of the "Children's Hour" on the radio, that period each afternoon when all the out island stations and boats checked in, reported the day's events. Captain Moxey of Hall's Pond Cay had arrived safely from Nassau that afternoon, in ballast. The motorsailer yacht *Adagio* lies at anchor in Georgetown, needing engine parts. Island to island, boat to boat, too. Big lobsters at Staniel. A record-breaking wahoo off Kit's Cay. In between these messages, loud bursts of Cuban Spanish from the fishing boats on the Banks south and west of Andros. Isolda, sitting quietly in the wheelhouse, heard one of them and rose quickly, rushed down to the chartroom to put her ear to the set. Normally I paid no mind to the Cuban transmissions, considered them mere interference. I slipped nearer, listened too. Yes, there it was again, Juan Mí's voice, almost devoid of consonants.

— Isolda, Isolda, Juan Mí. Él no viene mañana. Viene pasado mañana. Cambio.

So Marco wouldn't arrive until the day after tomorrow. That was all. The message was repeated after a few minutes, the same, plaintive *Cambio* at the end, Juan Mí hoping for an answer he'd never get. I heard Isolda translate it for Stan. Drinks then, the sun nearly down and the radio breaking up as the sky waves did their daily shift in the ether. Stan and I stayed in our sailing clothes. Isolda stayed in her white bikini, but added a long-sleeved shirt that tied under her breasts and was obviously made to go over that exact bikini. Havana Club rum, soda and ice, hers with a slice of lime. Stan brought out his guitar, sang some folk songs, one or two chanties. I piped in on the choruses, and Isolda laughed — a gloriously musical sound. Not for a single moment did she take her adoring eyes off Stan.

It got to be dinnertime, and as there was no shore power that meant we would have to face the terrible racket of the generator, no music possible. I did a shrimp and mushroom sauté, pasta, quick stuff, get that damned generator shut down. It echoed off the high coral formations around us, making its fifteen-minute run seem an hour.

The following silence was wonderful. We dined by lantern light and two dim twelve-volt bulbs. A bottle of Pouilly-Fuiseé. An orchestral arrangement of *El Amor Brujo* on a tape from the aft cabin. When we were finished I cleared, went to the galley to clean. The tape stopped. I went out on the deck with a neat rum and my cigarettes. Stan sang *Quiere me mucho,* and when the chorus came, *Cuando se quiere de veras,* Isolda sang with him in harmony. When they finished she was crying openly, and clung to him.

Sometime later I crawled down the fo'c'sle hatch so as not to disturb them. In my bunk I got through two pages of Gironella in Spanish before falling asleep.

"There are a number of ways to get from here to Staniel," Stan said over breakfast. "Normally, one would take the day here, enjoy the beach and the snorkeling on the coral heads, then run down for a few hours to

Warderick Wells, spend the night, dive and explore in the morning. Then island-hop the next day to Staniel. But we haven't that sort of time, do we?"

Isolda was playing with her pan tostada, perfectly coiffed and turned out in a tan bikini and a matching diaphanous wrap. I watched her fingers pinch the soft core of the bread, flick the crisp crumbs. It was how I kept myself from staring through the thin fabric that played across her breasts in the wafts of the light breeze. Neither of us answered Stan, I because I had no idea what to say.

"Isolda?" he asked.

She looked up at him for a moment as if she had forgotten her line. "I would like some time on the beach here today," she said at last.

He re-folded his chart, studied it for a time as if it were his morning paper. "We could take the day here, sail her down in the Sound tonight."

"How long would that take?" I asked.

"Most of the night, I'm afraid."

"Well, we've done that before."

We ate our pan tostadas and sipped Cuban coffee. The ship's clock emitted enough tings to tell us it was ten in the morning.

"Is that all right with you, Isolda?" Stan asked. "We'll get there fairly early in the morning."

"Yes. That will be fine."

"Right then. We'll go just after dinner."

This conversation sounded stilted and rehearsed, as if the plan had already been made and this discussion of it was solely for my benefit. The plan was fine with me, but I couldn't help feeling some resentment at the manner of its presentation. Oh well, fifteen bucks a day.

Breakfast done, I cleared the table and cleaned the galley. Stan came down, put together a picnic basket, gathered towels. "I'll take her over to the beach. Join us, if you like."

"No thanks. It's going to be a long night. Think I'll just stroll a little, read, nap."

I went up to the wheelhouse to see them off, watch Isolda walk. She walked differently that morning. She hugged a beach towel to her chest, head down, each step seeming tentative, her whole posture an expression of sadness. Stan lugged the basket and more towels and a big umbrella, so his walk wasn't all that sprightly either. Together they looked like a couple who had just received some terrible message and were on their way to face the consequences of it.

I took some time then to shower and shave, sit in the cool of the wheelhouse. Made some notes in my log, commentaries in Spanish about Gironella and what I might do for my thesis the coming year. Had a hard time keeping my mind on it.

Then the plane came. I stayed inside, ducked to watch it through the glass. It was the white one again. Buzzed *Brangaene* north to south, circled, buzzed the island, flew off to the west. Hated the damned things even when they were minding their own business, but this was out and out spying and intentional harassment. I longed for the cutter's fifty-caliber.

And I was afraid, for all of us. What if next time they came shooting? And what was it all about? Was it about the suitcase? The adultery? What?

Once the quiet had settled back in I went out onto the dock and walked up to the island. There was a little beach and a small boarded-up bar in a building adjacent to the quay. Beyond that, up a hill to the left, a few houses, a few trees. The road from the dock ran through a cut that had been carved out of the hill but it was still something of a climb. At the top a crushed-shell road crossed the cut. From there I could see Exuma Sound, deep and a blue near black, and hear the surf sobbing. I could also see Stan and Isolda sitting under the umbrella down on the beach, side by side, motionless, staring out to sea. I watched them until I recognized my envy of Stan and desire for Isolda and felt myself an ugly little voyeur and turned and went back to the boat.

Before I got there the red plane came over, low from the south. It passed over the boat, turned out over the Banks, disappeared. That one made me just as angry, but not as scared. I was pretty sure it carried Juan Mí and Paco.

At the boat I looked down into the water below her. It was amazing, so clear it appeared that the bottom was only inches below the surface, that every shell and urchin and clump of coral was within easy reach. A triggerfish swam out from under the hull, rolled to have a look at me. Other tiny, colorful fish scattered in every direction like jewels thrown into a fountain.

That cheered me a bit. I read for a time, napped for a time. It was while I was napping that Stan and Isolda returned. I stowed their beach gear while they took showers fore and aft. I took my book to my stateroom, settled in. Stan went aft. No more pretence, he would sleep with Isolda and didn't mind if I knew it. Which raised the question again: What had happened that night in Nassau? Why did she treat me as she did? Did I mean anything to her at all?

The sun was low when I got up. I went quietly to the

wheelhouse. Stan and Isolda were in the chartroom listening to the radio. It was well into Children's Hour, nearly six. When they came up, Stan said they hadn't heard another transmission from Juan Mí.

The white plane roared over again while we were having dinner. We all sat stiffly as the crescendo rose in the north, as the noise overhead shook us like rag dolls. None of us moved until the diminuendo went all the way to silence. "That will be their last one of the day," Stan said. "They'll accept that we're here for the night." The dinner had been nervous enough before. After that it was silent, desultory, and quick. We cleared and cleaned in relief that it was over.

Just at sunset Stan took the binoculars and hauled himself up to the spreaders. He scanned the Banks to the west and what he could see of the Sound and the string of cays to the south. He stayed there until there was little twilight left. Not until then did I quit listening for the red plane. It hadn't made a second run of the day.

"I know the way out," he told me back in the wheelhouse, "but it will have to be soon, as I will need a little light for it. See to your lines and fenders, would you? And then rig the main directly we're off the dock."

So we did it quickly, I leaving loose coils amidships and the fenders looped over the lifelines. While Stan backed her out I freed the stops on the main, saw that the sheet and halyard were properly led, went to the winch and stood by ready to haul. He turned her sharply to miss the end of the jetty, put her in forward and steered a course parallel to the shore. The engine echoed off the hill, deafening and threatening, until we passed the little point and could see Exuma Sound. There were several exposed coral heads on either side of the channel, but

Stan either could see them or had their positions memorized. In a few minutes we were clear of them and all the rest and punching over rollers. Stan signaled me to hoist the main. Once I had it up he bore off onto starboard tack, and I trimmed it board-flat. Her motion was better than it had been on the Banks, with the main to steady her and rollers instead of chop in her face. I cleared and coiled and stowed and she was a proper sea-going vessel again.

Venus showed herself on a rust velvet cushion, which gradually darkened to show a spray of diamonds around her. Warm night air swept the deck as I worked, clean and rich in my lungs. There is a numinous quality to such night air at sea, a reminder of something ancient and just out of mind's reach on a sea as much within as it is in the world. It whispers of joy and at the same time of loss, the sadness of being somehow alien to oneself. I held loosely to a shroud and clung too tightly to the feeling, squeezing it out and away.

I took one last deep inhalation of that sacred air and went aft, looked over the string of cays behind us. A faint glow showed from Norman's. That was all that marred the starlit sky.

It was dark in the wheelhouse, only the dim red of the binnacle light, and was crowded with the thump of the screw and growl of the engine. Isolda stood with her hip tucked into Stan's, an arm around his waist. He steered easily, small movements, letting *Brangaene* tell him what she wanted, how much. When he saw me he gently disengaged from Isolda, turned to me.

"Take her for a bit, will you?" he said. "Keep her right up on it."

I took the helm. He and Isolda moved behind me,

she to the settee, he to his charts.

"Running lights?" I asked him.

"Not yet. We won't need them for some time." Which struck me as dangerous, if not for us then for any Bahamian sloops out there. On the other hand, it did make for a better view of the night.

We were making a compass course a little south of east. *Brangaene* may not have been a particularly good powerboat, and she was a fine sailer as I've noted, but as a motorsailer she was superb. With the main up to steady her, the engine revs matched to the seas and about half of her centerboard down, she was making eight knots and doing it upwind with a smooth and gentle motion. Stan went out on deck with binoculars, moved forward and aft, starboard and port, scanning the sea. Came back in, went to his charts. He came to stand beside me, smelling of sea air mixed with diesel. "On this course we'll see the light at Eleuthera Point in about three hours," he said. "Assuming they've got it turned on, of course. In any event, in about three hours we'll tack over and put her under sail, see how she does to windward. Are you all right on the helm for now?"

"Yes, fine. It will be good to have the engine off."

He went aft. I couldn't see or hear any more of him or Isolda, just assumed they had retired. So the night and *Brangaene* were mine. Yes, she was superb as a motorsailer, but I'd never liked steering that way, jammed up closer to the wind than she could actually sail, not really feeling her, just keeping an eye glued to the compass. Not having running lights was a worry, too, making me want to scan the sea constantly, unable really to do so from inside. Coped with it, though, for about an hour.

Stan came up behind me, read the compass, stuck his head out to see if the wind had held steady. He reached up to the console and turned on the running lights, though not the masthead or steaming lights. I gave him a grateful nod. We'd been in the Sound about two hours altogether. That put us about sixteen miles out from the Exumas. I figured he wanted to be sure we couldn't be seen from any of the cays, at least until we were far enough off not to be identified as having left from Highbourne. But why? The white plane might not know we were going to Staniel, but surely Juan Mí in the red plane knew. Didn't he? Something about the timing, maybe. If we had waited until morning to go to Staniel down the inside under power, we would have arrived in the evening. This way we'd get there in the morning. But what difference would that make?

I held the course for another hour. Stan went out to the bowsprit again, scanned. Kept scanning for some time. Then he set to clearing the rigging for the jib, and with that done, went aft to clear the mizzen. When he came back in he lowered the centerboard all the way and throttled back. "Bloody light's out, as usual," he said. "Time to tack. Hoist or steer?"

"I'll hoist. Mizzen first?"

"Yes, straightaway. The jib as we pass through irons."

Out again in the fine night air, my mind cleared and put itself to the tasks at hand. I raised the mizzen, set its sheet and that of the main to where I guessed they'd be in good trim when she'd rounded. Dashed forward, cleared the last stop Stan had left on the jib, went to its halyard and hauled and winched as he put her about. He had its sheet almost right, so I took the time to coil halyards. Tweaked the main and mizzen sheets to get her full and by, then got the jib just right. Stan shut down the engine and kept the helm for a time, noting the course and speed she was making. "This is grand," he said. "Still eight knots and close enough to the course to have a sighting at first light, I would think. Take her for a few minutes, would you please? Log and dead reckoning to be done."

The one thing on a boat I did better than Stan was steer to windward. The only thing. Years in the dinghies as a child, I guess, while he'd seldom sailed any boat shorter than thirty feet. *Brangaene* took it well, heeled some fifteen degrees to leeward, responded in a dignified way to the helm. I was getting two degrees closer and a quarter of a knot faster than Stan had. I didn't mention that when he came back to relieve me.

Through all this Isolda reclined on the settee, eyes closed. She'd changed into blue slacks and another of her billowy shirts. Her hair and face were perfect, the nails on hands and feet perfectly shaped and polished. I asked both of them if they would like coffee. They said they would.

I'd found a small emergency stove aboard that ran on alcohol, not enough of one to cook a dinner but fine for boiling water. I pumped and lit it in the sink, stood there holding the pot over it while it heated. The motion wasn't bad, but enough to slosh an unsecured pot all over the galley. Isolda came down to help. There wasn't really anything for her to do, but she fiddled with milk, put more ground coffee into the cone.

"We make it differently in Cuba," she said in Spanish. The first words in days I could remember her addressing to me personally.

"Yes, I know. The heavy syrup left to cool, added to

the hot milk."

"Brendan," she said, in a way that forced me to look at her instead of the hot stove and pot. "I am sorry about what happened in Nassau. I know it was hard on you, and you have been very good about it."

It took me a while to answer. I looked back down at the pot, not at all sure what to say. How could you have made me fall in love with you, then take it all away? Hardly. Finally I managed a sound, though not a word.

"It was necessary. Juan Mí and Paco were watching us all the time, and those Americans."

"I see," I said, though it didn't seem to explain anything.

"You will say nothing to my husband?"

"Of course I will not."

"Oh, many, many thanks."

She gave my arm a squeeze and my cheek a sisterly peck. Then she was gone, before I could ask about the bad guys in Nassau, or what she planned to do in company with her husband for a month's cruise. Or about the suitcase hidden in the sail locker. Or how the hell she expected me to get over her.

Coffee made and served, I went out on deck to get a better feel of *Brangaene* upwind under sail. I went aft and stood near the weather rail, hands clasped behind my back, and let her thrust and dip and rise beneath my feet while I admired all the sights she offered as she drove into wind and sea. She looked like an etching or faded photograph of herself, the starlight showing no color, only shape and line, and even so she was beautiful in the long run of her teak deck, the tapered angle of her spruce spars, the elegant curves of her three leaches at one moment architectural, at another kinetic sculpture. The sheer beauty of her, of the night through which she sailed, washed self as clean as the sea.

Stan and I served her well through the dark morning, steering and trimming to sustain her joyful play with wind and waves. I was on the helm when the eastern horizon began to pale, still when the colors of ship and sea gradually brightened. To leeward the irregular shapes of the cays put a limit to the Sound, so I roused Stan and pointed to them. He went out with the binoculars, used them to scan the cays. He stayed out there for a long time. I held the course while Isolda slept on the settee, her lips parted, curled into a childlike ball.

"I can't tell yet for sure," he said, "but I think we're just off Warderick Wells now. I'll know in a bit. Cook or steer?"

"Steer, if you don't mind."

"Quite all right. I'm ravenous."

He freed the table to swing on its gimbals and gently wakened Isolda, who went aft to freshen up. Then he went to the galley. Soon he handed up café con leche laced with rum. A bit later he brought up a full English breakfast, bangers, eggs, underdone bacon and fried bread. Isolda reappeared in bikini and wrap. It was an entirely restorative breakfast.

Stan took the helm. I cleared and cleaned and used the head. I took it back when I'd finished with that so he could resume scanning the cays. This time he took a hand-held compass with him instead of the binoculars, and a chart folded small. He was again gone for quite a while. When he came back he said he'd got a fix between Warderick Wells and Little Major's, and that we'd have to hold the course a while longer. The clock rang off eight bells.

So close-hauled on port tack it was, with the breeze getting lighter and shifting a bit more south as we neared the warming cays. They lay not only to leeward anymore, but dead ahead and even showed a distant smudge to weather.

"It's time," Stan said, his head ducked into the starboard doorway. "I'll take in the mizzen now."

As he let the sail flutter and hauled it down I could feel her slow, feel the lee in her helm. The course fell away a few degrees and I could see waves breaking into surf ahead, not half a mile away. Stan came inside, took the helm and started the engine. "We'll round up now, turn her back into a powerboat."

"Centerboard now?"

"If you please."

Big sails, much flapping and flopping as *Brangaene's* bowsprit pointed into the wind's eye. I hauled and tucked furiously, pummeled by ill-tempered canvas. As soon as I had the main under some control Stan bore away and throttled up, putting the seas on her port quarter. He seemed to be steering straight for the surf. I furled and tied stops and was securing the last of her halyards as we passed the north end of the string of surf. It roared at us as if we were escaping prey. A rugged and worn coral cliff rose close by to starboard, reverberating with the cacophony of surf and engine.

Suddenly it was quiet. Stan throttled down, steered her into a bowl of soft emerald green beyond a small sandy bar. I went to the anchors, cleared them, looked aft for his signal. Starboard anchor first, upwind, then drift and maneuver downwind, set the second one. Lay her square between the two and make fast. Engine off. The sound of the surf returned, distant, plaintive, and benign.

Before I'd even dealt with the windward rode, Stan was already aft and clearing the motorboat for launching. I went to help him. "I'll get this, thanks," he said. "Would you go below and fetch up that hidden suitcase?"

I watched his back, his powerful shoulders, as he slowly paid out the lines of the tackle, lowering the boat with its heavy outboard motor from the davits. It was an eighteen-foot long skiff, squared bow and one big, powerful engine. I heard a sort of hum from far away, getting louder.

"What's this all about, Stan?"

He didn't pause, didn't turn. "No time now. Please bring the suitcase."

The humming grew louder. I turned to go for the suitcase and saw the red plane bearing down on us from the north. It roared over, continued south and banked.

"Please hurry, Brendan," Stan said. "Not a moment to be lost."

Mexico Beach, 2005

Not a moment to be lost, Ramona mimics. For us, too. Juanita will be here with the children in less than an hour. Caballeros, lunch is served.

It is a fine coastal lunch. At each setting an iced tray of three oysters on the half-shell and a cocktail of three enormous shrimp awaiting them. In easy reach is a hot baguette and a bowl of ghee. Three bottles of St. Pauli NA stand sweating beside frosty glasses.

Just a light snack today, Ramona says. No siesta, because the children are coming.

Grandchildren, Lee James says. Great grandchildren.

As they are finishing they hear voices and footsteps and the screen door opening and slamming, several times. Ramona rises and hurries to the door. Lee James sits unruffled, smearing ghee on the last heel of the baguette. Bren gathers dishes and silver, heads for the kitchen with his hands full. From there he hears joyful greetings, squeals and shouts, the patter of tiny bare feet running, he imagines, in circles. He returns, first to see Lee James with two colorful and squirming bundles in his lap, holding his head up and to the side, chewing and trying to swallow. Then to see the end of an embrace between Ramona and a tall woman, a lovely, blond, tanned, tall woman of about thirty. Her hair is not quite shoulder-length and curves in to frame a face with traces of Ramona in it. Ramona introduces him.

Juanita, this is our old friend, Brendan Harper. He's visiting with us for a few days.

Hi, she says, though it sounds more like Haeh. She offers her hand. He takes it, bows over it, says How do you do, hearing the phrase as absurd. And sees himself as absurd, seventy-five years old and as shy and abashed when meeting a beauty as ever he had been as a teen-ager.

The two little girls have finished mauling Lee James and are rifling through the beach bags on the floor near Juanita, who interrupts them to introduce him. This is Uncle Brendan, she tells them. Then to him, This is my daughter Elena, and her cousin Tyler. She says this in the slow, soft, vowel-rich tones of the Deep South. Elena says Haeh, just like her mother. Tyler says Hello. Then they are gone, with tiny buckets and shovels and balls.

I'd better ride herd, Juanita says.

I'll come out in a moment, Ramona says, and heads

for the kitchen.

I'll take care of that, Bren says. You go ahead.

Lee James wheels himself toward them. At least they're not squalling, he says. Juanita holds the door for him, follows him out onto the veranda.

Table cleared and kitchen cleaned, Bren goes out onto the veranda. He sees that Lee James has wheeled himself out onto the pier-like ramp he's had built to the dunes, and sits watching as the girls load shovels full of sand into their buckets. Ramona and Juanita lie on chaise longues near them, chatting. Bren takes a deck chair from the veranda, folds it and carries it down to sit next to Lee James. The day has cleared, the breeze has softened, the skirt of surf folds lazily onto the beach, the sandpipers take leisurely nips at its hem.

A smile twitches in Lee James's face as he watches his great grandchild and great grandniece. Even when it fades, Bren can just see that the smile stays in the corners of his eyes behind the sunglasses. Lee James has not acknowledged his arrival, so Bren says nothing, leaving his friend to his evident pleasure.

Sounds of a squabble rise from the dune. A squeal, a shout, a shovel clunking on a plastic bucket. The two little girls stand face to face for a moment, hands on hips. Abruptly, four-year-old Elena turns and strides purposefully toward the two old men, her three-year-old cousin in tow. She leaps into Lee James's lap, knocking out his air and putting his eyes wide, first with shock and then with suppressed laughter.

Bisabuelo? she says.

Sí, Guapa, he gasps, as soon as he has enough air.

My cousin Tyler wants to call you Bisabuelo too. She can't do that, can she?

Well, I guess she can call me that if she wants to.

Elena's face falls. She ponders for a while, then takes on a sly look. So she can call you that, but you won't really be her Bisabuelo, will you?

No, I'll still be her great granduncle.

Relief floods her face. She squeezes poor old Lee James's neck and he squeezes his eyes in pain. She finally lets him go, jumps to the deck and faces her cousin. Okay, Tyler, you can call him Bisabuelo if you want. She considers saying the rest of it but decides she doesn't have to rub it in. Tyler has missed the details of the deal, and so with a snaggle-toothed grin touching both ears, launches her own attack on Lee James, shouting Bisabuelo, Bisabuelo! Through which he can only sit, stunned and obviously hurting. Bren sits immobilized with a mixture of fear for and envy of his friend and can see nothing he can do to help either him or himself. Hoarsely, weakly, Lee James says, Go play now, darlins. It is some time before he can steady his breathing. He shakes his head.

Bisabuelo, he says.

Great Grandfather.

No, that's too long, too formal. Great Grandpa?

Great Gramps then? A pause. No. See what you mean. Then, Is there such a thing as a great granduncle?

No idea. Don't suppose it matters that much what they call you, Lee James says to close it.

No. It's all in how hard they hit your lap, I guess.

Or choke you, Lee James says, rubbing his graybeard throat. I guess the choking is . . . . He's laughing now, spotted hands drop from his throat and grip the wheels of his chair.

Yup, he goes on, it's those scrawny little arms cutting

off the last of your air. The chair rocks dangerously with his laughter.

Naw, he says when the laugh has finally settled into chuckles. No, you're dead right. That sudden blow to the chest. That's the best.

Out on the dune Juanita slips off her chaise and stretches. She is in a colorful bikini, her skin is a dark shade of brushed copper. She gives the old men a wave and a smile as white as breaking surf, turns from them and walks, almost glides, toward the Gulf.

The girl from Ipanema, Alabama, Lee James says. Bren is afraid to try to say anything. His throat is thickened with longing, the terrible sense that he has missed what is important in life and the sure knowledge that it is too late to find it now. Yes, he has a daughter and a granddaughter he seldom has seen and a great grandson he's seen only once, but nothing like this.

They sit watching the girls play with the balls now, something akin to miniature golf, using their shovels. Juanita returns, bends fetchingly to tidy the towel on her chaise before lying on it. Lee James seems to be nodding off.

Wheel you in? Bren asks through a yawn.

No. I guess I don't want to miss any of this. You go on up if you like.

Brendan decides that he will. Juanita is too beautiful, the girls are too cute, the day is too perfect, the confusion of his longings has tired him out. He excuses himself, folds his chair and carries it back up to the veranda. Inside, he goes to the liquor cabinet and takes a big slug straight from the bourbon bottle. This braces him for the climb up the stairs, but his hip hurts on the way nonetheless. In his room he decides he doesn't want to step out onto his little balcony, the beach scenes in his mind are already too much, no more, no more. He closes the louvered wooden panels over the glass sliding doors and undresses in the muted light.

In his bed on his back, pillows arranged to ease the pains in legs and back, he closes his eyes and waits, if not for clarity then at least for some orderly alignment of images. This doesn't come to him, but the images do fade, and he sleeps.

When he wakes he can tell that some hours have passed by the richer color of sunlight slipping in between the slats in the shutters. He unbends a knee a little, relieving a cramp. The idea of rising, dressing, seeing people, has no appeal. He closes his eyes again, casts himself adrift.

As for Juanita's beauty, well. He has encountered goddesses before, Elke, Isolda, Maya. All had scorned him, as goddesses necessarily must scorn merely human males. Still, her effect on him is ridiculous and embarrassing, absurd desire heating up in an ancient cripple. He squeezes his eyes, rolls his head back and forth on the pillow, feels himself blushing in shame. Old age is always disguising itself as illness or injury or exhaustion. You never feel old, just hurt or sick or tired. Not until a beautiful woman looks at you or looks away from you do you remember that you are old. Then it's always too late.

What is going on here in his room is far worse than the terrors downstairs might hold for him. He rises, goes through bathroom motions, dresses. He opens the shutters and looks out over his balcony.

The sun is no more than a palm's width above the Gulf and scatters pale blue shadows across the dunes.

Lee James still sits in his chair, head lolling. A large blue umbrella shades him. Ramona is bent over the sand as if it were a potato patch, collecting forgotten beach things. Juanita and the girls are not in sight. He gathers himself, straightens into what feels like a military posture, and leaves the room.

The house is quiet, no sign of children or a goddess. On the veranda Ramona places a plastic bucket in a corner, straightens spryly, gives him a smile. He wouldn't go in until they left, she says of Lee James. Then he fell asleep.

Shall I wheel him in?

Would you? I'll get the drink things.

The umbrella is an accessory to the wheelchair. Bren examines its various joints and latches, then uses them to fold it into its case on the back of the chair. Lee James yawns, breathes out a long jungle roar. Great nap. Is Bren up?

He's up.

Bren. How was yours?

Fine but for the waking. Wheel you up?

Sure. Juanita and the girls said to tell you goodbye.

Sorry I missed them.

Lee James helps with the wheels as Bren pushes the chair up the rise. At the top Bren hesitates, not sure whether to stop on the veranda or continue inside.

Here, Lee James says. The merry old sol is about to decree cocktail hour.

Ramona steps out with the drinks tray. In addition to the usual whiskey it holds a saucer glowing brightly with an arrangement of lemon wedges and a bottle of expensive British gin. I thought we'd make it special today, she says. They all take gin and lemon on the rocks.

Here's to quite a day, Lee James says, raising his glass.

Indeed, Ramona says. Then to Bren, I hope it wasn't too much of a strain on you.

Not at all. Lovely girls.

Juanita just glows with health, doesn't she?

Well, Lee James says, She certainly glows.

The sun just touches the horizon. The beach goes quiet in anticipation, the surf is momentarily speechless. The fiery orange changes from a ball to an oval, then two ovoids, one above the Gulf and one in it. Soon it is a spreading mass across the water with only a flaming knife blade above. Then all of its light leaps into the sky.

Tinkey-tinkey, Ramona says. They clink glasses and the two men repeat the phrase liturgically.

Leftovers tonight, I'm afraid, she says. with the children here all day. Picadillo, Morros y Christianos. I'll fry up some fresh plátanos maduros. It won't be long.

She builds herself another gin and lemon and heads for the kitchen. The men top off too, sit as the sky turns yellow, purple, then black, listening for the surf to return. It does, but only in a whisper.

After a time Lee James emits a low growl. When they play, he says, I play.

Brendan waits for more. When it's clear that's to be all, he says, I understand. He knows he does in a way, but he can't find a memory anywhere astern of the knowing. Dinner is a quiet affair, soft Cuban love songs on the hidden speakers, a bottle of Sangre de Toro. At the end Lee James declares himself a might tuckered out and asks that the rest of Brendan's yarn wait until morning, and then asks Ramona to wheel him to his room and give him a hand with things. Bren volunteers to do the clean-up. They wish one another a goodnight.

With the kitchen finished, Bren turns off the music and the lights, braves the stairs. He goes to his balcony, feels the night. The wind has risen, the surf voices dire warnings of a coming storm. He listens for a while, then closes the sliding glass. The closing of the door brings sudden quiet and a new sort of darkness. Flat, dull thunder out over the Gulf suggests that it won't be long in coming. He waits until he can see and hear the rain pound on the glass, then lies down, glad to find he can still hear it from the bed. He sleeps.

On his way down the staircase in the morning, dressed and shaved, Brendan sees Lee James and Ramona seated close to a crackling blaze in the big stone fireplace, coffee and pan tostadas on a small table between them. Both are packaged in rugs and sweaters and wear big, furry slippers. He glances out the window, sees it lashed by the continuing storm. They exchange good mornings, Lee James giving him a only a slow flip of the wrist, his eyes fixed on his damp newspaper. Brendan crosses the big room, picks up a dining chair and carries it up to the setting in front of the fire.

Lee James folds his paper, tosses it on a pile next to the hearth. Good morning to you, sir, he says.

And to you, sir.

Bren pours himself coffee, munches a pan tostada. Ramona leans forward, adds a log to the fire. I will call Julia this morning, she says. About Isolda Reyes. Please, Bren, take this chair. It is warm enough now in my room. I will call from there.

She leaves. Bren finishes his pan tostada, takes his coffee and sits at the hearth where he can send the smoke of his cigarette up the chimney with the rest.

Where were you last? Lee James asks.

Pardon?

In the yarn.

Oh yes. Staniel Cay, nineteen-sixty. We were leaving in the motorboat when the red plane came.

Before he can say any more Ramona returns. Julia is not at home. She will call this evening. She collects some of the breakfast things from the coffee table. Go on with your story, Bren. I won't listen in too much.

The Exuma Cays, 1960

"Not a moment to be lost." I dashed down to the sail locker, dug furiously for the spinnaker bag. Fumbled with the drawstring, pulled billows of white nylon out until the cabin was buried under surf or snow. Got the case free and scurried aft with it. When I reached the deck the red plane was fading away to the north and Isolda was sitting on the midships thwart of the dinghy, staring away at the island.

I handed the case down to Stan in the motorboat. "Come aboard," he said sharply. "Get the painter."

It was the first time I had heard Stan give a direct order. I stepped down, untied the line as ordered, sat to coil it. Stan gunned the engine and sped into a turn that pitched me off my seat and onto the floorboards. I hauled myself back up onto the thwart and craned around to see where we were going.

Not to the yacht club or the village. He threaded a course past a number of tiny cays, south and west on the Banks side. The houses of the village flew by as he rounded the point and steered south. In less than ten minutes we passed a long white beach. Near the end of it he slowed, aimed her inshore and beached her. I went over the bow with the little anchor and dug it into the sand, went back to help Isolda ashore. Stan handed me her luggage after she was afoot and moving toward a sandy rise inland. We followed her with the two suitcases and Stan's pack.

"Please tell me what it is we're doing," I said as we walked.

He didn't, not until we'd climbed the rise. I saw then that we were at the southwestern end of a packed shell airstrip, maybe half a mile long. Its windward side was protected by white cliffs rising fifty or sixty feet. Isolda strode ahead, moving well in her deck shoes. The cliffs broke the wind. It was hot and airless as we followed her. Stan spoke at last.

"You may have noticed that Isolda and I are close," he said.

"Yes."

Another ten or twelve paces.

"From Lauderdale, weeks back."

"I see."

"Well, Marco wanted this cruise for some purpose of his own. I don't know all of it, but it had something to do with collecting this suitcase in Nassau. I assume it is a large sum of money, smuggled out of Cuba."

"Seems likely. Does Isolda know?"

"I presume so."

My question was a mistake. At least twenty paces went by. "Please go on," I had to say. Another ten before he continued.

"When I left you in Nassau I didn't go to Miami. My green card is good for several more years. Actually, I flew to Georgetown to arrange for a plane to pick us up here. I radioed for it as soon as we anchored. It's due any moment."

"So you and Isolda are running off."

"Yes."

"With Marco's money."

"It's not that, you know it's not. It's that you can't be forever going off to sea without an anchor. You've got to have a home port somewhere. She's been that for me since the moment I met her. Bugger the money. If she feels she needs it I'll see she has it. That's all there is to it."

I thought about all that for several paces. The red plane never returned to Nassau. When we were at Highbourne Cay it went south. From where we were at Staniel it went north. There's only one airstrip between Highbourne and Staniel. "Marco is on Norman's, not here," I said.

"Yes. That's why we sailed out into the Sound last night. To bypass Norman's unseen."

"And why you staged that late-night conversation over the skylight in Nassau. So I wouldn't know that's what you were doing. Had that planned out already."

"Yes."

We were nearing the northeast end of the strip. I watched Isolda walking and realized that neither could I ask Stan about that part of it, nor could he tell me.

When we reached the end Isolda sat on one of the suitcases while Stan stared back at the runway. I looked out over the Banks, the amazing array of brilliant colors dancing and shimmering under the crystalline coating of constantly moving sea. Up there on the unrelieved white, sweating in the airless glare, I felt exiled and doomed.

We heard the plane and then saw it to the southeast, a speck above the cliffs. Soon it was close enough to have color and it was a relief to see it was a pale powder blue rather than red or white. Stan waved. The pilot wiggled the wings, banked. He landed it hard, propeller screaming in reverse, and barely managed to stop it before dumping it down the hill. Got it turned around. Stan and Isolda gathered their things and started walking toward it.

There was no way to hear the red plane with the blue one's engine so close by. It just suddenly appeared at the far end of the runway, bouncing angrily as it raced toward us. It stopped a few yards short of the blue plane, prop to prop, their slow rotations the twitching whiskers of cats snarling before a fight.

The first ones out of the red plane were Juan Mí and Paco. They wore olive drab fatigues and black berets with circular insignia. Both held pistols, aimed at me. They marched right toward me, several yards to the west of the planes. I raised my hands, one very scared Cap'n Bren, I'll tell you. Paco grabbed my arms with his free hand, plopped me down to sit on the ground. Juan Mí waved his pistol at Stan, had him sit next to me. Isolda stood and moved away from us, stared at the red plane.

A third man, one I'd never seen, got out of the red plane. He too wore fatigues and beret. He turned and pulled another man out, old and apparently crippled. Roughly dragged him toward us. pushed him down to sit next to me. I assumed him to be Marco Reyes. He stared at Isolda, first with wonder and then with, I thought, hatred. Isolda never even glanced at him. Or at any of us.

The third man held his gun on us while Paco put his

in his holster and picked up the suitcases. As Isolda and Juan Mí walked briskly toward the red plane, Paco went more slowly, backward. I glanced into the cockpit of the blue plane. The pilot sat with wide eyes, clearly without a hint of what was going on or about to happen. Isolda got into the red plane first, then Juan Mí. Paco handed up the suitcases. All of this without any words. With the engines of the two planes growling at one another nothing could be said.

The third man backed to the plane with his pistol still on us, got aboard just as Juan Mí got the plane turned around, gunned it and accelerated down the runway, sand-blasting us where we sat. The blue plane followed the red one into the sky, the pilot having seen enough of us and Cuban revolutionaries and their guns. The red plane veered off to the southwest, the blue to the southeast. In the silence after that I couldn't hear anything at all.

Stan and Marco and I sat in that silence, each of us wondering what this shift in our private worlds meant and would mean. We couldn't speak, couldn't look at one another, just sat stunned. As soon as I could hear the distant surf I gave it a try.

"Well, they didn't shoot us."

No response from either of them. They stared out over the pass. *Brangaene's* masts just showed above the rim. After a while Marco shifted a leg and groaned.

—Mierda, he said.

—¿Se duele la pierna? I asked him.

"Not just the leg, everything," he said. "Everything hurts."

More silence for a time. I pondered the nature of belief, faith, trust. Reached no conclusions.

Stan stood abruptly. "We might as well go."

The walk back to the beached motorboat went very slowly, with Marco having a bad time of it. We took turns helping him. By the time we got to the boat Marco's face was white and glossy with sweat. We helped him onto the main thwart. Stan went aft to the engine. I dug the anchor out of the sand, pushed her off, jumped aboard.

As soon as it was deep enough Stan cranked the engine and steered back toward *Brangaene* at a gentle pace. The breeze cooled and refreshed, the little dollops of spray coming aboard anointed us with elixir. Once alongside *Brangaene* I tied the bow line to a stanchion, then Stan and I helped Marco up to the deck. Stan guided him into the wheelhouse, stayed in attendance while I secured the motorboat in its davits.

"Take us out to sea," Marco said when I joined them in the wheelhouse. I didn't have to ask why. The white twin-engine buzzed us as we were getting underway.

We retraced the course Stan had taken getting her into the anchorage. When we'd cleared the line of surf we got the main and a jib up, shut down the engine and steered northeast for Eleuthera Point. There, because the plane had climbed high and could see the opening to the Atlantic between the point and Little Island and might think we were headed for it. They circled far above, keeping us in sight until they got bored or ran low on fuel. At four in the afternoon they headed west. With three hours of daylight left I figured they'd be back, and would stay with us well past sunset. That meant we would actually have to clear the point and sail into the Atlantic, set some sort of outward bound course until they left us. I'd been assuming that we'd go to Norman's once we'd shaken the plane, but didn't really know that.

Marco slept on the settee through the afternoon, so I couldn't ask him. Stan said he didn't know. He and I traded off at the helm. I went below, made sandwiches, fished out two bottles of beer. I realized I hadn't eaten since early in the morning, wolfed the food and guzzled the beer.

The plane showed up again half an hour before sunset, buzzed us once to make sure of who we were, then re-established its high, slow circle. The noise of the buzzing woke Marco. He made his painful way down to the aft cabin, with me assisting as best I could. When he was settled in he said he would like some coffee.

I made a pot, took it down to him. He sat up, sipped and after a few moments asked, "Do you have a plan for evading the airplane?"

"We might be able to do it after full dark. Not before then. You'll have to tell me where you want to go."

"Of course. Sorry, I forgot earlier. I would like to return to Norman's Cay, but now I don't know if I can trust anyone there. Where are we now?"

I pointed out to port. "Eleuthera is over there," I told him. "Little Island is off there to starboard. We'll be in the Atlantic soon. We've held a constant course since Staniel, showing them we're headed out that way. I'm hoping we can make them think we're headed east, to Puerto Rico or the Virgins or even somewhere in Europe."

"Could you actually sail this boat to Europe?"

"Sure."

He turned dreamy eyes forward, considering it. "No," he said, "I have my duty. We must go back to Norman's."

His duty to whom, I wondered. "All right," I said.

"Once we're clear of Eleuthera we'll put her upwind, as if headed east. Hold that until they go back for fuel. Then we'll darken the boat and sail back to Norman's."

"When will we get there?"

"Sometime in the morning. It depends on how long they stay with us."

He sipped his coffee, lit a cigar. I pulled out cigarettes, got us an ashtray from the console, one of those beanbag types that stay upright.

"Juan Mí told me that you were a help with the suitcase in Nassau," he said. "Why?"

I didn't tell him it was because I was in love with his wife. "It seemed the safest way to get it aboard, with those gunslingers around."

"And you're helping me now. Why?"

"I don't like airplanes. And I'd like to get *Brangaene* safely home."

"Good enough. If your plan works, you will. And if Norman's is still on my side."

The conversation had a relaxed and cordial feel to it, so I decided to take a chance. "May I ask a question?"

"Of course."

"What was in the suitcase?"

He squinted at me, assessing. "Get me back to Norman's and I'll tell you. It will be trusting you with a secret, and I'm not willing to do that here, now."

Fair enough, I guess. Just at sunset we left the point astern, lowered the centerboard and put her on the wind. She wanted the mizzen to balance the helm but we'd be slower without it, have less backtracking to do, so we let her yaw. The plane left us not long after we turned on the running lights. As soon as it was out of sight we turned them off again. We tacked her over and paid out the sheets, raised the board and reached back the way we'd just come. In less than an hour we cleared the point again and I set the course for Norman's. I left her to Stan and went to my bunk, fairly beat by a long night and day. He would rouse me when he got too tired to steer. I packed my kit before I lay down. It was the only thing I could think of to do to prepare for what might happen at Norman's.

Stan shook me awake in the dark. I flipped on the light. After a few minutes in the head I went aft, found stale coffee in the galley, took it up with me and relieved Stan. He sat on the settee with his guitar, picking out the melody of *Quando se quiere de veras.* I saw distant pinpoints of light ahead, and the sky was beginning to pale astern. We'd made a good run.

Steering in the quiet was very nice, the steady Tradewind just where it belonged, *Brangaene's* motion on the Sound's soft seas a lulling pleasure. I glanced rarely at the red glow of the compass but when I did it always confirmed the course, easy to hold in that weather. In less than an hour I was able to see it without the binnacle light, turned it off.

Just after sunrise I had to ask Stan to get the binoculars, take some bearings. He took the helm instead and let me do it.

Out on deck for the first time in many hours, the beauty of a fine little ship on a benign sea in warm moist air with a steady breeze abaft the beam, I was filled again with joy. I stood by the wheelhouse for a moment, admiring *Brangaene's* pristine sails and glowing spars and taut rigging, reveled in her lively motion. In that moment I was perfectly happy, all the rest was unimportant, I was grateful to be exactly where I was, doing exactly what I was doing. To be part of *Brangaene* was to partake of her beauty. I was part of her and so was, in that moment, beautiful myself.

But duty to her called. I had to glass the cays, find Norman's entrance, so we could put her in through the narrow slot without the scrape of coral or the crunch of sand. I went forward, took bearings and found we'd fallen about half a mile to the lee of the course. Not too bad.

I trimmed her up to compensate. Then I went forward again to watch for the yellow house with a gray roof. When it bore 265° we would round up, take in sail, put her under power, motor in and anchor, Stan at the helm, me forward at the winch.

The process was done Bristol fashion, as things always were with Stan aboard. We had her on her anchors a hundred yards off the dock at nine-thirty in the morning.

Marco was sitting in a corner of the wheelhouse when we finished. "Can't we go in to the dock?" he asked.

"No, sorry. Too shallow."

"All right. Can I use the radio to call my people? Perhaps I can find out if they still are my people."

"Sure."

Stan set him up in the chartroom, got the radio tuned up, found the frequency he wanted. We sat in the wheelhouse pretending not to listen. We heard the usual spate of squawks and crackles, short bursts of fast Cuban slang or code, Spanish I couldn't follow. Marco turned the radio off, stuck his head into the wheelhouse. "It is all right," he said. "They are still mine."

Stan and I went aft to lower the motorboat. I went

down into the boat, brought it alongside. Stan went into the wheelhouse. He was in there a long time. When he came out he said that Marco wanted a word with me.

We sat at the table. "I'm told that your Spanish is very good for a Yanqui, Mister Harper. Why?"

"I took it all through high school. Practiced it in Ybor City. Got my BA in Spanish. In the fall I'll do graduate work in Spanish Literature."

"How do you pay for this?"

"I have the GI Bill from the Coast Guard. I work summers and nights. I will be a graduate assistant in the fall."

"You are not involved with politics? With government?"

"No, sir."

I watched him think, decide.

"How much were you to be paid for the whole cruise?"

I had to figure. Fifteen dollars a day for thirty days. No, twenty-eight days. "Four hundred and twenty dollars," I said aloud.

He laughed at me. "And what will you do when you get back to Florida?"

"Work in a boatyard until the semester starts."

"All right," he said. He pulled out a fat wallet, counted bills. "Here is five thousand dollars." He handed me about half of his wad of cash. "Part of it is for serving me so well. The rest is for your silence. About all of this, all you have seen, about ever meeting me, of ever having seen Isolda. Is that clear?"

"Yes, sir."

"And especially about what I am going to tell you now. I promised I would tell you what was in the suitcase if I arrived here safely, no?"

"Yes, sir."

He grabbed my eyes with his, not squinting anymore, and held them for a long moment.

"The suitcase contained the freedom of Cuba and the death of Fidel Castro. Now it will be used to help him."

—Viva Cuba libre, I said.

His duty to whom was clear, then, and his reasons for secrecy. Not a thief or a drug runner, but a committed counter-revolutionary. I wasn't sure whether I admired him for that or not, as I'd given Cuba not the first thought since New Year's of '59. I think I did.

"And who are the gunmen in the white airplane?"

"They are pigs. They belong to the CIA, and pretend to work for freedom. But they kill and steal only for themselves. For profit. In Nassau they were following Isolda to find me, find the money. I told her to put herself on display, seem frivolous, so they wouldn't think she had the money with her." He sighed, looked out toward the island. Shook his head.

"She made fools of all of us, didn't she?"

"Yes sir."

We got him into the dinghy. I cranked up and steered in to the dock. Two of his people helped him out. He hobbled on his cane to a waiting jeep without saying goodbye.

Stan said we were to take the boat back to Lauderdale. We saw the white plane when we were westbound over the Banks. It circled and buzzed us for a while, then headed back to Nassau. Once we were clear of the Berrys it was a lovely sail back to Lauderdale, though Stan wouldn't say a word not necessary to the sailing. When *Brangaene* was docked in the canal and tidied up I asked Stan what he planned to do.

"Did he give you some money too?" he asked.

"Yeah. Plenty."

"Get out of this business," he said.

I think that was both advice and the answer to my question.

Mexico Beach, 2005

Even with the house shut tight against the chilly rain they hear the surf's ranting. The scrub oak fire glows. Lee James adds a log, though by now the room is warm. Too warm by the hearth for Brendan, who rises and walks stiffly to the windows. The covered veranda keeps the rain from pounding them, but they are stained with wind-driven seawater. Through one of them he can see the rain-pocked dunes, the high angry surf.

That's the end, I guess, he says. I bought an old Plymouth sedan for three hundred cash, the first car I'd owned since 'forty-seven. Drove to Gainesville and settled in, worked one of my old student jobs there, worked on notes for my thesis. Never again heard from Stan.

Ramona has moved from her chair near the kitchen, stands with her back to the fire. You never tried to find out what happened to any of them? she says, sounding incredulous.

He is stung by the tone of her question, finds himself shocked by it. She seems to imply that somehow he should have sought them out, have tried to uncover their stories. That he was a lesser man for not having done so.

No, he admits. I wondered sometimes, but no. I've lost track of lots of people.

I will try to call Julia again, she says coldly, and almost stomps down the hall. Lee James sits staring into the fire. Brendan joins him.

I was on the Tampa paper during the Bay of Pigs, followed it fairly closely, Lee James says. I know El Frente had a number of factions. Don't remember hearing of a Marco Reyes, though. Let me look him up on the Internet. He wheels himself down the hall to his study.

Brendan paces, looks out the window, decides to brave the storm. He takes his hat and jacket from the antique rack near the door, dons them, grabs his cane and steps quickly outside. The wind hammers him instantly, he has to turn his face away from the blowing sand. There is no lee on the beach side so he goes to the west end of the veranda, down the steps there to the street. He walks in the rain until he reaches the lee side of the house but it's flooded there so he can't stay. To hell with it, he faces the weather, walks to a space between the dunes and confronts the furious surf.

What did became of Isolda and Stan and Marco and how many others lost? Of *Femme Fatale, Lazy Drummer, Adagio, Capriole, Brangaene,* or any of the other wonderful boats?

What for that matter has become of Cap'n Bren, who never took the time to find out about any of them?

The surf roars, perhaps laughing at him but certainly offering no answers. What he thinks he hears is a reminder that all stories end in death, to quote the master roughly, or when a lovely old boat is broken up for scrap. It's just that some of our stories aren't over yet, and a few of those lovely boats are still afloat.

He goes back inside, removes coat and hat and soggy

shoes. The fire is welcome now, he sits and puts his wet socks to it. Pours coffee and sips. Lee James wheels himself back into place.

Anything? Brendan asks.

Some. Let's wait till Ramona's back.

They can hear her muffled voice from down the hall, rapid and indistinguishable Spanish. It seems she has reached Julia.

Care for a tot? Lee James asks. I know it's early, but I want to chase out the chill.

Might as well, Bren agrees. Later might be too late.

Lee James wheels to the liquor cabinet, returns with the bourbon bottle and two shot glasses. Ramona returns. Drinking so early. Cabrones.

Find out anything about Reyes or Isolda? Lee James asks. I got most of it on Marco over the Internet.

Okay, she says. Yes. But you first.

Well all right, Lee James drawls. He sips his whiskey, seems to gather himself up for some huge effort.

As you saw, Bren, Marco Reyes was in no condition for soldiering. But he stayed on a ranch near one of the training camps in Nicaragua. From there he tried to influence the course of the coming invasion, create a guerilla faction that would infiltrate rather than invade. His people were training in the 'Glades, with no CIA or US military behind them, planning to use the money you were to deliver to keep the effort supplied and secret. They still had a good bit from other sources, but it seems not enough to handle the 'secret' part.

Well, the spooks in Nicaragua got onto him, arrested him and his men and sent them to a prison camp with a bunch of other 'malcontents', as they called them. The invasion was a disaster as we know. When he heard of it he knew all hope was gone for his brigade too. He died less than a week after, on April 30th, of congestive heart failure, in that prison. He was fifty-three.

Poor man, Ramona says. Lost his wife, his money, his country. Everything. She goes to the liquor cabinet and brings back a bottle of Havana Club and a glass. Pours. Sips. Speaks.

Julia was a friend of Isolda's second cousin, Inez. They had heard that Isolda reached Cuba with the money, turned it over to Castro and won his trust. Inez said that Isolda thought of herself as the Cuban La Pasionaria. She heard that she was invited to the wedding of Antonio Gades and the Flamenco singer Marisol, with Fidel himself presiding or as best man. It was said that La Pasionaria herself was also there, so Isolda may actually have met her heroine. Julia wasn't sure exactly, but she thinks that Isolda went back to Spain with them and traveled Europe raising funds for the revolution.

The three of them stare into the fire. They have nothing left to say, it's all been said, What love hath wrought, that sort of thing. Brendan takes his mind off it, it's over, it's done.

Lee James clears his throat. I looked up T. Stanford Mallory, too, he says.

Find anything? Bren reluctantly asks.

This and that. A Tristan Stanford Mallory is still alive, in the British Virgins. Retired as head of sales for an English marine electronics firm. Could that be your man?

Tristan. Of course. What else could that T. have stood for? Bren tries to imagine how his T. Stan might have gone from dashing sea captain to retired salesman. He shakes his head, sighs heavily. Makes the story sadder yet somehow, doesn't it? he says.

They sip and stare the fire for a few more silent minutes. Then Ramona smiles suddenly and says, Look! The sun is breaking through. I will prepare a brunch.

Lee James and Brendan have another whiskey while Ramona bustles in the kitchen.

Brendan gets up and goes back to the window. The wind has gone westerly, making the surf even madder. The sun sends streaking shadows across the Gulf, and there are whitecaps out there as far as he can see.

AGNES OF GOD

Agnes of God

Brendan:

The bay dances in shimmering gold lamé. Long early pine shadows turn glimpses of it into flickering hand-cranked cinema. The Gulf, quiet and inviting out there today, the norther having blown itself out in the night. A clear horizon shines brightly beyond. The old man remembers how wild the Gulf had been in its mating rite with the wind from the Yucatan thirty years before. Thirty-three years, to be more accurate, June of '72. Seas higher than the bridge he's now crossing. He has heard that when it hit here it had been even worse than he'd seen in the Straits. Hard for him to believe.

After the bridge he drives into a dark tunnel of dense forest, tall pine, oak strangling in kudzu, oleander, wisteria, the occasional magnolia, none of it blooming this early in March. Magnolia. Maggie. His daughter's name.

He is tired and hungry when he reaches Palmetto, is confused by all the route signs there. He stops at a burger joint, painfully eases himself out of the car, remembers to lock it after removing his cane. He knows he will need the cane to walk into the place after so long sitting at the wheel. He will have to stand in line, carry his paper bag and styrofoam cup to a table, get up again, dump the lot in the trash, walk back out to the car, all that. A flash of anger at the inconvenience of convenience shopping.

It is bright inside, all plastics in primary colors and flooded with 'fifties rock and roll. Three teen-age boys and a girl watch his tortoise-pace, whisper. When he glances at them one of the boys tugs downward on the girl's tee shirt, showing some pretty cleavage and leering at him. The girl giggles. He decides to make it a to-go order.

He knows it's too early but he's no good for any more driving. He pulls off at a clean-looking motel, trudges to the office, registers, pays, drives to the parking space in front of his room. He is glad to see that it faces away from the highway and has a view of some old oaks beyond the asphalt lot. Spanish moss fans a soft breeze for them. He unlocks the door, leaves his bagged lunch and his cane, makes a second trip for his kit. Remembers again to lock the car.

The room is musty but clean. He opens the curtains, sits at the desk. Its writing surface is cluttered with a telephone, a rack of brochures and advertisements and a huge television set, leaving barely enough space for his burger and iced tea.

He would have thought such a room luxurious in the 'fifties, Bill Haley still rocking in his mind's ear. He remembers the band playing the tune the night a drunken fourteen-year old Maggie almost got herself gang-raped in the shrubbery lining the Clearwater Yacht Club docks. He'd heard the laughter of the crew from one of the racing yachts — not the one he'd sailed — saw the tussle from the dock where his boat was moored. He grabbed a winch handle and dashed up the dock, not knowing that their victim was Maggie but certain it was a drunk young girl much like her. What the hell do you think you're doing! he shouted. That's my daughter, you bastards! One or two of them took a fair taste of that winch handle as they fled.

She was dirty and what clothes she still wore were in tatters, and she was so drunk he couldn't tell if she laughed or cried. He half-carried her out to the boat, got her aboard, got coffee into her, helped her to puke in the sink. After a while she was able to use the head and wash. When she'd done that he bundled her shivering into a blanket and stretched her out on the settee and watched her sleep for an hour before crawling into his own bunk.

In the morning he cooked her breakfast, gave her aspirin, found her some sailing clothes. Asked her to promise to be more careful next time. She balked at that.

Of what? she asked sharply.

Who you drink with.

Okay, she said after thinking about it. If he'd suggested quantity rather than company he was sure she wouldn't have given in.

She hugged him when she left.

The old man sighs, chews the last of his burger,

sips the last of his tea. Afternoon sun glares in. He closes the curtains over the mossy oaks, loosens his clothing and eases himself onto the bed. Brief post-prandial, he orders himself, not even minding that he has skipped his after-dinner cigarette.

He is standing in a grove of Grandfather oaks draped with Spanish moss. There is a faint breeze, the light is dull gray. He wears his doctoral robe and cowl and his old Yalie yachting cap. He looks down at his polished shoes. They are placed on a well-kept gravel path. When he looks up from them he sees fourteen year-old Maggie before him. She too is in her academic robe, holding it closed across her breasts. I've graduated, Bren, she says in Spanish. They have never spoken in Spanish before, he doesn't think she has ever studied the language.

Congratulations, he says. On to college now.

No, Brendan. I've graduated from college.

He finds none of this surprising, the Spanish, the look of her at fourteen, that she has just graduated from college. He steps away and looks at himself. He is in his thirties, so it all makes its own kind of sense. What will you do now? he asks.

I will make love to you, and marry you, and leave you to die in agony. Saying this she opens her robe to reveal a tall, slim blond nude, not her own sturdy body. He looks at her face. This is no longer Maggie but Maya, who does not smile, just stares at him with a chilling malevolence.

He steps away and looks at himself again. He is no longer in academic regalia, but is seventy-five, sagging in wrinkled khakis and a filthy straw hat.

Oh Maya, he says, look at what you have done to

me.

Then the hurricane returns, he stares up into the perfect circle of clouds surrounding black velvet studded with stars, Maya's face with her sweep of long blond hair floats into it. Then a huge sea breaks over the stern and Maggie is swept away into the storm and he hears his own voice calling *Maaa* . . . . He wakes shivering, hearing the remnant of that ghostly moan filling the dark.

He lies there thinking what a mistake had been made when they started naming every other hurricane for a male. All his hurricanes have been entirely female, the angry spawn of *El Sol* and *La Mer*, casually destroying all in the way of their willfulness.

The drive is a concert of terrible fugues, Hurricane Maya. Maggie beautiful, face full of joy as she hugs him for the second time when he tells her she has enough money in the bank to go to college. Then the third hug on her graduation from USF, they'd really been in their robes and mortarboards that day in '65, he'd just finished his first term on the faculty. Then the tall, sultry blonde Maya of eighteen, less than half his age, leaning back in her chair in First-Year Spanish to appraise him with cool eyes. In bed with her in his apartment, awed by her sensuality, her abandon. Maya. Two years later they marry, she continues her eclectic classes in art, theater, dance. Plays fetchingly at the role of faculty wife.

Oh Maya, look what you have done to me.

He drives through palmetto and pine being bulldozed and burned to make way for more buildings out here where there once lived wild hog and quail and deer. Finally off the highways onto narrow asphalt, the bridge to Gasparilla Island. He finds Maggie's lovely old cypress house without any trouble.

The old man looks at her now as she sits in her worn and faded bikini, the shade of the big umbrella softening her features. He knows she is in her late fifties, but a salting of gray in her cropped cap of dark curls and the wear sun and seawater have scoured into her face are the only signs of her age. She is short and sturdy, shaped and toned, athletic and seductive. But for her face her skin is smooth and has tanned darker than five-star cognac.

Maggie:

You were slumped over the bar at Sloppy Joe's working on your second rum and soda before eleven o'clock in the morning. You stank. You were so thin I could have slung you out of there tucked under an elbow. That was over thirty years ago and I swear you look better today than you did then.

I remember, Maggie. Sort of.

It's none of your affair, but I'll tell you what I was doing in Sloppy Joe's myself before eleven o'clock in the morning. My crewman and I had dinner ashore the night before. He met an old girlfriend. I left him to her and made it an early night aboard. In the morning I packed his kit, rowed it ashore and left it with the bartender. That was what I was doing in Sloppy Joe's before eleven o'clock in the morning. I hauled you out of there, down to where I'd beached the dinghy, and rowed you out to *Nunnery* and doused you with seawater and detergent. You curled up on the cockpit grating and you covered your face and shivered and moaned and begged me to stop.

I remember, Maggie. Sort of.

All you would say for the first two days there at anchor was Lost wife, lost work, lost soul. I got you onto solid food and let you have one gin at sunset and one beer with dinner, and a day or so later you told me where to find your things. You'd been sleeping in the rotten hulk of a rowboat under an abandoned dock in the marina. I rowed over there and all that was left in the boat was a plastic sack with a logbook, a picture of that awful woman — she wasn't even pretty, Brendan, not even that! — and a soggy paperback of short stories by García Márquez in Spanish.

I remember, Maggie. Honestly, I remember all of it after that. But I still don't remember how I got to Key West in the first place.

Brendan:

— she wasn't even pretty, Brendan, not even that —

Not pretty? Maybe not, but the sexiest girl he'd seen since Maggie's mother. He remembers exactly how it had gone, exactly. He'd struggled all those years alone, worked summers in boatyards despite his damaged leg and spine, got his BA and finally a PhD in Spanish Literature and got a teaching job at USF. Maya, 1967, she was in one of his classes, the very paradigm of Mod: miniskirt, forever legs, blond hair to her waist, pert little breasts bobbing under bright psychedelic silks.

Maggie:

You were stronger by the end of that week, needed exercise. So we sailed *Nunnery* up to Boot Key. You still couldn't help much around the boat, but you were an angel at the helm upwind, still haven't seen anyone better at it. But under power in that narrow channel past the mangroves you dug a hole or two in the mud.

The marina there is gone, you know, part of a high-rise resort or condo. It's like that everywhere now, nowhere left to go, ten boats in every anchorage with room for no more than one, the cacophony of the little motorboats everywhere, water skiers weaving through the anchored boats, wakes jarring the hulls, football games on portable televisions at peak volume on Sunday afternoons aboard the cabin cruisers. No point in having a cruising boat anymore. I hear that it's like that all the way down to the Virgins. I saw an article in a travel magazine with pictures of Turks — I know you were there once — the harbor at Turks, dredged and walled and turned into a port for those floating hotels they call cruise ships. Can you imagine?

Brendan:

He tries to imagine Cockburn Harbour as it must be now, motorboats and skidoos, a golf course instead of salt ponds, air conditioning and swimming pools. He can't. Turks with its crushed-shell airstrip on the west-facing beach, small shops across from it on the other side of a crushed-shell street.

Maggie:

Wasn't *Nunnery* a lovely boat, though? I came on her in Lauderdale, a nasty, neglected hulk lying in cradles at an obscure boatyard way up the river. The yard wanted to sell her to pay the bills owed them, so they called the brokerage to list her. I went to have a look and fell in love with her immediately. I thought of you, how you would love her, the sort of boat you always talked about in the old days. I swear she *smelled* of you.

She looked pretty much a wreck, but I got the surveyor to go over her. She was built entirely of teak, not one rotten timber in her. I bought her for a song, and took two years re-fastening her with stainless, lightening her by trading her teak topsides for cedar, changing her heavy gas engine for the latest, lightest new diesel, changing from brass to stainless fittings everywhere. Gave her a new, state-of-the-art keel. I knew you wouldn't care for her new aluminum spars, the high-aspect ratio rig, the Dacron sails. But all of those things made her into one fast forty-two foot sloop.

Brendan:

She'd finished her bright, had even varnished the new cedar topsides. There were few such wooden boats left by then, and hers was as pretty as any of them, apart from the aluminum spars. He'd often sailed on her like, to Turks and a lot of other places. When young.

Maggie:

We stayed at Boot Key for several days, and you did all your exercises every day and together we got a fresh coat of varnish on her, all but her topsides, and the winches greased, and cleaned the creosote off all the fenders. You showed me how to sew a new grommet into the jib's clew. And I was good, too. I drank no more than I allowed you to drink. I smiled and chatted about everything except that damned woman Maya and what happened at the University. I never let you turn inside on that. I didn't flirt with any of the guys on the dock. I puffed you up by letting them think I was your girl, that I held you to be a better man than any of them even if you were seventeen years older. That cranked you up a bit. You ate like a horse and slept so as to keep the whole marina awake. I didn't mind that. I was proud of the recovery you were making.

Brendan:

I smiled and chatted about everything except that damned woman Maya and what happened at the University. I never let you turn inside on that.

He turns inside on that now, though. Their marriage, during which she continued as an undergraduate in various arts. She smoked marijuana and bedded classmates, came to know his faculty friends and bedded some of them who were in art and theatre. He returned from a lecture tour and she said, I've got to leave you. He asked why, and she said, I've done things I can't tell you about. The sight of her across the campus walking hand-in-hand with one of her scruffy artist types. The sudden fear blanking her face as he finds her in the pottery studio with her teacher — *my colleague!* — smearing clay on each others' cheeks, necks, breasts. The last of it was when he came home early from a cancelled faculty meeting to see a young musician hastily gathering clothes and jumping out their bedroom window.

Then the rumors, the glances aside from the friends

and colleagues she'd been with, smirks, conversations dropped to whispers when he neared. He couldn't take it, both losing her and all sense of his own worth and dignity. You don't have to do this, his dean said when he presented his resignation. It's not that bad, really. It will pass. Just take a leave for a while.

It didn't pass. He didn't take a leave. He resigned himself to the bottle. Somehow over the next few months he found himself broke and in Key West with no idea how he'd got there.

Maggie:

Things changed when that Stephens yawl docked up late in the afternoon, *Mary Jane,* out of Atlantic City, with the four guys aboard. Three of them were about my age, kind of greasy and sly-looking. They spoke with that godawful New Jersey accent, city boys. The fourth one was something else altogether. He was medium height and had all that 'seventies hair and sideburns, but was tanned and hard-bodied and moved with complete grace both on the boat and on the dock, and had the least touch of the South in his speech, though he didn't say much to any of them.

The bunch of them were walking down the dock about an hour before sunset, and this guy saw you and stopped and asked if you were Captain Brendan Harper. You told him you were and it turned out that he had worked for you seventeen years earlier in Fort Lauderdale on a boat called *Adagio.* It took you a moment but then you remembered him, Dante Rogers. He'd been fourteen then, wanted nothing in the world more than to sail with you on your next delivery or charter. That didn't work out of course, but he sailed nevertheless, whenever and wherever he could. He never called you anything but Captain Harper.

Brendan:

Could that have been a coincidence? Dante Rogers shows up seventeen years after working with me on *Adagio*. No, no. There was something more to it, *had* to be something more to it.

Maggie:

Naturally I laid it on. Thickly. How not? What did you expect? He was gorgeous. I'd just been dumped in Key West by that guy who was sailing with me. I'd been using every trick in my girl's bag to sell yachts for three years. I sold them big and slick and very, very expensive. I didn't get all that money by being shy and demure.

So Dante begged off from dinner with that crew and joined us for the evening. He came aboard, admired the boat, talked sailing. I shooed the two of you up into the cockpit so I could tart up. You talked, he talked. It was clear that you had been a hero to him, the very model of the seafaring captain that he had tried to live up to ever after. I listened from below, made some appetizers and rigged drinks. In a bikini, and with a bit of hastily applied make-up. He kept sending glances down as I worked, watching my dancer's moves from fridge to cutting board to the booze locker. I brought all that up and sat, crossed a leg as provocatively as I could. I bent to serve drinks, which was effective in that skimpy top, and let you have a second gin. Bad girl.

I could see that you were getting tired of his fawning, realizing that you had told him too much while you worked on old *Adagio*. You said you would cook. You hadn't done that so far on that trip, but I'd bought a couple of fresh mackerel fillets that afternoon and you wanted to sauté them in a Greek sauce. That was fine with me; you could do that better than I and it left me alone with gorgeous Dante.

Brendan:

He remembers that it wasn't exactly that he'd told Dante too much. It was that in hearing some of his own stories back from the lad he was reminded that he'd been a garrulous fellow then, and it embarrassed him. Not long after that, because of his increased burden of secrets, he had quit telling stories altogether.

Until he got to South America. But that was more about testing out his language skills, seeing if he could tell a story or a joke in Spanish. I have always loved reading *stories though, he thinks, taut as halyards, distilled as rum, polished as brass. Written, I still love them.*

Maggie:

So while you rattled your pots and pans, I poured him drinks and we chatted, mating ritual stuff. You put on a tape of classical music, I suppose to drown us out. I can't blame you. It was pretty puerile as conversation, but it definitely was working.

Anyway, it was cool enough below after sunset with the wind scoops and awnings rigged, so when you had it all together down there we ate at the table in the main cabin. It was good, the fish and the pilaf and the salad. I broke out a bottle of chilled Pinot Grigio and we toasted our meeting. Dinner lasted well into the night. Dante and I went up to the cockpit for after-dinner rums and cigarettes while you withdrew to clean up. When you'd finished you stuck your head out the companionway to say goodnight and that you would sleep in the v-berth forward. We stayed and talked, our voices low and intimate. We'd come a long way by then, footsie under the table and whatnot. I don't know how you felt about it, and at the time I sure didn't care.

His friends from the yawl came back late and loud and drunk, stopped to make some remarks. Bad guys, I thought. Mean. They looked at me as if I were meat, speaking only to Dante but with no respect for him. Look what the sailor boy has found for himself, the one they called The Sheik said. He wore skin-tight bell-bottoms in a dark color, shirt open to show gold chains tangled in coils of black chest hair. The other one, shorter, stocky, they called him Icy, muttered, Yeah, some little piece, some little piece, and laughed at what he said as if it were clever. The one called Lew held back some, if not ashamed then at least a bit embarrassed. They left us alone after too much of that.

Their yawl was docked around the corner behind the dockmaster's office and out of sight but for her mainmast above its roof. They made some noise for a while, but then settled in. You weren't snoring, thank Heaven. The quiet was wonderful, with just a few night birds scrabbling in the mangroves, the splash of the occasional mullet out in the basin. It was definitely romantic.

Well, I don't have to go into deep detail here. We went below to the starboard berth and consummated the evening, as it were, and after that Dante whispered close to my ear. They had stopped at Boot Key because their engine had blown an injector or something they had to replace. That yawl was a drug smuggler. They were on their way to Jamaica to pick up a ton of *ganja.* He would make five thousand dollars on delivery. The guys he was with were small-time gangsters from Teaneck, New Jersey and only one of them had sailed at all, Lew, just a guy he'd met at Dinner Key Marina. Dante didn't want to go through with it. I didn't want him to go through with it, either. I wanted us to sail away into the sunset.

Brendan:

Both of us hope that a declaration of some kind of an epiphany will be wrung from the other in the course of this exchange of stories. If such is to come it will have to be soon. Brendan is old. Damn old, and for too long his only solaces have been alcohol and tobacco.

That Dante, she says. She smiles to herself, then sends him a sparkling eye and they chuckle.

He remembers Dante in Lauderdale back in '56, a boy of fourteen in love with the boats. He'd got the job of helping Bren with the varnish aboard *Adagio,* that huge motorsailer he'd sat on in a boatyard for over two months. He didn't recognize him when he showed up at Boot Key in '72, tall and well-built and handsome at thirty-one. Dante recognized Bren though, and after a few minutes of chat Bren remembered him despite his big head of hair and bushy sideburns.

I didn't get all that money by being shy and demure.

This *versical* of hers brings the *respondum* of a silent *mea culpa.* He knows it is unwarranted, she speaks proudly. He searches her face for defiance, sees only her amusement at his discomfiture. This is Maggie, his daughter. For a moment he sees her mother at fifteen, the year before Maggie's birth, blond but just as tanned and with that same tilt to her head when she'd said something sharp. Sees her again with Maggie as an infant on her lap. Then he sees mother and daughter together at a regatta in Clearwater, Maggie at thirteen and her mother by then grossly fat and slatternly.

He sips his gin, looks out over the little bay. Across from Gasparilla Island is one tiny mangrove key left out there, shimmering with birds. The rest of its shore, once all mangroves, is now dredged and seawalled and lined with pretentious yachts docked in front of pretentious houses. Here on the outer shore, where they sit on Maggie's patio between her once-elegant house and her racy little sailboat at the dock, it is cool, with dense foliage shading them and hiding them from neighbors. The land under them had never been mangrove, but rather a sandy spit. He remembers it from before it was made into a housing tract in the late 'forties. A few houses had already been there, solid, silvered cypress, hers among them.

Maggie:

So he slipped out not long before sunrise and went to his yawl. If you would let me take him along, he'd pack his kit and sneak off. We'd have to be ready to sail before they got their engine part installed. We decided we'd sail for Isla Mujeres. That meant I'd have to get to the store in Marathon in the morning, after convincing you to let me take him on and to let him go with us. I didn't think you'd have much choice about that one. Well, it was my boat, wasn't it? I managed to sleep an hour or two once I'd remembered that.

You were up and had coffee ready when I finally awoke. I was slow that morning, so I decided on a shower up at the dockmaster's office and asked you to save me a cup. I washed my hair and generally luxuriated up there. There was a small window out of the ladies, with curtains. I peeked through at the yawl. Nothing stirred aboard her. I put on a fresh bikini and a big man's shirt and went back to *Nunnery*, loving the cool dampness as the breeze dried my skin and hair.

I joined you for coffee and a cigarette in the cockpit. The early sun and the light land breeze, your strong coffee and the smoke brought me around and I remembered what I had to do. The question was, do I tell you the whole of it, or just the part about wanting Dante to sail with us? You saved me the trouble. You said, Do you want him to sail with us?

And I was so grateful I almost broke down and cried. You asked me if I was sure he wanted to, and where we might go. I told you Isla Mujeres, and you grinned like a dolphin. You asked when, and I said as soon as I could buy stores and Dante could get clear of his bunch. You said okay, you'd get her ready to go.

So I dressed in more modest clothing and called a cab from the dockmaster's, hiked up the dock to the road. I figured Dante could tell you about the smuggling if he wanted to, once we were underway.

Dante was watching for me when I got back. He wheeled out one of the marina's rusty grocery carts and helped me unload the cab, wheeled the sacks back down the dock to the boat. On the way he told me that Lew, the one who could sail, had gone into Marathon to wait for the part at the bus station. He'd be back in a couple of hours. The other two were still aboard, so he hadn't been able to sneak his gear over to *Nunnery* yet. He said not to worry, it was all packed, he'd get the chance.

By then it was nearly eleven. The tide was about as high as it would get that day. You had the boat snugged to the dock and were waiting for us. Dante stayed to hand you grocery bags, I went below with the first of them and started making space in the lockers. Stowing all that stuff would take a good hour. You and Dante chatted. I wondered if he would tell you about the *ganja* run.

Of course he did. I knew it when you came storming below, kicking grocery bags around as if they were a pack of curs. Why didn't you tell me? you asked, once your fury had settled. What difference would that have made? I countered. Finally you saw my point and settled down. He just has to get his gear, I said. Then we can go. They won't be able to get underway until Lew gets back with the part.

You went back up to the cockpit and sat there stewing. Dante had gone over to the yawl. When I finished my stowage, I came up and sat with you. I was stewing a little myself. In a few minutes Lew came down the dock with a package under his arm. He said hello and waved as he passed. I let him disappear around the dockmaster's office, then went up there where I could see what was going on.

The other two guys left the yawl with towels and shave kits a few minutes after Lew went aboard. No sign of Dante. I heard the clank of a wrench from her engine room, then water running in the men's showers. I waited. And waited. The showers stopped running. Dante emerged with his kit, heaved it over the lifelines and stepped onto the dock. We hustled.

You had her hanging on her last two lines. When you saw us you cranked up the engine. Dante heaved his bag aboard forward, got that spring off the cleat and jumped aboard with it. I was slow with the aft spring line; the cleat was loose and it got jammed in the gap. The guys came out of the shower, saw us leaving with Dante, started shouting and ran for me. I got the line cleared, but when I leaped and grabbed the backstay, they grabbed the line and hung on. You were already in forward, about to gun us away. Dante saw what was happening and untied the other end of it. There was still enough tension on it to turn her bow in, but you managed to get her moving forward, skimming the dock. They ran alongside of us, yelling their heads off. One of them grabbed a shroud, made to jump aboard. Dante gave him a shove. He clung to the line, the idiot, banged into the last piling and finally let go. Just then you were clear of the docks, turned her sharply to starboard, and we were passing the yawl.

Lew apparently heard the ruckus and figured out what was happening. He was in the cockpit aiming a pistol at Dante. I shouted to warn him but he'd already seen it, flattened himself on the deck behind his bag.

The shot didn't come. Lew hollered the other two aboard and they prepared to sail off the dock. One of the guys went below, presumably to finish installing the engine part.

The tide was ebbing by then and the wind was

moderate out of the east, so they got her going pretty well into the marked channel by the mangroves before we'd got past the last marker. As soon as there was sea room to port, you rounded to it. I had the gaskets out of the main by then, and Dante had the jib up and drawing nicely. He went straight to the main halyard and in a single minute we were under full sail, you steering southwest for the Hawk Channel on a broad reach. Dante and I started rigging for the spinnaker.

It wasn't her best point of sail — she did better with the wind abeam or a little forward of it – but she had her new, modern keel, and the yawl had to drag her old-time full one. Besides, Dante assured us that without him they couldn't set their spinnaker. You shut down the engine of course, since it wouldn't help anyway with that breeze behind us. Dante and I went about tidying up the lines and fenders. He stowed his kit and relieved you at the helm. Then we set the spinnaker and furled the jib. It was after one by then, so I went below to fix lunch.

Brendan:

I remember.

I remember mainly the chill up my spine when I saw that pistol aimed at Dante. There at Boot Key as we got past the yawl and made for the channel my back, so badly injured that day at Tobago, was exposed to the gun and I remember how I cringed, waiting for the bullet to cripple me even further. It took half a lifetime to get out of pistol range. I'd never told her about Tobago. I wouldn't this time, either.

That was the only time I was scared that whole trip, Maggie. Truly.

But that wasn't strictly true. It was the only time

I'd been scared for myself, but I'd been scared sick for Maggie over and over.

Maggie:

I was too busy to be scared then, she says. Later I was really scared. Her eyes drift away from him, back to '72, he can tell.

I'd done some match racing in the dinghies, but never in a cruising class boat. That run down the Hawk Channel was pretty intense. They weren't ten minutes behind us at the start, and we increased our lead over the first couple of hours, being able to fly a spinnaker while they couldn't. But getting on toward sunset we started to get these little rainsqualls. The wind shifted in each of them, so we'd go from a broad reach to hard on the wind one minute, then sit in a calm while it rained itself out. Then it would gradually shift back to the east, and we'd be reaching again. We couldn't fly the spinnaker through stuff like that.

After the second squall they showed up just boat-lengths behind. We ran the engine whenever the wind dropped, but that little diesel didn't give us much. Theirs obviously was bigger, which meant that we couldn't possibly outrun them upwind. They'd just flatten the main, run the engine and drive right up our stern. So we had to keep them chasing us on broad reaches and runs. Apart from the squalls we were fine so long as the wind stayed up and stayed easterly.

It was a question whether to use the running lights once it got dark. The Hawk Channel was pretty well patrolled even then, what with the Cubans and the smugglers, so we went with the lights. So did they. We'd lose sight of them in the rains, but when it cleared they were always there, not more than a couple of hundred yards behind.

In the calm phase of what proved to be the last of the squalls, they put her bow to weather of our cockpit. They had put out their lights and with our engine running we didn't hear them. You were below then, I was steering. The Sheik was forward on the yawl, only a couple of yards away, waving the pistol. Get over here, he shouted at Dante. Get aboard this boat.

I ducked below the coaming and jammed the helm to port, down what little wind there was. Our transom almost hit her sheer. That threw him off balance, gave us a few seconds to make about twenty yards away from them, but he fired twice anyway, the shots sounding flat and dull in the rain. I guess you two were awake, because suddenly Dante was standing with the flare pistol in his hand. You must have loaded it very quickly and given it to him. I heard the whoosh as he aimed it over my head and fired. I looked up then and saw the world alight in an eerie red. The Sheik was on his knees, clinging to a lifeline with one hand, the other covering his head. I couldn't see the pistol. The jib behind him had a big black hole in the center of it, rimmed with flame. It reminded me of the circus, the ring of fire waiting for the horses to jump through.

Their helmsman must have been blinded, because they just curved away, clearly out of control. Dante turned off our lights and we re-trimmed and slipped southward from the channel. After a while the wind came back from the east stronger than before, and we could reach back up to our westerly course, turn off the engine, let the spinnaker fill and pull us almost gaily away from that danger. The firelight gradually faded behind us, then disappeared. We didn't see *Mary Jane* again that night.

We reached the Key West ship channel around eleven. We held a conference. One option was to sail in to the Coast Guard station there. Dante was against it, thinking it wouldn't really help. No one on the yawl had a record. It's not illegal even yet to have a gun on a boat in U. S. or International waters. They'd have a better chance at us ashore. So we decided to press on to sea, stay north of the reef as far as Rebecca Shoal light, then reach off to the Gulf Stream. It might take a day or two to lose sight of them, but once we did we could go any direction we wanted. Or so we thought at the time. That was on June twelfth.

Brendan:

They'd have a better chance at us ashore.

Dante was dead serious as we discussed our choices. These are very bad guys, he said. Lew maybe not so bad, I know you saw him with the pistol but it was just show. The other two, though. Not the first sign of anything like conscience in either of them.

I asked him how he'd fallen in with that crew. He shrugged. I was keeping a racing boat at Dinner Key, and bored to tears. It was a crack at some good sailing and an adventure with a prize. Lew said he'd done it before, got the stuff back, moved it in sailbags up the dock in broad daylight. Not as much of it as this time, but still, easy. I figured it was something you might have done yourself.

That put me aback. I realized he was probably right. There probably had been a time.

Maggie:

We cleared Rebecca Shoal before daylight. The wind was shifting, getting some north on it and picking up. We had to give up the spinnaker and set a high-clewed jib instead. We carried on to the west and were clearly losing them. Dante went up to the spreaders with the glasses once the sun was high enough to look back to the east. He said she was hull-down but he could still see the peak of her mainmast.

You cooked us a big breakfast, which we stretched out into a mid-morning brunch. By then we had to shorten down to the number two jib and reef the main. No huge seas, but quartering and hard to steer. Dante handled it best, using much less rudder than either of us could manage. After cleaning up, you ran the Loran signals, got a fix somewhere south of the Dry Tortugas. Told us the barometer was still at 29.90. You listened to the radio for storm warnings but didn't hear any. We put some south on the course, which seemed to steady her a touch. You said you needed to sleep. You lay down on the settee.

By afternoon the wind had gone back to due east and was blowing a good thirty knots. Suddenly it seemed the sun was gone behind a wall of rain and fog. The seas were getting confused, those driven from the south by the current bumping into the old ones from the east and creating a rotten chop. We double-reefed the main and changed down to the working jib. If we were to run, it would have to be southwest. We eased her off, which made it harder to steer but was better than banging into both wind and chop. It was all changing fast, only into what wasn't clear. For the worse, that was for sure.

Brendan:

Suddenly, it seemed, the sun was gone behind a wall of rain and fog.

It was more like a wall of fog we could see from where we sailed in sunlight, and we were heading right into it. It was nothing like the fog I'd seen once or twice in a calm on Long Island Sound. It reached upward, miles into the sky, and blotted out the sun in minutes.

The seas were getting confused, those driven from the south by the current bumping into the old ones from the east and creating a rotten chop.

He remembers what a sight that was, all around them the surface of the sea erupting into emerald spires, cathedral steeples made of seawater. He'd never seen the like of them before, twenty feet across at the base and rising thirty feet into the air, fountains of spume blowing off their tops, not just a few of them but everywhere as far as they could see. He was steering, and it was tough trying to dodge those spires. Maggie and Dante grappled with the main, battling to get the third reef into it. They were wearing life jackets and were hooked into lifelines, but there was nothing he could do to help them in that sea. He was terrified that one or both of them would go overboard, lifelines snapping, there would be no way in the world to go back for them. Maggie, my daughter, be safe, don't fall, don't you fall.

Maggie:

Come dark it hadn't eased off at all, in fact was producing gusts over fifty knots. The barometer was down to 29.85. I went below to fix dinner and got you up to relieve Dante at the helm. He was tiring badly, took to the settee, still in his life jacket and harness. He'd have to eat, I'd call him when it was ready.

I dug out some ground beef and a can of spaghetti sauce and put the pot on to boil. Thank heaven I'd spent the extra for the gimbaled stove. It sloshed when she pitched, but stayed steady enough when she rolled. I was dancing back and forth, up and down, her movement was bad for cooking, that's for sure. I browned and seasoned the beef, poured the sauce into it and was hanging onto the skillet as it simmered. I clung to a handrail next to the companionway with the other hand. It was a rough business.

I had to let go to drain the spaghetti, there was no way around it, as the colander was in the sink and it would take both hands. Just then she lurched something awful, and I poured boiling water all over my left hand. I couldn't let go, I just had to stand it, I had no choice. I got most of the spaghetti into the colander, but some of it went into the sink. I dropped the pot, which clanged off to leeward and hit the chart table. Another lurch and the sink, clogged with loose spaghetti, squirted hot water on my jeans and slimed across the pretty teak-and-holly cabin sole.

Well, eventually I got all the spaghetti back into the colander and picked up the pot. My hand hurt like hell, but there was nothing I could do for it at that point. I woke Dante, told him I needed help. He was slow to move.

I took the pot back to the stove, poured the spaghetti into it, scraped the sauce onto it and stirred. Dante asked what I wanted him to do. I sent him forward for the first-aid kit. What I guess I should have done was ask him to find plates, forks, cups, all that, but

I didn't. Anyway, we would clearly have to eat one at a time, so I was holding the pot in my bad hand, waiting for Dante to come aft, when she took a terrible roll to port. I reached up, with the big serving spoon still in my hand, trying to keep myself from banging into the cabinets over the stove. That was okay, I didn't hurt myself much then. But an instant later she rolled back to starboard just as badly, sending me and the pot and the spoon and all the damned spaghetti across to the lockers below the chart table. I took a bad crack to the head, almost went out. Maggie, I heard you shout, I think I just steered through a twister!

Dante showed up just then, dropped the first-aid kit on the settee and bent to help me up. Together we shoveled spaghetti back into the pot and got it onto the stove. Go up and help Brendan, I told Dante. I'll deal with this mess.

Well, Dante came back and said you were all right, he'd re-trimmed the sails for the new sea that followed the twister. *Nunnery* was all right, he didn't see anything wrong on deck or with the rig. I had him take out a plate and a cup, spooned spaghetti onto the plate, and poured wine into his cup. He went forward to sit and eat. I sat next to him and fiddled with the first-aid kit. In the end he had to help me to bind my hand. When he'd finished I had to lie down. I was seeing double from the crack on the head and my hand was on fire. I don't know how you two got through the night. I took a pill with some wine and went out of it entirely.

Brendan:

I didn't really steer through the twister. I clung to

the tiller with both hands, eyes stuck on the compass in amazement as it ran through a hundred and eighty degrees to port, then another one-eighty back to starboard. Working jib and double-reefed main never backed, she stayed in the same point of sail all the way around and back. I knew we should shorten down to storm jib and trysail, but with you hurt and Dante exhausted I didn't see how we could. Adrenalin kept me tireless for the next two hours, Dante sitting in the cockpit with me, dozing. We traded off then, and I went below. The galley was a mess, but everything was secured in one way or another. You lay still, or as still as was possible in that sea. I knelt and bent close to listen for your breathing. With all the noise on deck and the drafts blowing through the cabin I couldn't hear anything. Oh Maggie, please! Finally you moaned and my heart started again.

Maggie:

In the morning we shortened down to storm jib and trysail, with me steering. Once that was done *Nunnery* still bucked and twisted like a Brahma bull, but I had some control of her. We were all in harnesses and life jackets. We couldn't tell rain from spray, and everything tasted salty. She pitched and hammered and most of the time her lee rail was under water. I still wasn't in great shape, but the hand only hurt a little and my eyesight was clear.

We tried to get a fix from the Loran, but it was out. The antenna had survived the twister, but something had gone wrong, or the weather just wouldn't let us catch a signal. Our last sure position, late the afternoon before, was at Latitude 23°36′ North, Longitude 84°60′

West. We'd been steering southwest, and the knotmeter said we'd generally been doing seven knots, but that was really just guesswork. Dante went through the wiring, we cranked up the engine to make sure we had battery power. It all came to nothing. We would have only dead reckoning from there.

By mid-day or so we must either have turned a corner or the storm center had moved, because the seas steadied, driven by a single easterly wind. That made steering much easier, though it blew harder and harder, the wind gauge reading a steady fifty knots from the east. We took it on the port quarter, making good speed. You cooked something for us, then we took turns sleeping, steering, watching, keeping up the dead reckoning in the logbook. It was a wild ride, but it was beginning to seem natural, as if we had never seen or sailed in any other kind of weather.

It was nearing sunset — not that there was any sun — when the first bird banged into the trysail and fell to the deck. It got caught under the lashings for the liferaft, lay there fluttering. It was some sort of finch. The next one was a dove. It clung to one of the gaskets on the furled main, rocked there in the wind hanging on, its eyes closed. We watched it teetering until it tired and was blown overboard. Then another and another, finches, sparrows, doves, small parrots. These were land birds, driven from the trees and fields of western Cuba. Some died on impact, some lasted for a few minutes, some clung shivering in the lee of the deckhouse until she put a rail under and the sea washed them away. One hit you on the shoulder, fell into the cockpit. It had died on impact, so you threw it over the side. We watched this happening for an hour at least, and after full dark we still could hear them as they hit the sails or the rigging or the deckhouse. By then we were getting sixty knots of sustained wind, with gusts over seventy. One gust pegged the gauge at ninety knots and broke it.

Brendan:

The birds were so sad, little girls driven out into the storm, seeking sanctuary in a convent. I wanted to gather the living ones, put them below out of the wind, and actually tried it with one little sparrow. Cupped it gently between my palms, got it to perch on the rim of a plastic cup in the sink. When I went back below a few minutes later it lay dead in the cup and I had to throw it over the side.

Maggie:

The noise! We couldn't speak to one another without shouting, the wind blowing the words out of our mouths, howling in the rigging, the sea itself roaring at us. I had to ask Dante to steer, I was dead out of it, my vision doubling again, my shoulders shaking from the strain of the helm, my burned hand throbbing. I huddled in the lee corner of the cockpit, not really out of the wind but with Dante's bulk protecting me some. You went below after dark to make us something to eat. After rummaging a while down there you hollered up that we had to start the engine, the fridge was losing its cold, we'd lose all our stores. Dante turned the key. It started all right, but after a few minutes he said that the temperature gauge was soaring, he'd have to shut down or we'd burn it up. I screamed down to you and explained. You nodded and ducked into the engine room.

We'd lost suction in the seawater intake for the cooling system. Her port quarter, where the intake was, kept being lifted out of the water, so it couldn't draw. There was nothing to be done until she could settle enough to keep it under. So you opened cans of tuna, made sandwiches on soggy bread and passed us beers. Heavenly. Then you told us that the barometer had fallen to 29.79. I asked what that meant. You said, It means it's getting worse.

Well, we knew that. It didn't matter much to me, as after the sandwich and the beer I absolutely had to sleep.

Brendan:

Scared for you hardly says it. Worried to death is more like it. You reeled down the companionway, clinging to handrails, lockers. I did what I could to help you to the starboard settee, tipped you into it, rigged the safety board to hold you in. Your eyes were glazed, you shook your head when you closed them. I gave the galley a rudimentary tidy-up, knowing I would have to relieve Dante at the helm. My hip was trying to kill me by then. None of us was in very good shape, were we?

I struggled up the companionway and was hit by so much wind it blew the breath right out of me. It had reached the point where I couldn't tell if it were actually blowing harder or just seemed to be after being below and out of it for a while. I watched Dante steer for a minute or so. He wasn't letting her go peg to peg, but he sure wasn't managing the narrow arcs he had an hour earlier. He looked awful.

So we switched. It took a while to get the feel of her back, and I soon knew that it was definitely blowing harder. Dante huddled in the lee corner where you'd been, eyes closed, hugging himself. I knew we'd have to take in the trysail soon, dreaded asking him. *Nunnery* kept trying to bury her bows as she sledded down into the troughs.

She did it a few minutes later, just stuck her nose into the bottom of one, swam through it. Dead birds cascaded with the wash as it poured into the cockpit, sloshing bucketsful down the companionway into the cabin despite the slats I'd slipped into it. Dante came up sputtering, said it for me, We've got to douse the trysail. He got up, shook himself like a wet retriever and started the slow, dangerous crawl forward. Good lad, good lad, God help us all.

There was nothing I could do to help him. If I released the sheet he'd never be able to tug down the luff. If I flattened it, she'd yaw to weather and I'd never be able to hold her when the next big one came to capsize her. Nothing I could do but steer them best I could, try to keep her head out of the water when she reached the troughs.

Tug by tug, pull by pull, he got the sail down. I steered through dozens of seas, maybe even hundreds, before he had it down, madly flapping but no longer drawing. She quieted a little and no longer did her diving act. He got a couple of stops around it but it clearly wouldn't be possible for him to furl it properly, get it off the mast.

Great work! I shouted at him when he'd made it back aft. She's much better now! He nodded briefly, curled back up into his corner.

So we ran from it, surfing down from the crests, the storm jib keeping us just ahead of it. I was just as happy for the darkness, didn't really want to see how high the crests were, how deep the troughs.

Maggie:

When I woke up it was asphalt black in the cabin. I had no idea of the time. Her motion was better than I remembered it when I'd gone to sleep. It was still just as noisy, though, and I gradually became aware that I was smelling bilegewater. Under the sounds of the hull creak and rigging moan and sea roar I heard something else, something new. I listened, lying still, holding my breath. Yes, it was bilgewater all right, sloshing all over my expensive teak-and-holly cabin sole. I rolled over, put my bandaged hand down to touch it. It came up drenched to the elbow. I found a light switch and turned it on. It was dim, even flickered. I saw that the cabin was awash with gallons of seawater.

First I went aft to find a flashlight. Then I went forward, lifting bilge hatches, shining the light into every cranny. I found the leak in the head. The sink and the john were full and pouring into her. I crawled into the cramped space under the sink, found the seacocks and the valve for the drain and closed them. Then I closed the cocks behind the john. That was when I found the main leak. She had a two-inch hole in her where the through-hull drain fitting had broken away. I stuffed a towel into it, knew it wouldn't stay.

The important thing was to tell you about it so you could start pumping. She had an electric pump of course, but that wasn't going to be any help with the engine out. She had a big hand pump with its handle in the cockpit. It would be up to you.

You were steering, Dante was dozing. I shook him awake, shouted the news, told him where the pump handle was, under the seat on the port side. He nodded and set himself to it. I went forward again to see what I could do about the leak.

I made my way through there, ankle deep sometimes and sometimes knee deep in it when she pitched, clinging to whatever came to one hand, gripping the flashlight with the other. I turned off the light over the settee when I got that far, knowing we'd need every ounce of juice to start the engine once we had fixed the intake and could do it at all. Cushions were floating, I kept kicking into pieces of loose gear that were moving underwater and underfoot. Finally I got back to the head. The towel I'd stuffed into the hole was gone, somewhere in the general mess. I would have to come up with something a lot better than that. Duct tape was my first thought, naturally, but knew it would have to be something more than that, since it was all underwater. What?

I crouched in that miserably cramped space holding another towel over the hole, tried to think what was cylindrical and about two inches in diameter that I could stuff in there and make hold with tape. Or something. Something. Once in a while, when other sounds abated, I could hear the pump working. It would take a long time to empty her, and I couldn't stay there like the little Dutch boy forever.

A plastic cup would be about the right size. I pulled the towel away and aimed the flashlight at the hole. Tape wouldn't do it. I thought I might be able to wire something on there somehow. Yes. There was a fragment of the fitting still screwed to the hull, and a seacock for the john was only about eight or nine inches away. So I stuffed the towel back in there and went aft again, to find wire and pliers and a plastic coffee cup.

It took ages. The water level wasn't noticeably different as I lurched toward the galley. And where the devil had I stowed the spare wire, the pliers? I rummaged. You steered. Dante pumped.

Finally I found some fishing leaders and the little wire-cutters we used to set up trolling lines. I found a set of measuring cups hung together on a ring. I thought the biggest one would be big enough, but tucked a coffee cup in my shirt with it, just in case. Then I made the lurching crawl forward again. The leak had gained on Dante's pumping. It was deeper for sure. I couldn't see how she would stay up much longer if I didn't get at it, she would dive into one of those endless troughs and just stay down. I hurried, which meant that I was making the speed of a conch dragging itself across a reef.

Well, I crawled back in there and fitted the measuring cup over the hole. It was a little small, so I wrapped it in a washcloth, banged it in there with my hand. My burned hand, because I couldn't get to it with the other one. Of course it popped out when I went to work rigging the wiring to hold it in place. I dropped the flashlight. I found it again and jammed it into an armpit. I couldn't aim it properly, had to work by feel. I got one end of the wiring fixed at last, hooked the other loosely to the seacock. Then I had to fish around in the muck to find the cup with the washcloth around it. Then I felt her dive, and waited for the rise. It didn't come. In a moment

I was completely underwater, stuck in that corner, unable to move. I heard the pump stop.

Brendan:

That was what you would call scary, I guess. She was getting sluggish, not answering the helm at all well. She came up out of one trough with the forward half of her clean out of the water, then took the next crest with her transom under, filling the cockpit. When it had passed, her rudder came clean out and I was trying to steer her in air instead of water. She broached I think, though I couldn't really see. When she went into that next trough she just wallowed there, as if she were an exhausted fighter, just couldn't get up from the mat one more time. Dante had seen it coming, let go the pump handle and clutched the nearest winch with both hands. I sat there just clinging to the tiller and watching. I had no idea if she would ever get her head up again.

Maggie:

I held what breath I had left as long as I could, then had to start blowing bubbles. How long was she down like that? I had no idea. I felt as if I were trying to set an underwater record. Then I heard the pump start again, and she rolled off to starboard a little, draining the compartment. I sucked air fiercely, waiting for her to roll back and bury me again. She didn't. I went back to work on the leak, hands slow and numb, all of me shaking. I don't know how long it took, but I got the cup to stay in the hole and the wires snugged down tight. Then I just stayed there for a while. Hearing the pump now and then was all I had to give me any hope. Not much hope, but some. It was a while before my hand started hurting again, and when it did I realized that both of them hurt. I'd cut them up pretty badly with the fishing leaders. Couldn't see any blood, all of it had washed away in the bilgewater.

When I could move at last it was in increments, a limb at a time. The flashlight was fading, but it didn't matter much. I was wondering if there might be a way to hook all the flashlight batteries into the system to help crank the engine, if ever it would be time to crank the engine. I absurdly thought about what sort of engineering that would take as I crawled out of the head and aft. I couldn't tell if the water level was any lower, but decided it had to be. I'd fixed the leak, hadn't I?

Brendan:

She rose of course. Had she not we'd not be here talking. She wallowed, the cockpit full of water, but I could feel she had some life in her, answering the helm reluctantly, but answering. Once the cockpit had drained to a point where he could, Dante resumed pumping. I steered as small as I could. Speech was impossible in all that wind, not that either of us could think of anything to say. Just to breathe was hard enough. Dante pumped, I steered. For hours. My back was going, legs were shaking. I changed from sitting to standing often, moving the pain from one part of me to another. No choice. Dante had to pump, I had to steer. For hours.

Graylight finally showed us sea and sky, a bleak start to our fifth day of gale force winds. The pallid light made the steering a bit easier, though I can't say why, as the wind didn't slacken. The pump growled its announcement that her bilges were finally empty. Dante put away the pump handle and half-lay on the grating, head on his arms, entirely used up. I worried about you. How had you fared below in all that water?

Dante stirred, sat up, looked out at the sea with an empty face. Suddenly he stood, glared to windward and shouted, You won't kill us, damn you! You will not kill us! I took that as a good sign, though it occurred to me that it might have been quite the opposite. He glared at the sea for another minute, then turned and went below. I could see his head above the companionway slats as he did something in the galley. For the next half hour I cursed him silently for not telling me how you were doing. Then he brought up a cup of coffee and said you were sleeping and took the helm and I felt ashamed for having cursed him.

He remembers then going forward to the mast, clinging to halyards, leaning into the edge of the trysail, staring or perhaps gazing into the wind into the sea tasting and smelling and listening to the wind and the sea, the beauty of it, the purity of it, and feeling calm and absolutely joyful at once. He disappeared into the wind and the sea knowing he would never return to any world at all like the one that disappeared with him in that moment. He would from then on be in the wind and the sea and inseparable from the wind and the sea and would set sails so that the boat of his life would be just like this one, rising and plunging and at ease in the vastness of wind and sea exactly as she now was doing with her storm jib and trysail as happy as he was and would be from that moment. This is something he can't describe to Maggie or anyone else. It will have to remain a secret between Father Wind and Mother Sea and this old man Brendan for the rest of his life.

I sat on the lee bench, rested my back on the bulkhead, huddled over my coffee. Numb. Better than pain. Dante steered. I slumped.

I guess I drifted off, because the smell of bacon frying seemed to waft up from the galley only a minute later. Dante was still at the helm, so I realized that you had to be up and cooking. I got to my feet, found I was still clutching my coffee cup gone cold. I bumbled down the companionway, saw you propped in a corner between the port side settee and the stove, hanging onto the frying pan and holding a fork. You didn't look your best, in your foul weathers and life jacket and harness, but were a beautiful sight anyway. You even smiled.

Everything below was wet, soggy, and smelling of bilge. The way *Nunnery* was tossing herself around it was pointless to try to clean her up. I sat at the chart table and did what I could with the dead reckoning. The way it came out worried me; I was pretty sure we were too far west to be safe to leeward. I went over it again, decided we had another twenty hours or so before Mexico showed up to shatter us. Nothing we could do about it anyway. The barometer was still falling, 29.08. Jeez.

Scrambled eggs and bacon wrapped in a soggy tortilla. Wonderful. You went up and relieved Dante. He came below, sat, ate, toppled over onto the settee and was dead asleep in an instant. I went up to sit with you, watch you steer. You were doing well, lining her up to take the crests squarely, holding her steady as she plunged into the troughs. I watched as long as I could. Not very long, I'm afraid. Didn't sleep long, either, though long enough for you to get so tired you missed one and woke me. I relieved you as soon as I could move, sent you below.

Maggie:

I have no idea how long I slept. It seemed like an instant to me, but I'm sure you and Dante thought of it as an eternity. However long it was — four or five hours, I suppose — I woke from it renewed, ready to hand, reef, and steer, to cook and clean, make myself irresistible. How I was to do the latter in soggy foulweathers wasn't clear. Surely I could cook.

The boat was such a mess, everything was scattered everywhere, and soaking wet. I tidied things just enough to get to the galley without tripping. The cooking didn't seem any harder that it had in the last St. Pete to Lauderdale race when we were close-hauled against a norther in the Stream, and the gusto with which you two ate your breakfast was most cheering. I poured Dante a fat rum with his so he would sleep. It probably wasn't necessary, but again, was cheering. I took a small swallow myself.

Steering in that wind and sea was exhilarating for the first half hour, but gradually wore me back down to pre-sleep debility. You huddled in your corner, sleeping or drifting, obviously not in good shape yourself. You woke, stood, turned your back to me and pissed in the cockpit. That reminded me that I wanted to pee too, and had nowhere to do it decently, what with the head being out of commission. Of course I could just do it in the cockpit as you had — it was self-flushing after all, with great quantities of spray — but turning my back to do it would hardly amount to privacy.

Anyway, you went below, brought up the rum bottle, took a swallow and took the helm. I took a swallow, tucked the bottle in the rack beside the companionway, and took my pee. Don't look, I shouted, and you laughed. At least Dante didn't get to see it. What a damned nuisance it is to be a woman sometimes, especially in a foul weather suit.

It was near mid-day by then, and as bright as it would get. I looked over her deck and rig. The deck seemed all right, just a tangle of line here and there, but the rig was a mess where Dante hadn't been able to furl the trysail properly. The wind instruments at the masthead were simply gone, the wiring whipping its shredded strands off to leeward and angrily scratching at the mast up there. But all the shrouds and stays seemed solid, the main safely furled, stops holding, all the rest okay. That tiny storm jib pulled *Nunnery* forward with a power that awed. As a sailboat, if not as a floating RV, she was in fine shape indeed. Standing there aft of the cabin I watched as she stuck her bow out over the crests and the long, deep caverns that opened below her down to the troughs ahead. She would hover there, then glide in a rush down into that hole, where she would shiver, then raise her pretty butt to the next crest like a cat in heat.

We traded off at the helm for the next three or four hours while Dante slept. The sea and wind stayed the same, sixty to seventy knots we guessed, we couldn't really know with the windspeed dial stuck at ninety. You did your dead reckoning, again figured us to be too far west. You said that when Dante came up we should try to drop the jib, heave to on the trysail. You asked me if there was a sea anchor aboard. I told you there wasn't. You thought we might be able to rig some sort of a drogue to slow her down.

When he woke, Dante agreed with you about heaving to, rigging a drogue. But when he went forward to lower the jib, he couldn't. The halyard had jumped the sheave, there was no way to lower that jib but to go to the masthead and clear it, and that couldn't be done until she lay in quieter water. We did rig a clever drogue astern, a long bight of line with two life jackets lashed to the middle of it. It didn't slow us much, but it did seem to make the steering a little easier.

I made us one-handed cold sandwiches, mostly cheese. The fridge was definitely starting to smell. We took turns eating, steering. Dante went down into the engine room to see if he could do anything with the cooling system, came up after half an hour to say he couldn't. We plowed on, sleep, steer, sleep, steer, even into the dark, the masthead light dimming hour by hour. The wind backed to the northeast for a time, but we were all too tired to try to take much advantage of it. Nor would the sea have allowed it; we could go only where it drove us.

Then suddenly the wind stopped. Just stopped, went to dead calm on a sloppy sea. I looked up and above us were stars surrounded by a ring of cloud, a perfect circle of cloud. That was June seventeenth.

Brendan:

When the calm came I knew what had happened. We had sailed her right into the eye of a hurricane. I dashed below to read the barometer. 28.90. Jeez. You said, It's over. I had to say, No, it's not. This won't last long, and it will be worse as we get the back side of it.

How long? Dante asked. I had to tell him I didn't know. Minutes. Not an hour.

As it turned out there was enough time for him to

go up the mast and clear the jib halyard. Normally I would have winched him up on one of the other halyards, but we couldn't get any of them to move, so he just went up hand over hand. Brave lad. If the weather had come back while he was up there we would have lost him for sure. Once he was up he lashed himself to some fitting, maybe the spar itself. He found all four of her halyards had fouled in the sheaves the same way, and we struggled to clear them, he up there, I on deck with the winches. Then we tidied up the sheets and halyards and furled the storm jib and trysail. I took in the drogue. Both life jackets had been torn off of it. Dante tried again to fix the cooling system, couldn't. We then just waited, rested, still in our harnesses. For about ten minutes.

Maggie:

We were so lucky, getting all that gear cleared in time, because when it came it came suddenly, and from the southeast. Even with no sail up at all, *Nunnery* lurched and heeled to bury her lee rail. I don't know if the wind was worse than it had been before the eye of the hurricane , but it sure seemed to be. The sea behind it was confused at first, and we just wallowed and banged, heard all the gear below clanging and bashing as it chewed up my lovely teak joinery. You clung to the helm, Dante and I clung to whatever came to hand and to each other. But after a while it steadied into huge rollers, huge, bigger than any we'd seen before. You shouted Trysail, several times, and finally Dante and I clawed our way forward, freed the gaskets, got it up and sheeted home. You put her as close to that wind and sea as you could, laid her off them just enough.

Brendan:

Thanks be that they weren't curling. The wind blew spray off the crests, but they rolled, didn't curl. If even one of them had curled we would have been lost. As it was, your boat found equanimity if not peace with the helm hard over and the trysail trimmed close. There wasn't any steering to do really, with her set up like that. Once you were both back into the cockpit I lashed the helm with a bit of mainsheet tail and sat back, watching and feeling her. She was nearly becalmed in the troughs, the waves setting up a lee to protect her. On the crests she bore away a little, put her rail into the water, but recovered quickly with each new trough. I didn't time the waves, but they were long, not crowded. Couldn't actually see them either, which I thought was just as well.

Maggie:

When the light came, the sight of those waves shook me. I sat at the helm with you for a while and was terrified. From there behind the helm I could look up from a trough and see the next crest *above* the masthead. *Above* it. I tried doing the math, the height of the mast, the distance from where we sat to the maststep and so on, and figured they had to be at least ninety feet from crest to trough. Neither of us tried to say anything. There was nothing to say.

Dante made his way forward, clung to the mast,

watching. He came back after a while and shouted that he thought we could use the drogue again from the bows. You shrugged. He shrugged back, went forward again. The next time he came aft he was in a hurry.

Freighter! he yelled, and pointed to the port bow. We stood, and on the next crest we could see her, not much more than a hundred yards ahead and bearing down on us.

Ease the trysail, you shouted back, freeing the tiller from its lashing. We'll try to bear off.

Dante freed the sheet from its cleat and handed me the tail. He slowly slacked the line by turning it over the winch. You held the helm down until she turned in a trough. She climbed sidewise like a crab up the next wall of water, heeled dangerously as the wind at the crest hit her, but she held. I caught a glimpse of the freighter looming over us, not fifty yards away now. *Nunnery* drove away to the west, inches at a time, slowed and steadied as you surfed her down into the next trough. Minutes — could it have been minutes? — later, as she rose to the next crest, the freighter was not twenty yards away, but we weren't seeing her head-on anymore. As she passed we could smell the diesel stink of her, see a man standing in a companionway high on her superstructure, watching us.

It took a long time for her to pass. We could hear her engines and generators, and the stink that followed her turned my stomach. Godawful stench, and such an ugly sort of ship, rust-streaked, paint peeling. We could see her superstructure even in the troughs. She plowed into the next crest, shuddering with the impact, even though she was driving downwind.

Once she was past we saw that she was dragging

a long towline. At first I thought she was using it as a drogue, as we had. But then, on the next, or the next, crest, I saw what she was towing. It was *Mary Jane*, the drug boat from Marathon, half her mainmast lashed at an ugly angle where it had broken below the spreaders, mizzen gone entirely, deckhouse crushed by her heavy, fallen boom. She lurched and tugged against the towline, and I truly thought I could hear her screaming.

Dante told me later that he raved inside, whipped himself, that he clung to the sheet of the trysail and watched the passing of the behemoth, — so huge, an ugly skyscraper above us, our mast barely as high as the rails of her hull, her superstructure rising like a dirty slum, tilting into the sky, — that lovely old Stevens yawl ignominious in her wake. He said he saw her story whole — *Mary Jane,* what a name for a *ganja* boat — yes, her whole story. He knew it would have been different had he been with her, he would have been on watch, at the helm, would have had her trimmed right, would have seen the great ugly behemoth in time, or if not would at least have saved her mainmast.

Oh, he could see it all right, two lubber gangsters and poor Lew, who had been to sea only on those behemoths, who really knew nothing of sail, and of the sea only what view you had of it from a giant floating truck, a perverse monster, so ugly, that is not knowing the sea.

Oh, he said, he could see it all right, a tired Lew or tired gangster at the helm, holding to the weather just as *Nunnery* had, somehow driven more south than west the last few days, no way in those seas to see even a behemoth more than a minute or two ahead, a pair of eyes closed against wind and spray on a crest, still closed and lulled in a trough, maybe two, and then there is the behemoth, taking away her mizzen and lifelines, perhaps some other gear, Lew and his gangsters in panic, the behemoth giving them a lee and then rolling down onto her, pounding her mainmast into her while Lew wants only to be aboard the behemoth, assured by her size, the rusty, safe bulk of her iron, her likeness to a New Jersey factory, a floating truck, all that familiar and safe to him.

Dante said he saw himself as the last man aboard the yawl, charged with hauling the heavy cordage across from the freighter, tying it to the stub of the mainmast, lashing it onto the bow, then tying a lighter line around himself and having himself dragged as the others had been across the sea into the bowels of the behemoth.

No, he said. If he had been aboard her he would have saved her mainmast, and he would never have tied that foul cordage to her or to himself, he would have faced the storm alone and saved that lovely Stephens yawl the indignities of the tow and probably worse to come.

He said he thought of the dreams you had instilled in him back in Lauderdale just by being the man you seemed to be then, who had been to the islands and across the seas, that he followed you, he followed you, and what it had come to was this poor, sad, damaged, imprisoned Stevens yawl, his fault forever. And of me, no Island maiden, any sort of maiden, he saw me as the toughest of tough cookies, said he couldn't tell me from a man in my foulweathers.

He said that as he watched the vile behemoth and its prisoner plod and plough northward, he looked aft at you, his hero and exemplar, and at me, his ill-named seductress and then at the shambles of *Nunnery*, my ill-named vessel, — he never liked my name, he thought I should have had a fire-name, and didn't like my boat's name, either — anyway he looked at us and thought that he had served worse people and far lesser boats and felt his guilt somewhat assuaged by his determination to get us all safely home.

Wages of sin, was all he said at the time. Pure hell on a fine boat, was all you said.

Brendan:

I wonder if they're alive, was all you said, Maggie.

The old man knows that Dante would not have saved the yawl. He knows that Dante would have died if he'd stayed aboard her, that he and Maggie would never have sailed into Hurricane Agnes if he had stayed aboard her, that he and she would not have had this private rite of yarning and Agnes his granddaughter would not have been born and his great grandson would not have been born and that the coincidence of Dante showing up at Boot Key wasn't a coincidence at all but an absolute historical necessity because this present depended upon it absolutely. He is completely aware of his faulty logic in this but nevertheless he knows, he knows.

Maggie:

We put her back up onto the wind and I lashed the helm and we took turns watching through the rest of that day and the next night.

And the wind gradually slacked and by morning it was less than thirty knots — the Trades returned — and we could have talked again but didn't have anything to say.

I remember your saying, Now it really is over.

That evening we actually saw a sunset, and stars in the night. We rested the next day, hove to as the seas gradually settled down to the Caribbean you would generally expect. The world sparkled, but *Nunnery* certainly did not. Dante got the engine right, we built battery power, still had to deep six most of the meat in the fridge. Then he went to work on the broken hose fitting in the head, somehow got that to work again, too. You cleared the deck, still finding dead birds, and got the storm jib and trysail folded and stowed and we got plain sail up and got a good Loran reading and put her on a reach for Isla Mujeres while I cleaned below and tidied and cooked us something. We took watches through the night and slept and slept.

Brendan:

Yes, Maggie, I remember. It was fine sailing. I was so glad to be sailing with you.

She rises, takes his glass, and he watches her walk her fine walk as she goes to the cooler. Watches her pose as she bends to it, a 19th century pose with no flowing dress or frilly bonnet, close enough to nude to make him think of even earlier painting. The clink of ice in the glasses, the lovely walk back. The scent of lemon, the dry-sweet taste of the gin. They light cigarettes.

Maggie:

That was the end of Hurricane Agnes for us, but it wasn't quite the end of our adventure, she says, not looking directly at him.

She waits, sips. She wants him to say more, he knows it. Finally he says, Why did you name your boat

Nunnery?

She drills him with sad eyes for a long moment. Then she breaks it off, laughs to herself, shakes her head, shakes off her disappointment.

The short answer is, as a joke I gathered an all-girl crew, bikinis except when it was cold, then shiny red skin-tight wetsuits. We posed and razzed the macho boats, partied hard back at the Yacht Clubs, had a grand old time. We didn't always win, but hardly ever got less than third. A boatload of women, not at all like nuns. Hence *Nunnery.*

She looks away, at a lot of past, not all grand old times. That's true enough, but of course there's a longer version, she says at last.

I was a pretty wild kid, as you know. Joe and Mother had just about nothing, though he came from money; had been disinherited. I was able to join a sailing club and have the Moth, though Joe and I more or less had to build it together out of scraps. No way that family could have been members of the Yacht Club. Wild or not, I kept winning. But the talk behind my back was never about the winning, only about the booze and the boys.

I got serious, though, when I went to college. I was able to supplement what you gave me with a sailing scholarship, inter-collegiate racing in Lasers, Europes, whatever they had. I didn't spend any more than I had to, but it meant I didn't have to waitress.

Anyway, after college I went to Lauderdale, got my broker's license, joined the Yacht Club, started making lots of money. But you know how the racing circuit is, everybody knows everybody, that old reputation followed me down the Gulf, through the Keys and right up to Bahia Mar. I had two choices: try to hide from it, or flaunt it. I carefully and conscientiously played the unattainable slut. Very theatrical. Very flirty. It worked to get me big sales, because the guys at the brokerage knew me better, knew I could close with the older men who were buying the big, gold-plated yachts.

I had always wanted older men, anyway. Somehow they knew it. I never actually bedded any of them until after all the papers were signed, and then just the ones who appealed to me. Not that many of them, really.

So when I'd finished re-building and re-rigging and re-finishing *Nunnery* I took her back over to Clearwater, got my all-girl crew and raised hell there, jamming it all into their faces. Kept my apartment in Lauderdale and kept working, selling. Back in Clearwater they knew nothing of my life and work, just had this party girl strutting and out of reach of any of them. But at the end of the day, *Nunnery* was my private refuge when I was on that coast, and so the name was apt in that way, too.

He can see that she is shifting in time, now, thinking of something, sometime, else. She dribbles a bit of gin into her glass, squeezes a lemon wedge over it. The sun has just fallen below the scalloped rim of the umbrella and filters through the leaves of one of her punk trees, striking her face with a complex of light and shadow, creating a portrait of deep mystery.

Until that guy I took with me to Key West. He was younger, seemed okay, a pretty good sailor. I guess he was disappointed when I proved not to be quite the slut I appeared in Clearwater. And then Dante showed up, and everything was different after that.

That Dante, she says. He got me pregnant on that

cruise, I'm not sure whether it was at Boot Key or underway or at Isla Mujeres. We married when we got back, once I knew. Of course he couldn't stay. After Agnes was born he went sailing again, naturally. He was like the wind. He'd be back for a few days or a week between boats, but there were lots of other girls in other ports. We divorced after a year or two. That was when I sold *Nunnery*, bought this old house, gave up Lauderdale and the rat race, just kept this little sloop to teach Agnes how to sail. Now that she's married and away I seldom use it. On a day with a good breeze I'll take a couple of hours to sail out to the Boca Grande sea buoy, flash the sportsmen in the Pass chasing tarpon for the tournament, zip back in here feeling young. But it's not the same anymore.

She touches the fine lines around her left eye, then her right. Examines the scars on her hands from the wires that had cut her during the hurricane.

That Dante just never could bring himself to care much about Agnes, though I think he sometimes tried. She was never happy when he was home.

I remember, Maggie. I visited once when he was home.

You were good with her, if a bit distant. She wasn't very warm with you, but then you weren't very warm with her, either.

That's true. I felt warm, but couldn't show it. Afraid, I guess.

He was too, I suppose. Felt he had to stay free.

Brendan:

The old man ponders this, isn't sure what to say. Isn't

sure what it is he'd felt toward his granddaughter. He'd taken delight in her, he's sure of that. But he can't say why he'd held his distance. Certainly not from feeling he had to stay free.

I didn't want to burden her, I think.

Burden her? Do you think you've been a burden to me? Don't you think you could have stayed nearby, seen us more often?

I couldn't, Maggie. Not then.

Because of that awful woman. What you let her do to you.

That's a way to put it, yes.

So you ran off to South America and left us alone.

That's a way to put it, yes. Mainly I had to put a lot of sea room between Maya and myself. I had to find women, my Carmens and Salomes, as many of them as it would take to insulate me from the memory of those horrors. And of course, I had to make a living.

She glares at him for a moment, slugs down her gin, slams down her glass. Damn you, Brendan Harper, she says coldly. She rises, turns, strides rapidly to the door of the house. This is not her pretty walk. She is hunched, drives her heels into the deckboards.

She slams the door behind her. He sits stunned, unmoving. He thinks about what South America had done for him, everything he had hoped; he had found work teaching English, had met the poets whose work he translated, saw one of those translations become successful, the writer become famous, so he got more work translating, not only poets but novelists too. And the women, lots of them, finally healing the wounds Maya had inflicted on him. Now, however, he has to admit that the price of this was time with his daughter and his granddaughter, and now a great grandson he's seen only once, and that the price may have been too high.

He stands, bracing himself with the table, the back of the chair. Grabs his cane. Limps around the perimeter of the patio, touches the leaves of a bougainvillea, the soft bark of a punk tree. While the feel of these plants is vaguely pleasant, he is iced inside, terrified that what he has said or has not said has lost her to him forever. Out on the dock he looks down into the water, notes that the tide has risen, listens to the gentle way it licks at the pilings, the seawall. He smells the weed on it, the plankton, the crustacea, the salt, the fish. Now, with the tide high, he can see much more of her racy little sailboat, the varnish gleaming in the last of the day's sunlight, all her lines fresh and perfectly coiled. She turns a little on her slackened moorings and a wafting of air, and he sees for the first time her varnished transom and the name carved into it. She has named her boat *Electra.*

He returns to the table, pours half an inch of gin onto the ice remaining in his glass, sips. He thinks of how he might have lost her during the hurricane, sees her again struggling with the trysail, getting drenched at the helm as a wave breaks over *Nunnery*'s quarter. To have lost her that way would have been worse, much worse. Still. If I lose her, this will be a rotten way to do it too.

Maggie returns. Her face has a scrubbed look, she has applied a little make up. Sorry. It just makes me so mad sometimes. Agnes wasn't enough for you? Either the hurricane or granddaughter? I wasn't enough for you, you ran to that awful woman, during that time I never even saw you, and then I find you drunk and filthy in Sloppy Joe's and sober you up and nurse you and sail through a hurricane with you, and. . . .

If only. . . . he begins to say, then stops, all the if onlys overwhelm him, sitting there in the fading light of day he cannot stop them, the night-sweat litany of his if onlys.

And about Maya, if only, if only. If only I'd understood then what I have come to understand now, why she did what she did. She'd had no time on her own, just a semester or two in a dorm. She craved freedom, as it was understood in those heady days of revolution. She went from being her parents' child to being my child bride and surrogate daughter without ever having been herself. She had to do things she couldn't tell me about in order to get free. I understand that now, way too late, but if only I had understood it then.

If only.

If only what? Maggie asks.

He considers. If only I'd been able to stick with your mother? No, It doesn't answer. All his if onlys are long in his wake, nothing compared to this immediate, blistering *fact* of Maggie, right here requiring resolution, his absolutely correct *respondum*. He shakes his head.

Not if only. That distance I have kept I have thought of as a way of loving, and it often seemed the only way to love you. A kind of fender rigged over the side to protect the varnish spread over a life. I slipped my moorings, spent years of my life adrift and didn't even know it.

He looks down, has no idea how to connect this to all that needs saying. He lets the gin float him into his memory. He finds nothing there of any use in this.

I'm your father, Maggie, he says. You're my daughter. That's all there is to say. All there is to it.

She smiles, bows her head. Then looks up at him, eyes glittering. She reaches across the table, takes his hand and squeezes it.

Tell me how it went, please, she says.

Are you sure you want to hear it?

She nods.

When your mother was pregnant, all I wanted in the world was to be with the two of you, live any way we could, a shack at a boatyard, a trailer behind a gas station. At seventeen and not even out of high school, how could I hope for anything better than that? Still, anything, anywhere.

But there is one other part of that, Maggie, of which I am much ashamed.

He clears his throat, bows his head.

To this day I don't know if I would have stuck even if she'd said she was willing to. I believed much of what I was taught, that one had to be educated, one could not waste a life on boatyards or boats, gas stations or cars. I know now that all that isn't true, such a life would not have been a waste, I spent a lot of it on boats and I could never say it was wasted. In the end it was just about my father's pride and his desperate fear. I didn't know that then.

Maggie looks away from him now, out over the bay, lights on the houses and docks coming on, ruining the twilight. But did you love her? she asks.

Oh yes. In the only way a sixteen-year old knows love. Perhaps the most pure and simple way a male loves a female. She was almost as beautiful as you at that age, Maggie. She made me feel blessed, brilliant, beautiful myself. As do you.

They sip. She doesn't look at him, stares at her

glass. Sips. He is afraid to say anything else, can't.

I had a pretty good stepfather anyway, she says at last. Joe Teller was a drunk, yes, but he was a lot more than that. He loved Mother and he loved me and he loved the Bays, Boca Ciega Bay most of all, and suffered horribly as he watched its destruction.

He had this collection of old charts, 1942, '50, '55, some older. He would pull them out sometimes when he was drinking, show me where there had been grass flats that he'd fished and scalloped, mangroves he'd poled through catching snapper, netting mullet and bait fish. That was on the older charts. Then he'd show me the newer ones, the dredged, ugly fingers of artificial land where those flats and mangroves had been, looking like that crap over there. She tosses her head contemptuously toward the opposite shore.

It hurt him especially because his family was behind a lot of it and making a fortune out of it. He came back from the Army and was furious at what he saw they'd done to it, refused to have anything to do with them. That's how he came to be disinherited. He'd never have taken a penny from them anyway. He fished, worked in marinas, boatyards. Gave us the sort of life you would have, I guess, at least as far as the money went. I don't suppose you'd have done it any better. Being ten years younger and so middle-class I doubt you'd have done as well.

She falls silent, examines the water and the lights just coming on across the bay as twilight begins. Finally raises her glass, slugs the last of her gin. Time for me to start dinner, she says, stands. I'll call you when it's ready. As she goes inside he can make no guess as to her feelings, there is not enough light now for him to see the quality of her walk.

He knows she's right, he wouldn't have done it as well as Joe Teller. He could not have gone on for Maggie's sake alone, he'd left the squalor behind and taken the guilt with him. If he hadn't he'd have had to carry even more of it than he has carried as it is. He'd never have learned his Spanish, sailed those grand old wooden boats. Might never have got the money to send Maggie to college. Might never have brought the work of his South American writers into the English speaking world.

He stews and squirms. He smokes. He sips. Though the evening is sweet, the light breeze redolent of near-forgotten desires, he shivers with cold or with fear. What will she think of me now?

He hears the occasional clatter of a pan from inside the house, dinner seems to be taking an awfully long time. Finally he hears the sliding door, sees Maggie silhouetted in it. Dinner is served, she says.

He rises, enters, closes the door behind him. The dining area is to the right, dimly lit with candles. The light from the kitchen is brighter. He looks in there, sees her at the stove, her back to him. She is dressed in a tight white sheath, wears red spike heels. He remembers her mother dressed exactly that way almost sixty years ago, exactly but for Maggie's much higher hemline and heels now red instead of white.

She turns toward him. She is made up now as for a night out in London or Paris or New York or Milan, say Donatella Versace but for the hair, with which little or nothing can be done. He wants to cry. She smiles at him. He chokes.

So we're still all right? he asks.

Sure we are.

You truly don't mind that I couldn't be your father then? That I left her?

Of course not, Brendan. The only thing I mind is that I never got to see enough of you through the years.

Same for me, he says. I thank you for what times we have had.

I have not lost her. She forgives me. Gratitude, gratitude.

She comes to him, grasps his arms, embraces him carefully, he can tell she knows how fragile he is. Come and sit down, Brendan, she says. Pour the wine. I'll be right there.

She leads him to the table, seats him. He pours the chilled white wine. She is just turning twenty in the candlelight, her eyes sparkle. They talk about other things, but he is thinking about coincidences, his certainty that they are not coincidences at all but something else altogether. An idea is forming as he listens to her talk about her daughter and her son-in-law and her grandson, perhaps not an idea but just a notion, perhaps not even a notion but an intuition. Then suddenly he has it, he sees it whole, it lies in the sum of all our perceptions, all consciousness. This is the clarity sought in our yarning, we are father and daughter now, truly.

It's about cordage, Maggie, he says. Lines between ships and docks, ships and sails, ships and ships, ships and men. But yet another kind of cordage exists, an invisible skein of lines connecting hearts, minds, spirits or perhaps souls. There has always been a stout, taut length of line between us, between father and daughter. And it's of the finest, old-time manila three-strand.

Maggie:

They go to work clearing the table, then tidying the kitchen. He moves very slowly now, his limp very bad, he can't seem to straighten his back. She does most of it, tells him to sit, but he refuses, they wash dishes together. He often touches her arm or hip with his arm or hip, and she returns these touches and they laugh.

Kitchen done, she dims the lights and takes him to his bedroom, her arm around his waist, her head on his shoulder. He tells her goodnight, but she stays, helping him undress, asking about his pills, what else he might need. Then she opens the covers and helps him to arrange all his pillows and covers him when he's down and ready. He tells her goodnight again, but she puts out the lights without answering and kicks off her shoes and crawls into the bed with him, puts her arm around his shoulders and just lies there holding him. It's all right, Brendan. You're my father now, she says.

Really, she thinks, as he snuffles and then snorts and then settles into the raspy breath of sleep, really there's not much dear about him anymore, just the private history. He smells like the old man he is, I look at him and see only what he was, not what he's become, oh, but he could steer to windward, I'll never forget that, and was hurt and weak and ruined by that awful woman, but I think Agnes would have killed us if he hadn't been there. And I might have died that night when that drunken crew had me, he may have saved my life that night too, and then there was the money for college that put me on a fair course with the rig in reasonable trim so I didn't have to founder as my mother and poor old Joe did. Joe helped me with the Moth, he tried to be a father to me and never hurt me, even skunk-drunk and maybe, just maybe old Captain Brendan Harper, with his Spanish poets and skills or inspirations passed to Dante, — that Dante, that damned Dante, Dante the Damned — and whatever else that crazy old drunken reprobate Captain Brendan Harper — *my father!* — may have done in his life, skills and inspirations, oh damn it I never learned any Spanish I wouldn't know one of his Spanish poems from a recipe but maybe that stinking old drunk I dragged out of Sloppy Joe's at eleven in the morning did something with his ragged, damaged life, something of some sort of lasting value, even if it cost me.

Cost him.

Well, cost all of us.

She tries to imagine the affair between her mother and Bren, the late 'forties, how daring, exciting, dangerous it must have been, and a new admiration for her mother's courage in her skin-tight white sheath and high heels — at *fifteen*! — floods her. She has only known her mother as a gross, slovenly, fat blob with an angry mouth. What an adventuress she must once have been, though, to have seduced Captain Brendan Harper, well he wasn't a captain yet but surely there were even then signs of what he would someday be, and there must have been much more to her than I ever saw.

He's right about the cordage, isn't he? Strained, attenuated though it has often been, even when these two frail vessels have been tossed on violent seas and out of sight of one another, still that length of line has held fast to the cleats in his heart and in mine, and never parted, no matter how many crests or troughs between us.

Who has ever been so true to me?

To whom have I ever been so true?

Myself, damn it.

Just like poor old Cap'n Bren.

She clings to the old man, not minding his smell so much now, sad that he is so diminished that they won't have any more adventures together but determined to keep him with her this time for as long as she can. I will see that he gets to know his granddaughter too, and to play with his great grandson, and we'll all learn Spanish and he'll read his poets to us and he and I, just the two of us, will remember Hurricane Agnes and hold fiercely to our length of three-strand cordage, right to the end.

Author's Note

I have been working on *Three-Strand Cordage* since 1972. I started it in Tampa, stuck ashore after Hurricane Agnes for a time, yachting having been brought to rather a standstill by that event. The stories have been through at least three entirely different versions since then. I put it aside several times, my focus changing, writing other books, immersing myself in Japanese arts, language and culture. These other activities significantly changed the form of the book when, this year at last, I felt free to return to work on it.

Some years ago I sent a version to Bill Baynes, author of *Bunt*, who critiqued it with great accuracy, and sought and got several other reactions, perhaps less perceptive than Bill's. It took three years of my clearing the decks of other pressing work for me to return to it. During that time I was in touch with Peter Matthiessen, who, though he didn't read the book, was most encouraging and was kind enough to give me permission to use the quote from *Far Tortuga* for its colophon. *Far Tortuga* was a particular inspiration for *Three-Strand Cordage*. Other writers also inspired the shape and style of it: Joseph Conrad, of course; Rudyard Kipling's *The Man Who Would Be King*, which largely set the narrative point of view in *Pirates*; Alan Villiers; Cormac McCarthy and Kent Haruf, who freed American fiction from the essentially journalistic convention of quotation marks; and in a roundabout way, the *haiku* of Matsuō Bashō, which set a world standard for minimalism. Jim Harrison, too; the success of his *Legends of the Fall* lent new legitimacy to the collection of three novellas in one volume, and his *After Ikku* showed how Zen influence could be beautifully melded into literature in English.

Readers will note that I broke pattern and used quotation marks in the main story in *Brangaene.* I did so for this reason: There was quite a bit of Spanish dialogue in the narrative, which I felt required the Spanish forms of punctuation, so English quotation marks were needed to be consistent.

Choosing names for fictional characters is one of the cheeriest parts of the writing process, and here I could name not only characters, but boats, too. The reader may have noticed that *Femme Fatale* was recently so named, but had previously been *Allegretto* and kept that name in an earlier version. *Capriole* was about to be re-named *Rondo,* and already had that name in the earlier version. *Adagio* kept her name in all the versions. The earlier version of *Pirates of Penance* was subtitled *Sonatina for Sea and Sails.*

Brendan was named for a medieval Irish monk, believed to have been the first European to sail to North America. "Harper" was because itinerant, usually anonymous, harpers were the storytellers in Ireland (and Europe generally). "Jack," from "Jack Tar," because he was crew. "Morgan" for the famous pirates, Henry Morgan and J.P. Lady Caroline was named for Horatio Nelson's lover. The Thorssens, I confess, were just off the top of my head, except for Elke, who looked to me like a tanned version of the actress, Elke Sommer. Maya was named for the Hindu goddess of illusion.

The whole story of *Brangaene* was based loosely on Wagner's libretto of *Tristan and Isolde* and Malory's *Tristan and Isault,* so those names were all rather obvious. Those in the frame story are to emphasize the Southern and Cuban backgrounds of the characters. The title *Agnes of God* was consciously intended to refer back to the play of the same name, in order to emphasize the different ways people react to deities and "acts of God." In *Agnes,* the boat names are explained in the course of the yarn. "Dante" was because he more or less led them into the hell of a hurricane. "Rogers" because "to roger" was an 18th century British term for sexual conquest.

The dating of the stories also went through several changes. I placed *Pirates* in the 50s, because that was the heyday of the last of the great wooden sailing yachts. I placed *Brangane* in 1960 because I needed the Cuban revolution and its counterrevolution for the action and characters to make historical sense. Because I sailed through Hurricane Agnes much as described, and her passage through the Yucatan is clearly documented, I had no choice but to place the yarn in June of 1972.

For all this to work I had to make Brendan ten years older than I am. He could have sailed the Caicos and the Virgins at age twenty-five as easily as at thirty-one, my age when I did it. He could have sailed the Gulf Stream and the Bahamas as well at thirty in 1960 as I did in '71, and I thought it wasn't too much of a stretch for him to have sailed through Hurricane Agnes in his forties rather than his thirties, as I did.

I started sailing at age nine in dinghies (Haggerty Seashells and Y-Flyers) and later in Herreshoff Fish and a Rhodes Bantam. I let go of it for the most part from 1956 to 1970. I want to assure those of my readers who are sailing buffs that the descriptions of sea and wind conditions, courses and fixes, all that, are accurate and factual, although placed in different times, and sometimes different places, from my actual experiences. All the events and characters in *Three-Strand Cordage* are fictional or used fictionally.

M. J. Sullivan
Tōshoin, 2014

Off Norfolk, ca. 1971
author photo by David Parkinson

M. J. Sullivan has been a concert guitarist, a teacher, a sailing yacht captain and an artist. He has a BA in Humanities and an MA in Asian Studies. *WAZA*, his first novel about Japanese Buddhism and the martial arts, received the CoVisions Recognition Award for Literature. *Three-Strand Cordage* is loosely based on some of his sailing adventures.

He earned the name Seihō and his teacher's license in calligraphy from Nippon Shuji Kyoiku Zaidan, and wrote the English language versions of their textbooks. He was made an Honorary Citizen of Takamatsu and one year was the *nidan* level swordsmanship champion of Kagawa Prefecture.

Deeply involved with Zen and Japanese culture, he paints and writes at Tōshoin (洞書 院 , Cave Writing Hall), his studio in the Colorado Rocky Mountains.

www.ingramcontent.com/pod-product-compliance
Lightning Source LLC
Chambersburg PA
CBHW060555310726
48982CB00008B/1130/J
* 9 7 8 0 9 8 2 9 9 2 0 6 7 *